# Temporarily Out of Luck

## by

## Vicki Batman

*A Hattie Cooks Mystery*

**Temporarily Out of Luck**

Cover Art by *Debbie Taylor*

The Wild Rose Press, Inc.
PO Box 708
Adams Basin, NY 14410-0708
Visit us at www.thewildrosepress.com

Publishing History
First Crimson Rose Edition, 2021
Trade Paperback ISBN 978-1-5092-3337-3
Digital ISBN 978-1-5092-3338-0

*A Hattie Cooks Mystery*
Published in the United States of America

Sometimes, I felt like a small white mouse housed in a cage with lots of small white mice, whose playground activities involved eating, sleeping, and continually revolving on the exercise wheel. Just like one rodent friend—who I named Mr. Happy-Go-Lucky, having a field day back-flipping from the top of the spinning wheel—something happened. Unexpectedly, I found myself airborne.

Not hurt, a sense of disappointment overcame me, plus a bit of confusion, and a whole lot of colorful adjectives too numerous to list. I, mostly known as Hattie Cooks, shook off the pine shavings and joined the rat race. Sometimes, life sucked.

*But wallowing?* Not a good solution.

*Being positive?* A better one.

In most cases, a pitstop was a good idea, and I found comfort in my chocolate stockpile. And in most cases, I found empty shelves, for I had little dough to supply my habit due to the loss of my adored job as an assistant buyer at Sommerville's top-class department store, Tucker's, and the subsequent low-paying temporary ones I reluctantly took in the interim. Due to the expenses of rent, food, utilities, budgeting became my new compadré. However, for my recent birthday, Mom suggested friends and family provide me with treats. They were generous—gifting lots and lots of my favorite M&Ms in vast colors and flavors.

## Dedication

To Handsome: Every second, every minute, every hour of every day.

~

To New Baby! I can't wait to be your VB.

Chapter One

Sometimes, I felt like a small white mouse housed in a cage with lots of small white mice, whose playground activities involved eating, sleeping, and continually revolving on the exercise wheel. Just like one rodent friend—who I named Mr. Happy-Go-Lucky, having a field day back-flipping from the top of the spinning wheel—something happened. Unexpectedly, I found myself airborne.

Not hurt, a sense of disappointment overcame me, plus a bit of confusion, and a whole lot of colorful adjectives too numerous to list. I, mostly known as Hattie Cooks, shook off the pine shavings and joined the rat race. Sometimes, life sucked.

*But wallowing?* Not a good solution.

*Being positive?* A better one.

In most cases, a pitstop was a good idea, and I found comfort in my chocolate stockpile. And in most cases, I found empty shelves, for I had little dough to supply my habit due to the loss of my adored job as an assistant buyer at Sommerville's top-class department store, Tucker's, and the subsequent low-paying temporary ones I reluctantly took in the interim. Due to the expenses of rent, food, utilities, budgeting became my new compadré. However, for my recent birthday, Mom suggested friends and family provide me with treats. They were generous—gifting lots and lots of my favorite M&Ms in vast colors and flavors.

Mom's idea totally rocked as the best birthday gift ever.

From outside my door, I heard Allan Wellborn smack the doorframe.

"You know how to find me."

I roused from my ruminations and banged the back of my head against the door. The tone Allan used upset me. A headache pounded in my temples, and acid reflux climbed in my esophagus.

Yup, I did know how to find Allan Wellborn, hunky cop, brother of my grade-school best friend, and on occasion, my wanna-be boyfriend. Most days, I drove right past his townhome or the Sommerville Police station, where he worked as a detective. But I cruised by not in a creepy, stalking, devious manner. Just drove my normal, everyday, routine route.

"I've had enough of this…whatever it is…with the slamming the door thing, sweetheart," he said.

*Sweetheart?* Snort.

"You need to face your fears. I came here hoping…things would be better between us. Since you aren't talking, I feel…stupid. Adios."

Not surprising, he expressed his dissatisfaction over our substandard reunion.

Because we had no reunion.

Because I told him, "No."

I skimmed up the front door to squint through the peephole only to see him stomp toward his granite 4-Runner. I flattened my hands against the wooden surface and stared at his well-formed body.

Allan yanked open the truck's door and flung himself inside. He cranked over the engine.

With that, the man of few words, the one I really adored, departed. My soul cracked. *God. Will we ever???*

I set my hand to my chest, shaking my head. Even though I cared for him deeply, I said "no" for a very good reason. My heart nearly shattered in a bazillion pieces when Allan was shot. I blamed myself for the incident, even though someone else was the responsible party.

I hadn't pulled the trigger.

Blonde Bimbo had. One hole drilled into his shoulder.

What Allan asked took a great deal of courage—to *get lucky*—although I understood he wanted us to explore the couple course. From firsthand experience, a whole lotta guts were required to ask the question 'cause several months back, I'd asked him to *choose me*.

After I had been nearly stabbed.

After I had determined he used me for information.

After we nearly had almost wild, almost sex.

*Sex would have been good.* Remembering, I set a finger to my lower lip, letting my mouth curve at the corners. *Everybody knows sex is a good thing.*

When I asked Allan to choose me over Blonde Bimbo, aka Cathy Bartholomew, he said *no*. This silly girl thought he meant we would carry on in our respective, separate lives. Only I didn't understand he categorically meant he was undercover investigating-slash-dating her. Unbeknownst to anyone, my former Northside, Lancaster, and Brookside co-worker turned out to be crazy insane.

I could add a few other descriptive words.

Today, he returned, asking me to choose him, translated to "get lucky." The kind of lucky where one howls at the moon and basks in the afterglow for all eternity.

No question I desired Allan. I did—badder than badly. Even now, just thinking about almost wild, almost sex made my girl parts squirmy and throb. But too many things happened recently, and I hadn't—for lack of a better word—*coped* well. I wanted him in a normal-relationship way without people-trying-to-kill-us way.

*Am I foolish to think that?*

I crammed my fists into my temples, grinding them into my skin. Somehow, I missed a critical memo.

With a disgusted sigh, I turned and paced from the entry to the space in front of the television and back, pleating my forehead with my fingers. Most likely, I had blown it again. I didn't know what to do. My life was up in the air. I felt…tossed aside…like the small white mouse.

My brains, scrambled like eggs, frustrated me. I pressed my backside to the door and slid to the floor. Propping an arm on my bent knee, I cradled my cheek. Part of me wanted to run after Allan and grab and start…something…somewhere. The past few months of on-again, off-again, on-again, off-again tortured me. Frankly, I deserved a rest like a month-long stay at an exclusive, five-star resort with a top-notch spa and attentive cabana boys ferrying champagne cocktails and high-quality chocolate.

*Everyone knows champagne and chocolate cure everything.*

Jenny Arbothnot, my BFF and roomie, popped out

of her room. She evaporated when Allan showed and appropriated the M&Ms he included in his usual Get-Well gift bag shaped like a pot of flowers.

By the way she bounced on her toes, I knew her insides were hopping up and down while witnessing all firsthand. My friend had a running Big Top sideshow of "Romantic Encounters with Hattie and Allan," showcased in the middle arena—the apartment we shared. However, we probably wouldn't be roommates much longer as Mr. Who-Uses-All-The-Hot-Water would more than likely be proposing soon.

Leaving me roommate-less for the second time in four years. Knowing I wouldn't have a job and the dough which came with one to support myself meant I had only one option left—to return to the *intima parentes*.

Pea-green nausea roiled in my tummy. *No, thank you.*

With her nearly finished bag of peanut candies in hand, Jenny sat alongside me, mimicking my pose. She didn't utter a word, just tossed back a treat and munched.

I sent her a sideways glance.

"Harriet Lee Cooks, you should be ashamed of yourself."

Feeling like a deadhead combined with her calm and measured tone of voice, I glared. "You sound like my mother. Hand over the chocolate or—"

Jenny popped another M&M in her mouth. "Or what?"

"D-I-E."

She pressed her hands against her small bosom. "I'm so worried. How will you do me in? Arsenic?"

5

Flattening her lips, she shook her head. "No, maybe strychnine? No—"

I leveled my finger in her face. "Be scared, my friend. I'll think of something, something totally evil. Maybe rats." I want to think the threatening note in my voice might have sounded intimidating because Jenny—willingly—passed the whole candy package.

With an arched brow, she studied me as if I would do something irrational.

Like I had anything irrational stockpiled. Nothing. I was dead-dog, bone tired.

Jenny grunted.

"You're staring exactly the same way my mother does."

"I feel like your mother. You're lucky she isn't here to pontificate on her favorite subject—Allan Wellborn, whom we all know and love as Mr. Saintly." Her lip twitched. "Why would you do something so unbelievably stupid like sending Allan away?"

Stupid—the perfect descriptive for my relationship with him. I excelled at stupid.

After shaking the candy bag, I noted its lightness. I palmed the remaining crunchy crumbs. What I tasted…disappointing. Despite what the commercial stated, two or three treats and bits of coating crumbles would never be satisfying.

Standing, Jenny snatched the empty bag dangling from my fingertips, rolling it into a twist. She pointed the trash-shaped light saber in my direction. "He might throw in the towel and won't come back. He did a few months ago. Look what happened then. Aren't you worried he'll hook up with another bimbo?"

I rested my forehead on my knees and murmured in

my cave, "I don't know what I was saying. I didn't know having a relationship with Allan could be so difficult. College boy had been so easy. No killings, knifings, or shootings. Just plain ol' fun…and handholding…and great sex. Why me?" I raised my head to find Jenny nodding. "I need to regroup."

"Lots of people endorse regrouping. Wouldn't hurt to think on it."

Occasionally, Jenny supplied good advice.

My best buds, the Funsisters, supported me like real sisters. We shared all our naughty bits and good pieces. Ran to the rescue when needed. Friends for life. I could never live without Kellar, Trixie, and Maggie. They more than understood the emotional trauma I experienced over the last few months. I was stabbed by a crazy insane woman, and Allan was shot by a jealous, insane woman. Both insane people murdered other people.

Here was what I discovered—things like this—i.e., murder and mayhem—didn't happen to everyday human beings in the big wide world.

Jenny pulled me to my feet, and I found my way to my secret hiding spot in the kitchen pantry—which most certainly would never be much of a secret—for more of my favorite cure-all. Funsister Maggie found an article stating chocolate held restorative and curative powers, and oh boy, did I consume my daily share to cure something. If nothing happened, I would chase the treat with my favorite soda. If nothing worked, I would order a pizza, fully loaded with Canadian bacon and crispy bacon. *Doesn't everyone think lots of cholesterol is a bonus?*

When friends and family gifted me with my

preferred chocolate treat on my birthday, I felt my heart flower with trills of delight. Mom would've never given me vast quantities of chocolate when I was a kid. Not ever-ever. She confiscated our Halloween chocolate and repeated lectures about developing diabetes or cavities. However, her birthday surprise lacked variety and, frankly, could be on the verge of boring.

Snagging an unopened bag, I propped a hip against the kitchen counter and munched on a few candies, not tasting them. While I pondered my next move, I passed the package to Jenny, who dumped her trash and observed me. Perhaps, she believed eloquent words would spill from my lips, but she would have been wrong. My ability to speak had dissolved.

She poured a handful of rainbow gems in her palm, then chucked the package on the countertop. "I think I'll go read our book for book club. Although the heroine is batty, she's getting more sex than you." She pushed off the counter and disappeared down the hall.

*Great. You do that. Abandon me in my hour of need.* Jenny and I belonged to a book club with our Funsister friends. For our next meeting, Jenny submersed herself in our selection, which featured a wacky girl's pitiful attempts to solve a mystery.

*The character could take a few pointers from me— mostly on the lack of orgasm part.*

Taking the yellow candy bag to the living area, I flopped on the khaki couch and, out of habit, powered on the television. I surfed through some channels, but no program captured my attention, not even a new episode of a home improvement show I regularly viewed. I landed on a local network, my attention diverted with the highly rated program, *Celebrity*

*Corner*, which dished gossip morsels about Sommerville citizens.

"Breaking news: For all you ladies who seek a wealthy stunner of a local heart-throb"—the red-headed anchor leaned forward and shook her curly head—"he's no more. Jonson Leggett the Third is officially off the market."

Choking, I sat upright and suppressed the urge to regurgitate a hairball, like the one Allan's cat, Lucky, produced after a grooming session. *Did she say Jonson Legett the Third?* Not him.

"You heard it here first." The reporter looked at her co-host. "Well, rats for me."

"Rats is right. However, the bride-to-be is a former beauty pageant contestant. She's tough competition." The male anchor adjusted his tortoiseshell glasses as he rotated to face the camera.

To the left of the program host, a window appeared with a picture of the newly engaged couple surrounded by her parents. Beams of love, similar to colorful rays of sunlight after a thunderstorm, radiated from her body. A close-up of her with a tiara anchored on her head followed.

Did they post a photo of Jonson's family? No way, but not shocking. Based on what I knew of his past, he probably murdered them or spent all their money, and then murdered them.

The woman anchor shuffled her papers. "In a few months, Jonson Leggett the Third and Barbara Louise—whom Sommervillians know and love as Barbie—Fenster, daughter of lumber store magnate and his wife, Fenley and Faith Fenster, will tie the knot."

"Hopefully, he can keep his johnson in his pants."

The male anchor slapped the table as he smirked.

*What a lame joke.*

"Oops," the redhead said from behind her hand. "The censors might ding you for using *that* word."

"I couldn't help it." He chuckled. "The gag wrote itself."

The label Horrible-Nasty-Awful-Dreaded-Appalling-Terrible-Bad-Vile-Disgusting-Marriage-Material should have been stapled to Jonson Leggett the Third's forehead. I more than detested him and with good reason. Honestly, *couldn't* someone *do away with him?* Raise a little dough. Call in the Russian Mafia. *Finito.*

The male anchor gave a hearty smile. "Stay tuned to *Celebrity Corner* for extra-breaking news about Sommerville's darling couple."

I would never, ever call Jonson Leggett the Third "darling." Certainly demonic. Devil incarnate. Diabolic. These descriptives sounded best.

To purge all notions of Jonson from my mind, I picked up the remote to toggle to another station. I landed on the Home Improvement channel, where I longed to be one of those crafty people featured in the programs.

Commercials ruled the airwaves, and the current advertisement airing profiled a renovated strip shopping center in Sommerville. Several new businesses were highlighted. The background voice stated a couple of the chic boutiques sought experienced employees—

*Whoa!* A big revelation smacked me right between the eyes. Experienced employee? In retail? *Whoa. Whoa. I AM an experienced employee in retail.* I desperately needed a job as there were few pennies in my piggy bank.

I upped the volume to listen for further details. One of the stores, Miss Anastasia's Wedding Wonderland, desired to hire someone as an assistant to a wedding planner.

Not every day did the perfect job opportunity land in one's lap. An excited, unknown something-something stirred in my chest. I dropped the remote on the couch and gripped my knees, leaning in. *I could BE that employee.* At State Technological University, I majored in Clothing and Textiles, with an emphasis on Fashion Merchandising from the School of Home Economics. I took a job after college with Tuckers, which, coincidentally, happened to be my mother's favorite place to shop.

My extensive background in retail made me over-qualified for the position at Wedding Wonderland, except for the part about the wedding stuff. But I could learn fast and work hard. I could do the job with my hands tied behind my back.

My retail career began at one of Tuckers' smaller store locations where I managed the women's and children's clothing areas. I shifted to new stores and became known as a New Store Specialist, readying the latest in the chain's launch. Approximately a year later, I landed the job as the assistant buyer in men's sportswear, where I blossomed like a flower amongst a garden of macho types.

Those guys itched and scratched in unmentionable places and cursing like sailors seemed commonplace.

I had fun. I worked in the buying office for three years, and when the handbag buyer relocated to Atlanta for her husband's new job, the timing looked promising for my promotion up the corporate ladder. Instead, Tuckers' management reorganized the buying staff and laid me off due to an economic downturn.

Based on another friend's recommendation, I called my Funsister friend, Trixie, who ran the employment agency, Jobs Inc. I needed an income stream, and she found temporary positions while I waited for the perfect buying job to appear magically.

At Buy Rite Automobile Insurance Agency, I did data entry and office work, only to have the boss's assistant brandish her trusty letter opener in a threatening way when I uncovered the embezzling scam our larger-than-life superior operated.

A position at Button & Bows Stationery Company followed where I inadvertently messed up an important and significant wedding order, and ultimately, resulted in the owners asking me—very politely—not to return the next day. Nor the next. I didn't blame them for my firing as I made a terrible, horrible mistake on the invitations. Occasionally, I had a problem with spelling unusual names—which could happen to anyone.

I scrubbed my palms over my thighs. Trixie found me a third short-term job with Northside, Lancaster & Brookside, Certified Public Accountants, as the Administrative Assistant to the firm's Managing Partner. Unfortunately, another jealous Administrative Assistant—the Triple Threat Blonde Bimbo, whom I assumed Allan Wellborn was friendly under covers with—tried to kill him because of his affection for me.

After the police carted her off to the station, my desire to return to NLB vanished. The partners intimated they didn't want me to stay anyway.

The overwhelming hunger to work at the bridal

salon encompassed my head. I could do the job. Wouldn't hurt to try. Surely, I would ace the interview. Who would murder someone at a bridal salon—*right?* Because of the upcoming nuptials, every customer would be in a state of pre-wedded bliss. Of course, considering the possibility to encounter bridezillas— *yikes.* In those television programs, I'd seen a lot of vitriolic hate displayed, and all the viewers wanted to do away with them.

Possibly, the owner of Wedding Wonderland would say *no*, which wouldn't be the end of the world. Lately, I learned to live with rejection. The whole rejection thingy and I were like close buddies— unfortunately. I determined being extra charming and selling myself to be the best path.

Optimistic, I grabbed a scrap pad someone dropped on the coffee table and scribbled the store's name and contact information. For a long while, I stared at the words, buoying myself with upbeat phrases like "you can do this," and "you're a retail rock star." I collected the ticket to my future, headed to my room, and booted up my laptop to search the Internet for any details about Wedding Wonderland by Miss Anastasia I might have missed.

As I settled on my bed, computer in my lap, I recollected a famous Southern belle said something like, "The next day is a new day."

*Has my day arrived?*

Chapter Two

The subsequent morning, I tossed my tote and handbag in my Jeep. I paused for a moment to admire my surroundings—a glorious autumn day rose over Sommerville. Crisp, clean mid-sixties were ideal weather conditions. An embracing briskness encompassed the air, but the sun promised warmth. No clouds. No rain.

I slid on my sunglasses, ready to conquer unemployment, and scooted inside my car. With a crank of the engine, I shifted in gear and took off.

Because of the accessibility to nearby larger cities, Sommerville became a fashionable place to reside. We enjoyed small-town amenities with big town convenience. Many considered our corner of the world to be exclusive by some, old money by others, and sought after by everyone.

My mom, Elaine, and my dad, Harry, raised my sister, Tracey, and me in Sommerville. We lived in a classic two-story Tudor house, which sat on a half-acre lot with a pool in the back yard and a couple of massive red oak trees in the front.

In grade school days, I became a close friend with Sarah Ann Wellborn, Allan's younger sister. I still count her as a BFF today. Back then, we—occasionally—pretended to be twins. To help us realize our goal, our mothers stitched us matching sundresses in a cutesy flowery print. Unfortunately, many classmates believed we were beyond silly stupid and laughed. Pointing fingers were involved, too.

We all knew things changed, and even though I lost jobs before, I had to shift forward, not be stuck in the past, and embrace the new life adventures thrown at me with a positive mental attitude. I slapped the steering wheel in affirmation.

According to the Internet article I discovered, apparently, Sommerville embraced a new future, too. A developer bought a dilapidated shopping center near my favorite mall and flattened the buildings overnight. An upscale strip center with limestone facades and dark oak doors rose from the concrete crumbs. The owner found success in enticing new businesses to the area.

I drove to the shopping center. Next door to Stan's Haberdashery, I located the boutique, Miss Anastasia's Wedding Wonderland. I berthed my car in a space in front of Wonderland. I smiled as I noted the other stores were putting on the finishing touches for their grand opening as well. Muy exciting! Construction trucks and utility company vehicles filled the alley and street. With brushes in hand, painters perfected doorways and trim. A landscaping company spread mulch and created river-rock borders in flower beds.

Positive note—if the wedding job didn't pan out, I could hit on the men's establishment.

Before I exited the car, I checked out Wedding Wonderland's storefront. Temporarily, brown craft paper partially covered the upper part of the display windows. The name of the salon flowed across the bottom of the pane in fancy, black calligraphy, shadowed with old gold. Beautiful wood and beveled glass french doors secured the entryway. Urn-style cement planters stuffed with velvety purple and white pansies and dark green ivy stood adjacent to the portal and evoked a special-things-to-come aura to the customers who entered.

After closing the car door, I paused. With one last glance, I noted how professionally dressed I looked for the prospective interview in my best Chanel-styled knock-off, a navy-blue wool suit with a white tailored shirt. I fastened to my jacket's left lapel an enameled flower pin once belonging to my grandmother. I'd slipped my feet into dark red kitten heels and slid a matching handbag over my arm. A leather initial "H" dangled from the handbag handles. The fashion mavens declared initials to be the season's hot stuff.

A sizable silk scarf tossed over my shoulders as a dramatic accessory provided warmth in case of an unpredicted chill. The computer bag I carried contained an updated resume for the interview, references—not many considering some of my former employers were dead or didn't have ideal things to report—paper, pen, and an electronic tablet loaded with e-books—all the accoutrements of a hopefully soon-to-be-employed girl.

The store owner would see a five-foot, eight-inch, slender gal with lightly layered, shoulder-length brown hair, highlighted with dark blonde, and brown, friendly eyes. When I checked my slim-fitting skirt, the only flaw I discovered—wrinkles from the seatbelt fastened around my hips. I ironed them flat with my hands.

Optimism buoyed my spirits. I searched for other retail jobs while in tempo limbo, but I desired more than a position scanning merchandise gliding past via a conveyor belt. Nor did I want to organize clothing "just so" on the display racks at the local superstore. Who would be excited about the mess the customers left on the floor in the dressing rooms? Not me. A bridal salon required an employee with extensive retail experience and the person—I squared my shoulders in determination—would be me.

I depressed the latch to Wedding Wonderland's door and pushed, but it didn't budge. *Probably locked.* So, after I tried a second time with no results, I knocked boldly.

About two minutes later, a woman cracked open the door.

Through the slit, I observed a questioning lift shaping her brow.

"Yes?" she asked.

Before she could slam the door in my face, I took a quick breath. "Hi…I'm Hattie Cooks…I saw an advertisement on television about how some of the stores…in this shopping center…want to hire employees…and I wanted to speak with you about…a possible position." I took several deep breaths after spitting out all the information in rapid-fire bursts.

She opened the door wider, clutching a giant screwdriver against her chest.

The woman appeared to be approximately sixty-five. Sturdy navy pumps on her feet lifted her height to nearly mine.

Tilting her gray head, she scanned me from head to toe. "Do you have any retail experience?"

"Plenty," I affirmed with a nod. I set a palm to my heaving chest and took a calming breath. "I worked as an assistant menswear buyer for Tuckers."

"Impressive. Tuckers is a very reputable

establishment." She rubbed a finger over her chin. "However, I don't see how your past employment as a menswear buyer will help me. After all, I *am* a wedding planner, and the store *is* a bridal salon. Do you have any bridal experience?"

"No, ma'am." I shook my head. Her dismissal of my previous employment at Tuckers stung some. Obviously, she forgot retail basics easily transferred from one department to another. "I haven't been one."

Her forehead crimped into a *V*. "Been one?"

The whole conversation perplexed me. "No, ma'am. I haven't been a bride."

"Oh my." She threw back her head and laughed. "I mean, have you *worked* in a bridal salon before?"

*What a silly mistake.* Did I feel brainless! I snorted at the faux pas entre nous. "No, I haven't worked in the wedding industry before now, but I'm a fast learner. Look, I didn't know anything about insurance either, but I did fine." *Kinda. Sorta. In the "not being killed" way.*

Gripping and releasing the screwdriver's handle, she studied me for a minute longer.

While she considered, multiple please-please-pleases swirled through my head. "Please," I nearly begged, "let me come inside so we can talk. You can read my resume. I believe I'm the person you want to hire."

"Then, we should chat." She opened the door all the way.

I entered quietly, unsure of what to expect.

She closed the door and turned the lock behind me. To my unasked question, she lifted the screwdriver. "Security. I spend most days alone in the store. I lock the door and carry something for protection. The whole stranger-danger thing, you know?"

"I get it." I took a few steps farther inside. I roved my gaze to the display fixtures, and then, moved to the barely pink walls glazed with a shimmery hint of silver. Shadows and sparkles from the humongous crystal chandelier flitted across the ceiling to the back area where a raised carpeted platform took center stage. Three of the largest floor-to-ceiling mirrors surrounded the platform area. All looked top-notch.

The store owner swept past, deposited the screwdriver on a table, and indicated two ivory-covered armchairs arranged not far from the front door and next to a French Provincial-style desk adapted into a check-out counter. "Won't you have a seat?"

She extended her right hand. "I apologize for omitting to introduce myself. Anastasia Fernholly, owner of Wedding Wonderland. I prefer to be called Miss A."

Her hand felt plump and warm in my grasp. "Nice to meet you, Miss A."

Miss Anastasia Fernholly, aka Miss A., stood approximately five feet, six inches tall with overly permed, white pin curls. Her body type leaned to a roly-poly kind, sorta like a grandmother. However, extensive business experience filled her round cobalt eyes.

Over powder blue slacks and a crisp white shirt, she wore a lab coat style of jacket also in white with large patch pockets sewn two inches above the hemline. "Miss A" was inscribed in royal blue script below her left shoulder.

*Note to self—blue could be her favorite color.* I sat and retrieved a notebook from my tote.

Miss A. selected a pen from a decorative pencil jar on the desk, then rounded the table and took a seat.

I handed her my resumé.

All quieted as she shoved on a pair of blue marbled bifocals studded with rhinestones, which glittered when she turned her head.

I stayed still as she perused my work history, clamping the urge to explain.

She occasionally paused to peek over the top rim of her glasses. She scribbled notations.

Too much time passed, causing my foot to jiggle. I had to say something. I cleared my throat. "As I said, Tuckers employed me as an assistant buyer for men's sportswear. My responsibilities included inventory control, to track best sellers, spot trends, pricing for sales, and to place orders. I visited stores and, on many occasions, worked the floor, even tagged merchandise in the warehouse. And if need be, hand-delivered the goods to stores."

I paused to gauge how she received the information—all looked good. Her body slightly tilted forward as she listened. "As a department manager, I stocked merchandise quickly, managed staff, set up displays, and processed the inventory. I dress well, and other employers consider me to be highly organized. Those skills will transfer to most retail jobs. I can do what you need and more."

"Hmm." She lowered the paper and shoved her specs to the top of her head, where they nestled in her white cotton curls. "If you were well-suited to the job, why did your employment at Tucker's end?"

Mentally, I paged to my go-to answer. "Reduction of staff due to an economic downturn."

"Hmm." She tapped her cheek. "Tucker's let you go because of cash flow?"

I pressed together my lips. To this day, my heart still ached because I loved the lost job. "Unfortunately, yes."

"Such things do happen." She bobbed her head. "Our economy ebbs and flows."

"Yes, it does. If you want, my boss at Tucker's would be happy to give you a reference." *Because he owes me big time.*

After a while, she pushed her bifocals on her nose and resumed reading. "You've worked several temporary jobs. Nor were you employed with them for very long."

"True." Honesty—the best policy. Explaining my weird work history felt strange, even to me. "In a town the size of Sommerville, finding the perfect retail job has been…a challenge. In the interim, I asked a friend to place me in temporary jobs. She deemed the additional experience would be beneficial. More opportunities would open up, and I might acquire more skills."

Boy, I sounded super good. However, the need for mucho dinero drove my mouth.

"I like what I see here," Miss A. mused, quirking one side of her cheek while she scratched notations on the paper. "You have good experience, great deportment, and a nice disposition. You sound intelligent. You're—"

I gripped my pencil tighter. *Come on. Come on.*

"—hired."

*Yippee!!* Immense relief swept through my body. The heavy "unemployed with serious deficit load" I carried vanished in the wind. "Really?"

With a broad smile, she nodded.

My entire being grew lighter than a feather. "Thank you, Miss A. You won't have any regrets."

"You're welcome. I believe in you."

Her genial smile caused me to feel accepted, too.

"However, I cannot pay a lot. Not until we reach specific significant sales—which we will. I'm determined to be a success—at all costs. You see, I'm old-fashioned about marriage, and I believe in true happy ever after."

The hourly wage Miss A. mentioned sounded standard for the times and desirable over nothing. I could cinch my budget tighter and make do for a while.

We chatted a little longer to get to know one another better. Miss A. explained she lived elsewhere, until recently, when she decided to relocate to Sommerville, a familiar stomping ground from younger days. She revealed her prior retail experience in women's clothing, and after working in a wedding salon in the Northwest, she desired to open a store of her own.

"Good news," I said. "I have a potential customer."

Miss A raised her brow. "You're a fast worker."

"My sister." I nodded, happy to share. "Her 'I Do' day is months away. And she needs major help."

"Excellent. I look forward to meeting her. An influential couple has an appointment in the store in a few days to plan their wedding, too."

"Influential couple" caused an image of Jonson Leggett the Third and Barbie Fenster to pop in my head. Silently, I prayed "anyone but him."

Miss A. shifted forward to set aside my paperwork

on an adjacent table. With a tug, she adjusted her jacket placket into place. "Now, if you don't mind, I suggest—for the store's purposes—we call you Miss Hattie."

*Weird. Me being called Miss Hattie sounded weird, like* what-I-called-my-Sunday-School-teachers *weird.* I twerked my mouth sideways. Didn't matter. If "Miss Hattie" was my store name, "Miss Hattie" it would be. My main goal, other than pleasing her, was to keep the job; so, naturally, I would agree to most anything— within reason. Like knifing and maiming wouldn't be a part of the job, except in self-defense, which shouldn't be a problem in a wedding salon. "Of course."

"Excellent. You have plenty of expertise which will easily transfer to my line of business," Miss A. said. "I can teach you about the wedding industry. You appear eager to learn."

Confidence swelled in my chest, nearly busting my shirt's buttons. "I am."

"So, how about starting tomorrow? The store opens at ten in the morning and closes at six in the evening, except for Thursday and Friday when we close at nine. We aren't open on Mondays either, except for now while we stock the store. If you could arrive a bit before ten tomorrow—perfect."

"I'd be happy to."

"Wonderful." Miss A. stood and, with a wave of her hand, indicated the way to the front door.

When I arrived at the door, I set my hand on the handle and paused. One question plagued me about the opportunity. "By the way, Miss A—"

"Yes, dearie?"

"Does Wedding Wonderland sell invitations?"

"But of course." She patted my shoulder in a grandmotherly fashion. "I have contracted a specific printing company to work with."

An "uh-oh" sensation sank to my feet.

"Everything is done on-line. You'll learn the ins and outs."

Based on my not-so-good past job at Button and Bows Stationery Company, I felt duty-bound to bone up on my proofreading skills. I couldn't lose another job because of misspelled names similar to female body parts.

Chapter Three

At my recent birthday bash held at my parents' house, I introduced my sister, Tracey, to her fiancé, Stuart Steems. I watched love blossom at first bite.

Sitting off to one side at a table covered in a red-checkered tablecloth, Stuart munched on chips, which he liberally dunked in Mom's tasty cream cheese picante dip. In an admirable way, he maneuvered a whole triangular chip in his mouth without any mishaps.

Stuart worked at Northside, Lancaster, & Brookside Accountants as a senior Audit manager. He interviewed me for the temporary administrative assistant's job for the firm's managing partner. Near the end of the interview, he invited himself to accompany me to my birthday party.

I didn't want to take him based on his geeky look plus his "interesting" social skills; however, despite his excessive begging, I followed a page from one of Mom's lengthy lectures on "politeness" and succumbed to his puppy dog expression. I did outline dating boundaries.

He stood a little less than six feet with spikey short black hair, startling blue eyes, and wore rectangular, wire-framed glasses in black he purchased specifically for the occasion.

Sister Tracey, who dressed like the artsy type and

also was employed as an accountant, rolled in more savings than moi. At every opportunity, Mom sang lofty praises about her youngest daughter's career choice, which caused me sometimes to feel less than adequate, non-intelligent, dumb.

Luckily, Tracey would be well-prepared to care for our mother in her advanced dotage.

Tracey had zeroed in on Stuart seated across the patio, calmly eating and drinking. "Who is the gorgeous hunk?"

Her scream pierced my eardrum. I pursed my mouth and wondered if her babbling referred to someone else. I thought, *oh no, missy.* Any hunk at my birthday party belonged to me—not her. *Me.* After many pointing fingers, I determined "the hunk" was Stuart who'd caught her fancy.

*Can anyone spell relief?*

A tiny part of me held sympathy for my sissie. Tracey didn't connect with men easily. She lacked confidence. I implemented some of my wily moves— read skillful manipulation—and introduced them. They've been inseparable ever since.

Subsequently, Stuart's wardrobe improved immensely when he began dating Tracey, thanks to expert fashion advice from me via her.

*Ta-daaa.* A curtsy would be in order.

A record speed-breaking courtship ensued. While on his death bed after an unfortunate incident where our NLB colleague, Cathy Bartholomew—aka the Blonde Bimbo—shoved him down the stairwell, Stuart asked Tracey to marry him.

I was shocked, but I wasn't the only one.

When told about the prospective union, Mother

acted more than floored, like "required-a-pitcher-of-martinis" floored, but she recovered instantly and plunged into the BIG plans up to her elbows. After all, mothers wanted to see their offspring happily married ever after. No take-backs. And my mom wanted to make sure the fête would be the ultimate in perfection, worthy of a two-page newspaper spread in the society section of the *Sommerville Express*. The gossip tongues would wag for decades.

Flipping my blinker, I steered onto Boston Avenue, took a quick right on a side street, and continued. Tracey's and Stuart's imminent nuptials took the pressure off me. Mom didn't have enough hobbies like World Peace or Save the Whales to keep her busy. Distracting her shifted all focus off my back to match me with Allan Wellborn. She focused on her youngest daughter.

Truthfully, Tracey and Stuart compiled a lot of questionable ideas for their "I Do's" and needed a professional other than Mom to corral them. Miss A. would be a huge help in this department.

I slowed my Jeep at the stoplight, studying the cars to my left and right while waiting for the light to switch back to green. Because of Stuart's ballroom dancing hobby, the couple wanted the wedding party, along with a few select friends, to take dance lessons, specifically to perform the tango during the reception—sorta like a Fred Astaire and Ginger Rogers floor show. Except for one thing—Tracey didn't tango. In actuality, none of us did, apart from Stuart. Everyone agreed—very, very reluctantly—to their wishes for the special day. If we looked silly, we did so in a group where everyone looked silly.

I dreaded tonight's activity.

This evening marked our first lesson, which took place at the studio where Stuart and his regular partner—his mother—practiced. Locating the studio, I parked my Jeep and flew across the parking lot, flung open the door, and oriented myself. Most of us had shown on time and ventured into the rehearsal room, where we shuffled into a semi-circle to face the instructor, Ms. Yolanda.

Ginormous mirrors lined the walls. The mirror ball fixture sparkled. Our footsteps on the hardwood floors squeaked.

Ms. Yolanda dressed in a long silky caftan worn over black leggings. Her ebony hair was highlighted with one thick white streak originating at her widow's peak.

Stuart presented his teacher, and in turn, he introduced each of us to explain our role in the wedding. As sister to the bride, I was designated Maid-of-Honor by default.

After the introductions, Ms. Yolanda shifted us into two lines—girls on one side and boys on the other—to pair us with a partner.

For today's lesson," she said in a sing-song voice, "don't worry about who is matched with whom. Since the girls' line is longer, you at the end"—she pointed my way—"are left without someone. Doesn't matter. All will work out."

"No worries, Hattie." Stuart threw an arm across my shoulders and squeezed. "He'll be here shortly."

*He?* I stared. *Who the heck is* he? Probably some nerdy accountant co-worker. *Rats.* I would forever be doomed to spend my life with geeks and dweebs.

Stuart flicked a wave and abandoned me to join my sister.

I wished not having a partner gave me an excuse to leave, but I didn't. My sister's future happiness depended on her big day being perfect. From behind me, the entry door banged, and with quick steps, somebody approached.

Everyone swiveled to see the new arrival.

Allan Wellborn. My mouth crooked aside. Not much of a surprise. But my heart did beat faster.

"Come in. Come in." Ms. Yolanda's hands beckoned him forward, a large toothy smile shaped her mouth. "Your partner is the pretty girl." Her directing finger indicated…me.

Snickers emanated from the various quadrants of the room.

I rolled my eyes. I should have known Allan was asked to dance. I didn't bother to glare Stuart's or Tracey's way. Even though preparing and interviewing for the new job exhausted me, I wasn't dense. Me thinketh someone deemed it funny-eth to play matchmaker.

Miss Yolanda guided Allan in the space opposite me. "Such a handsome young man," she gushed while patting his lapels. "So glad you could join us. We'll have you performing the tango in three easy steps."

*Do three easy steps mean one easy lesson?*

After Allan tossed his sport coat on a chair, he turned his gaze toward me and stepped on his spot. He grinned.

His sleek smile sparked the attractive sparkle in his eyes and possessed the ability to drive me crazy. Leaning slightly back, I located my sister and scrunched my brow. I couldn't smack her since she stood conveniently out of boxing range. I cupped the side of my face and mouthed, *"What the hell are you doing?"*

Tracey experienced this question lots of times. Ever since her toddler years, the things she did made our family wonder "what the hell she was doing."

She shrugged, ignored me, and pivoted to whisper in Stuart's ear. Their shoulders bobbed as they giggled.

I stored one itty bitty word, one tiny thought for her—*later*. Later, I would make her pay, just like I did when we were kids, and I solemnly convinced her the mud-covered ants she'd eaten were real chocolate-coated treats.

I should have taken her allowance, too.

With a sigh reaching all corners of my body, I stared at Allan. A crinkle of his nose mimicked the fun exchange between Nick and Nora Charles from *The Thin Man* movies. I loved the films and the characters' banter.

But he knew that.

If I wasn't so pissed, I might have laughed and scrunched my nose in return. Instead, I turned my attention to the toes of my shoes. I hadn't spoken to Allan since our "door encounter" when neither of us got lucky. Through my lashes, I stole a look and grasped what I missed. Simply said, he was too big to ignore. Seventy-three inches and one hundred ninety pounds of lean—not mean—gorgeous man. My fingers itched to shove through his crisp, dark brown hair. I balled my hands. His eyes were the color of chocolate, my favorite food group. His towering size alone commanded attention. The bad guys he arrested were

30

intimidated.

Besides, if Mom found out I was rude to her favorite project, she would have lectured me with the "Wouldn't Be Polite" discourse. A long speech, one dispensed many times, usually about him.

"Hi, Hattie," he said. "Long time no see."

I looked his way. Obviously, he scored nicer on the meter than me. I couldn't classify "seeing me a day ago" as a "long time." "Hmm."

"You look spiffy today. New outfit?"

*Spiffy?* Spiffy was not a guy word. I wore my interview clothes, nothing special for dancing.

He scrubbed his palms as his gaze roved the studio. "Here we are. The tango in three easy steps."

From my throat came an unladylike sound.

"Not buying it? You don't believe—what's the teacher's name again? Miss—"

My grunt sounded more like a laugh. "Miss Yolanda, stupid."

He shook a finger in front of my nose. "Your mother wouldn't like you calling anyone stupid."

Ha. I knocked away his finger. "Neither would yours—"

Ms. Yolanda clapped for our attention. My friends and I rotated her way. "Class," she said. "You need to get used to the movement and rhythm. Girls, place your hands on your partners' shoulders, and gentlemen, place your hands on the girls' waists. Perfect you two tall people at the end. Beautiful."

Quite possibly, her reference to "tall people" meant Allan and me. I certainly didn't feel "perfect" nor "beautiful." I *did* feel annoyed, like roughed and irritated.

31

I was all too aware of his hands when they circled my waist; I did feel squirmy with the profound nearness of him. The man-heat his body emanated my way made me want to fan my face. I swallowed deeply. *Lordy.* Dancing with him? *Sexy.*

Recognizable tango music commenced. *Daaa dum dum dum dummm, dadada dada, dum da dumdum, da dada, dum da dum dum.* The class followed Ms. Yolanda's lead. Allan and I stepped to his right and whipped to the left. Over and over, we familiarized ourselves with the sequence so it would become second nature.

My fingertips tingled with a hyper-awareness of Allan's muscular arms and smooth movements. Without a doubt, he lifted weights and ran every day. In middle school, his mother enrolled his sister and him in deportment classes, which included dance lessons. Based on his past, quite possibly, Allan was already familiar with the tango. Two beats later, he stepped on my toes—*er, maybe he wasn't.*

Surprisingly, Mom hadn't forced me to attend the classes. The mystery of how I avoided the torture sessions would go to Mom's grave. The best of friends, my mother and Mrs. Wellborn agreed on everything. I had, however, attended classes in Teen Scene where young ladies learned how to apply deodorant, clean their combs and brushes, pluck their eyebrows into perfect arches, and walk with a book balanced on their heads.

A while back at an engagement party, I danced with Allan, and at the time, my body melted into a puddle. He scraped me off the floor and took me to his place for a memorable evening where both of us believed—wanted—we'd have almost wild, almost sex. Only de rien happened because his cellphone interrupted, which left quite an unfavorable impression.

When I checked on him, I found a pensive look pinned on me.

"You okay?" he asked.

To preserve my sanity, I would answer just enough to get by. My defense mechanism would keep him at arm's length. "Yep."

He and I maneuvered through a set of steps. "So," he said. "Stuart and Tracey are taking their vows."

"Yep."

"The wedding party is here to learn a dance for the big day."

"Yep."

He tilted his head. "Are you talking to me?"

I coupled my hand with his. I felt my palm grow sweaty. "Yep."

He sighed. "Hard to converse with someone when the someone only speaks one word at a time."

I firmed my lips. I summoned everything I possessed not to laugh.

I concentrated on the instructions. My foot slipped wrongly, and I screwed up our turn. My shoulder bumped Allan's left shoulder, the one where Blonde Bimbo shot him.

Instantly, his right hand massaged the spot.

Horrified with what I'd done, I took a few steps back and slapped my hands to my cheeks. *Stupid.* He might still be in pain. *Stupid-stupid-stupid.* "I'm so-so-so sorry, Allan. God, I'm so clumsy. I didn't mean to bump your owie. Did I hurt you? Do you need anything?" As I lightly fingered his shirt sleeve, my hand trembled.

"Hattie, I'm fine," he said low and slow, his right hand captured mine and brought it to his chest. "No worries. Everything has healed. Just a small scar."

His heart beat a steady rhythm against my palm. I didn't remember a small scar. I remembered a large puckered hole leaking scarlet. My eyes filled with hot tears, and I shifted my gaze to the studio window. I blinked and brushed my cheeks.

His finger turned my chin to face him. "Are you okay?"

I nodded "yes," but truth be told, anxiety had buried in my soul over how Blonde Bimbo shot him and the responsibility I encompassed because of his injury. When the Bimbo finally comprehended Allan cared more about me than her, which didn't jibe with her game plan to reel him to the altar hook-line-and-sinker, she hatched a new strategy—no one would get him. She also stole my undies, poisoned two co-workers, and shoved Stuart down a flight of stairs, almost killing him.

When someone I cared about hurt, I hurt. Maybe my emotions had taken over. Maybe I should be healing better than this.

Guys tended not to express emotions and the ilk out loud. Most of the news I acquired filtered through the Mothers Always Know Network.

I shook my head to purge the emotional trauma which swirled in my brain. Directing my attention on the divot at the base of his neck, I leveled my shoulders and returned my hands to the designated spots for coupling with my partner. "Let's try again."

Allan and I repeated the steps Ms. Yolanda taught

us. Something coalesced in my head and transitioned to what he said a few seconds earlier. He commented about the wedding party learning the dance—

*Wedding party?* I stiffened. Wait a freakin' minute. Was Allan an official member of THE wedding party? *Who voted for that?*

The idea never occurred to me Allan would be asked to participate in the wedding party. Neither Tracey nor Stuart had said anything, which surprised me as Tracey was terrible at keeping secrets. I grouped Allan as a friend of the bride's family. That friend sat in a pew on the designated bride's side with his parents. Not as a groomsman.

Abruptly, I halted. I raised my index finger. "Hold on a sec. I need some clarification." I rubbed the length of my nose. "You're in the wedding party?"

"I am."

"You are?"

"I am."

"You might be mistaken. I helped with the guest list. I'm pretty sure you're classified as a friend of the family."

"I am, but like all good things, they changed. I'm"—he puffed his chest slightly when his shoulders drew back—"the best man."

"You're what?" My explosive query drew unwanted attention from the rest of the dancing group who stopped and looked our way. I shook my head to deny his statement. "You can't be the best man. No way. My mom or my sister would have told me. You don't even know Stuart. Not his best friend. Not family. Not a co-worker."

Allan regripped my hand. "Tracey suggested Stuart

ask me. We've raised a few beers since. He may be geeky, but he's a nice guy and truly loves your sister. Besides, your cousin's husband from Bayston is a groomsman—"

"Nice try, Sherlock. He's related through marriage."

"If he can be one, I can be the best man."

"You're a family friend—a huge difference."

Taking my hands, he guided us to his right. "You're beating a dead horse here. What's your point?"

I crinkled my nose. "A friend is not family." *Touché and grasping at straws.*

"Sometimes, friends can be."

I stared hard.

"You've been my sister's best friend since grade school," he said. *"As you well know, my parents and yours are good friends. Just. Like. Family."*

His explanation speared me like a sword. My head conjured images of our mothers at Super Saver Grocery store where they exchanged gossip over parsnips via the Mothers Always Know Network. *Our families are close. Sometimes, too close.*

"Doesn't matter," Allan said. "He asked, and I said yes. Simple. Stuart doesn't have many men friends. I'm honored to be a part of the wedding. He said I took a bullet for him." He bent closer. "Besides, I have an ulterior motive—as best man, I get to be near you, the maid of honor. Thrilled?"

I bit into my lip. "Best man…for real?"

"Best man," he whispered.

Allan's breath brushed my ear. Shivers skated along my spine. Fluttery sensations made me feel off balance.

"For real," he said.

Secretly, I did like him. However, I alternated between wanting to wring my hands or savoring every inch of my body against his—-torture without the torture rack.

Suddenly, all became clearer. Every little thing revealed. They—my friends and family and my soon-to-be brother-in-law—hatched a scheme, a master plot, behind my back to match Allan with me. A Conspiracy Theory.

I gritted my teeth. *God,* I wished I was devious enough to pull together my own "get even" plan.

*I know. I could quit.* Quit my sister's wedding. Chuck the whole enchilada.

But not participating could never be an option. Mother would be…aghast. Tracey would be distraught.

I couldn't get ejected from the wedding unless on my deathbed, and even after my body was embalmed, Mom would stuff me in the pre-selected bridesmaid's dress fashioned from silk in Tracey's favorite color and complemented my skin tone. Utilizing a furniture dolly, Mom would wheel me into the designated spot by the altar railing. I would be propped upright in a ghoulish way, and not one guest would discern any difference.

With a flip of my fingers, I said, "As they say—"

He pulled us tummy to tummy. "Takes two to tango."

I set my hand on his chest and thrust him about four inches. "Y-yes."

"Lovely, couple at the end." Ms. Yolanda flicked her long tail over her shoulder. "Now, best man, step to your right. Perfect. Seize her with fiery intent, lunge, and drape her over your thigh."

Before I could protest, I sensed Allan take charge with "fiery intent" and sweep my body across his bent left leg. I fastened on him my unparalleled evil eye glare and received the "got you, babe" one back.

I would show him.

I would show them all.

I played along by fluttering my eyelids shut, and in slow, tiny increments, I lifted my left arm in a delicate ballet arc over my head. My fingernails barely teased the floor.

Ms. Yolanda clapped. "Wonderful! Wonderful! Class, come over, and let's study their lines."

Occasionally, rebellion created problems. Opening my eyes, I wanted to stand, but Allan held me in the position.

Stuart bounded to my side. "Hattie. Allan. You're naturals."

I rolled my eyes. *Great. I passed the tango test.* Allan chuckled.

I stayed in position for what seemed like hours but most likely were five loonnng minutes. My lower back spasmed, which caused me to grimace. Allan pulled ever-so-gently and restored me to my feet. I removed my hands from his. Moisture coated my palms, and sweat dripped down my back along my spine. I was a wreck.

"Thank you so much, couple." A beaming Ms. Yolanda rotated. "I'm impressed by your length and beauty."

*Length and beauty*—my ass.

"Let's regroup here tomorrow, shall we?"

I walked to the chair where I'd dumped my black trench coat and crammed an arm in one sleeve. From the corner of my eye, I noticed Allan drawing nearer. *Won't he ever get the message and leave me alone?*

*Not likely.* I stuck my other arm in the second sleeve. *And wouldn't if I couldn't sort out my affections for him.*

He faced me, his fingers grasped my lapels and jerked them into place.

I looped the belt tight.

"Wanna go for a drink?"

Did I hear optimism in his question? I batted his hands and shoved my handbag on my arm. "Can't."

"Can't?" He lifted one eyebrow. "Or won't?"

I sighed. "Can't. C-A-N apostrophe T."

After the longest studious look on record, he said, "Chick-en."

"Not hardly."

"So, go."

"As I said, I can't."

"Okay. How about we go play with Lucky?"

Lucky—the large gray cat he'd rescued and the one I babysat occasionally. "Still can't—"

"Can't. Brock-brock-brock-brock."

I didn't take his bait. With a smile, I tucked my handbag handle into the crook of my arm.

He slung his coat over his shoulder.

"Believe what you want. The bald truth is I have to go to bed early because I start a new job tomorrow."

"Another new job? How many have you had?" His gaze circled to the ceiling, followed by a shake of his head. "Will you burn the place down?"

I pinned my best slitty eye look on him. "As much fun as your idea sounds, I won't do it…deliberately. Or maybe I will. Who knows? A cute fireman riding to the rescue would be fun."

Allan lifted the right side of his mouth. "I'll notify the fire department."

I gritted my teeth. *Why does he always infuriate me?* "Aren't you Mr. Helpful?"

"Can be. I possess many talents. Moves you've never seen."

I shoved his arm, then skirted him and all his helpfulness, talents, and "moves," and headed to the exit.

He fell in line next to me. "Where's your new job?"

I snorted. "As if you care."

Allan pulled open the door. "Hey, I care."

"If you must know, Miss Anastasia's Wedding Wonderland." I passed through the exit. "The newly revitalized strip center across from the mall. Don't feel compelled to visit."

"Brrr." He shimmied his shoulders. The door shut behind us. "Bound to be an icy reception." He shrugged on his jacket.

Once outside, I paused to study the sky. The moon—a bare sliver of a golden bowl in the inky blue-blackness.

"Sweetheart, instead of star-gazing, you should keep your eyes peeled and make sure the walk to your car is safe."

*Yadayadayada.* Safety always first with this man. I pursed my lips. I would put sex first. Or chocolate like the three-pounder of chocolate-covered peanut-y treats he gave me for my birthday.

I didn't comment—because, *well, why?*—and strolled toward my Jeep. I climbed in and started the engine. When I looked at the studio, I found the overhead light illuminated Allan still in place. His hands fastened on his hips. I fluttered my fingers and shifted into gear.

He shook his head and walked to his truck.

*Tracey's wedding is gonna be the death of me.*

Chapter Four

I woke the next morning, reflecting on the night before. I had informed the Funsisters about my new position at Wedding Wonderland, and my girlfriends and I rejoiced over the most excellent news. Mostly, Trixie acted the most ecstatic. Visible relief glowed on her face. She helped me find jobs and wasn't keen on helping me find others. After three strikes, she lost her loving feeling.

"Hattie." Tracey snagged my sleeve. "Since I *am* your beloved sissie, and you *are* my maid of honor, could you use your employee discount to buy my dress and accessories? Pretty please?"

I hadn't been on the clock for long, and my sister took advantage of me. "Um, I'll need to check on the store policy first."

She nodded. "You do that. You know how Stuart's all about saving for his, soon-to-be *our*, 401K."

*Oh boy.* Stuart's interesting hobbies—ballroom dancing and financial investing.

"Told Allan?" Jenny cruised by and lobbed her question over her shoulder.

"What?"

"About the job."

"Why should I?"

She walked backward, shrugging. "Maybe Allan would like to know."

He would love to bug me.

****

After a shower, I dressed carefully. I waffled about the perfect outfit to wear and had nearly been late. I didn't think jeans would be appropriate clothing for the store. I settled on black slacks, a nice T-shirt, and tossed over my shoulders a pale gray sweater embroidered with flowers and beads in a variety of colors.

I arrived a squish before ten A.M. for my first day at Miss Anastasia's Wedding Wonderland. Miss A. opened the door at my knock. I greeted her cheerfully as I entered the store. Since my interview, many nouveau things took place overnight. I circled about to study what Miss A. accomplished. She transformed the store into the ultimate in wedding wonderland. Stunning, like a magic fairy swept her wand and beauty abounded.

"Miss A., the store is…exquisite," I couldn't help but say. "Removing the paper from the windows and the dust covers brought in a light which enhances the understated silvery swirl in the carpet and on the walls. Well done, you."

A happy countenance captured Miss A.'s face. "Thank you, Hattie. I worked late last night. I became totally immersed and couldn't stop. The store is coming together, and I'm pleased with the results."

How enthusiastic she sounded. Her white-enameled smile and her about-to-bust-a-button demeanor broadcasted her excitement. I said, "I should have brought you a cup of coffee."

"I have an empty pot in my office. I feel like I'm running on jet fuel."

*Hmm.* Probably not the jet fuel from high school days. I was familiar with a concoction of a powdered drink mix and grain alcohol. I doubted Miss A. ever imbibed anything like that. "Did you get any sleep?"

"A little. In the office. I couldn't help myself. My eyes shut on their own. My forehead dropped to my desk. I think I drooled." She threw back her shoulders and bobbed her head from side to side. The kinks in her back let loose with a pop-pop-pop. "Itching to get to work?"

I clapped my hands and bounced on my toes. "I am. I am."

"Let's get to it."

My journey began at the check-out desk. I trailed a finger over the pecan-stained wood. A brand-spanking-new monitor and laptop sat on top. The matching credenza was positioned along the wall behind the desk with a printer, the ready light glowing green. Comfy cushioned armchairs created two waiting areas to the left and right of the reception area. Glass-covered tables sat between the chairs. Floral arrangements featuring my favorite flower, stargazer lilies, along with other colorful blossoms, were artfully assembled in cut-glass vases.

Throughout the space, chrome-and-acrylic shelf units lined the walls. A mixture of stand-up advertisements featured local suppliers like makeup artists and hairdressers. Jewelry, gloves, shoes, and other accessories filled some of the shelves. Framed portraits of beautiful brides posed in their finery adorned the walls.

Only an idiot couldn't find anything to purchase in here.

I proceeded to the staging area and sat on the built-in banquette. I floated my hand over the softness of the dark blue velvet upholstery. Blue carpet covered the raised platform and the rest of the store. I noted my reflection in the mirrors, which she polished streak-free. Miss A. placed additional silk arrangements on pedestals positioned next to the end mirrors. As far as my experienced eye could tell, she skimped on nothing for the store.

I rested my head against the tufted seat back and clasped my hands to my breastbone. "I can't wait to see brides modeling their dresses and family and friends celebrating with them. What a joyous occasion. Will we hold a grand opening? Serve champagne and chocolates?"

"I love your party ideas," Miss A. said. "Any recommendations?"

"One favorite chocolate is made locally and a tiny bit expensive, but I believe they make mini versions. Perhaps, we could cut a deal with the store and fill trays with individually wrapped ones. As for the champagne…maybe we could consult with a liquor store, and if we order regularly, we probably can negotiate a discount."

Miss A. scribbled on a notepad. "Another good idea. I'll add small bottles of water and paper napkins printed with our store name." She looked up. "Anything else?"

"Sparkling apple cider is festive. Add a slice of lemon and orange with a splash of ginger ale—party time!"

"I like where you're headed, but no red wine." She tossed her head.

"I agree. Red wine makes for a nasty mess." With a wince, I sympathized. The thought of the undesirable stains on gowns and carpet—*ick. I am happy she likes my ideas. I sure hope I have others stockpiled.* "Let's do champagne and water only. Keeps things simple."

"I had a fabric protectant sprayed everywhere; however, if a discoloration sits, it could be difficult to remove," Miss A. said.

"Helpful Hanna's Home Advice column addressed the topic in last week's *Sommerville Express*. What did she say?" I snapped my fingers. "I remember. Blot. Dilute with water. Blot. Top with a baking soda paste."

Miss A. bobbed her head. "I'll check into the remedy just in case because you can never say never."

"Add cake. Every festive occasion has cake. Your bakery vendors can supply petit fours. They're miniature cakes."

"Cake is a good thing." She scrubbed her palms. "You have perfect ideas, Hattie. I believe we're off to a great start."

Across from the reception area, she had heavy-duty six-foot-high rods hung from the walls for the bride's, bridesmaid's, mother's, mother-in-law's, and other attendants' gowns. Behind the mirrored platform, two large dressing rooms with wide doors were built. To the left of the platform area stood a storage room-slash-office for Miss A.

Not a huge shop, but she had covered almost everything related to weddings. And if the business grew as she hoped and more space might be needed down the road, footage could be rented from the vacant retail unit sandwiched between Wedding Wonderland and the men's store.

Miss A. peered through the reading glasses balanced on the tip of her nose. "Shall we talk about the computer program?"

I picked up my tablet for notetaking. "Absolutely."

I situated myself in front of the computer. Miss A. pulled a chair next to me. She explained how the latest in technology had infiltrated the wedding industry. She purchased special software containing a step-by-step program necessary to plan the big event from months out to zero hour, organized through a calendar with the specified time frame for each bride to order invitations, schedule fittings, flowers, etc.

Every morning, a prompt appeared on Wedding Wonderland's computer with brides' names and their respective notifications. The bride could log-in and use her account to access the information, too. I could check the program first thing in the morning to see which brides needed to do what and remind them by email or text in case they forgot to look at their account. All appeared simple, mostly data entry, and the computer took over. *Not tough.*

Miss A. and I reviewed what seemed like the whole shebang. Dividing the duties, we decided most of her responsibilities would focus on the planning and gown selection, especially with fitting.

She tapped the computer. "Are you comfortable with the software, Hattie?"

"I can do the data entry—no problem. My experience from my days at Tucker's will be helpful. I want to play around with the program for a while, but over time, I'll be fine." Tonight, I could review the voluminous notes I'd taken.

Later, Miss A. shoved aside the mouse, her glasses

to the top of her head, and tucked a white curl behind her ear. She stood, and, with her palm along her spine, she stretched her back. "You look exhausted, dearie. I know I am. A change of scenery will do us good. Go. Eat lunch. Come back in an hour or so."

"I'm hungry. I'm starving." Wedding brain dead, I came to my feet. I rummaged through the credenza, where I stored my handbag in a locked drawer. "Do you want me to grab a sandwich for you?"

"No, thank you, dearie." Miss A. tousled her short hair. "I need to run errands. I seem to have misplaced the hammer and must hang some pictures—which reminds me. I want to purchase picture hooks for large frames. Start a list for me, please." She rustled a sticky notepad from the drawer.

I scrambled for a pencil tucked in a pen jar.

"Take your time."

"Sorry." *Miss A. is gracious. Not a mean bone in her body. The kind of employer I admired. Works hard. Considerate. Educated.* I scribbled "hammer" and "picture hooks."

"Anything else?" I asked.

"I don't think so. Maybe if I carry the note, something will come to mind. Have a nice lunch, dearie."

After saying "bye," I exited the store and hopped in my ride. I drove to my favorite fast food joint, where I grabbed a chicken Caesar salad and diet soda. I parked the car and killed the engine. I took a long slug of my drink, so long, nearly half disappeared. I let the back of my head drop against the headrest and closed my eyes. The buzz from my phone caught my ear, making me snap upright. A check of my watch told me I napped roughly fifteen minutes.

"H-Hello?"

"Hey," Jenny said. "How's the first day?"

*She sounds way too cheerful.* I drank a small swallow, then squeezed dressing on the salad. I stirred my fork through the lettuce for a more even coating. "I've never been so tired, not even at Tucker's when we opened new stores," I said in between chomps. "Am eating lunch now."

"I hear."

I paused mid-crunch. "Sorry."

"Working late?"

"Don't know. Why?"

"I'm not surprised you dis-remembered. Tango lesson number twoooo. Ring a bell?"

*Crap.* I'd forgotten. Another torture session.

The previous night's dance resurfaced, and through only God knew how, merged with the wedding salon and the dream I'd had. Dressed in a lacey, V-neck confection, which billowed at my ankles, I swayed in time with the music. At first, the man's image eluded me, but even in my imaginings, I sensed him to be Allan.

"Hattttiiieee???"

*Jenny.* I sucked the rest of my drink to the ice crumbles. "You don't have to yell."

"You vanished."

"I heard you."

"Are you coming? You'll be with...your favorite...partner. Again."

Jenny's singing dialogue maddened me. "Don't remind me."

I crisscrossed the fork through the romaine and

parmesan shavings for hidden chicken and crouton bits. Some bacon would have rounded out the salad nicely because everything food-related tasted better with bacon.

"I have four words for you—"

*I can't wait to hear this.* "That would be?"

"It's. Only. A. Dance. Moron."

*Huh.* Not every day a BFF called her BFF a moron. "Five words. Your counting is off."

She hung up.

I mouthed *moron* at the screen because, well, just because, and tossed the phone to the passenger seat where it landed next to my handbag. Closing the takeaway lid, I set the container on the floorboard and started the car.

*Lordy.* Tango lessons. *What's a girl to do?*

****

Back at the shop, Miss A. and I unpacked bridal gowns from exceedingly big white boxes we removed from larger cardboard shipping boxes. She lightly steamed the dresses, and when finished, I suspended the garment on a padded hanger. The dresses were encased in clear plastic garment bags and then were hung on the rods.

"I order each style from the manufacturer in a size ten," Miss A. explained. "We use these." She showed me two-inch binder clips, the black kind sold at office supply stores. "The bride tries on her dress to see if the style suits, and if need be, we can adjust for fit with the clips. We order other sizes from the manufacturer, which is why a shipment can take so long. Or alter."

"I see." I rubbed my chin. "Do we have an in-house alteration staff?"

"Not yet." She shook a no. "That is, not a permanent one. I found someone local who does alterations and is available to work with us. We'll test her before making her permanent."

"Sounds good."

By six, exhaustion ruled. "We've hung about half the gowns," Miss A. said. "Tomorrow, I will provide a white jacket embroidered with your name which will identify you as Wedding Wonderland staff. What is your favorite color, dearie?"

"Light pink."

She squeezed her brows. "Do you think light pink lettering would be hard to read? Would dark pink be more visible?"

I guessed the store didn't have a hard and fast signature color, and I truly appreciated her asking my preference. "What about fuchsia? Or hot pink? Shrimp? Flamingo?"

Miss A.'s laugh tinkled. "Very well, your name on the jacket will be embroidered in a readable shade of pink. And tomorrow, we can hang the bridesmaids' and flower girls' gowns."

*Oh, God, my shoulders ached.* I overlapped my arms and massaged my biceps. Lifting eight to ten pounds over and over made them throb. "No need to go home and lift weights."

"I agree. Some dresses are heavy due to the decorative goodies, like beading and crystals. You will be relieved to know we won't carry very many mother-of-the-bride and little girl ones. Those can be ordered from a catalog and modified after arrival—thank God."

Miss A. retrieved her belongings from her office. I pulled my handbag from the credenza. After she secured the premises for the day, I walked to my car. I couldn't wait to get settled at my apartment and trade my shoes for comfy ones or none at all.

She paused in the parking lot. "We need to plan more of the opening day festivities."

"That'll be fun."

"Any more ideas?"

In front of my Jeep, I paused and leaned against the front bumper and slipped off my shoe so I could rub my toes. "A basket of trinkets for giveaways. The drinks, cakes, and chocolates we talked about earlier. Perhaps, some postcards with discounts."

"I like your suggestions"—Miss A. stroked the Jeep's fender—"and your style, dearie. A very cool ride."

"I love my fun car. My mother believed a four-door sedan more sensible, but I rebelled, and I'm glad I did. I love my baby." After slipping on my low-heeled flat, I clicked open the lock and looked over my shoulder. "See you tomorrow, Miss A."

"Hattie."

I straightened with my foot propped on the running board. "Yes, ma'am?"

"I'm so grateful you interviewed." She stepped closer and embraced me.

Her powdery rose scent teased my nose.

"I don't know what I would do without you."

*How nice to be liked and valued for my contribution—for once.* I smiled. "My pleasure."

\*\*\*\*

I could hardly concentrate on the drive to mi casa. Drained. Ravenous. Weak. Overjoyed with Miss. A.'s compliment.

"Honey," I drawled as I opened the apartment door. "I'm home."

Jenny popped out of her room. "You look awful."

"I strive to please." I tossed my handbag on the sofa and pointed to my bathroom. "You can find me in the tub. Covered in bubbles."

"Seriously?" she asked with a huff. Her hands hit her hips. "We have to leave in thirty minutes for Dancing with the Wedding Party lessons, my friend."

My head went from side to side. "Not just a no, but a big NO."

"Mighty sassy language."

"No."

"Why not?"

"First, my entire body has never hurt like this before. Second, I want food before I go anywhere. If I'm late, I'm late. Maybe Ms. Yolanda can be the maid of honor. She already knows the tango." I toed off my shoes, unhooked my pants, and by the time I hit my bedroom door, I had unbuttoned my blouse.

"Thanks for asking about my great day buying luggage for Tucker's," Jenny said from the kitchen. "Want me to fix you anything?"

"Whatever. I'm too tired to care." I shut the bathroom door and set the water to steamy. I poured a drop of lavender oil in the tub and inhaled deeply when the incredible scent enveloped the room. After I tugged the shower curtain into place for privacy, I let my body slink into the bubbly depths.

Jenny rapped lightly and cracked open the hallway door to my bathroom. "Naked?"

"Yup."

"I'll look the other way."

Something clattered on the solid surface counter. "Appetizer," she said.

"Appetizer?" I peeked past the curtain's edge to find she'd set a bowl of peanut M&Ms next to the sink. *How considerate.*

The door closed. I heard her ask, "How did the rest of your day go?"

"Great. I like my new job." I snaked my arm around the curtain and stretched to grab five candies. "Miss A.'s the best kind of employer. Very professional and desperately needs help—yay for me."

"How is she professional?"

"One who doesn't kill anybody." I slid deeper into the warm water. The heat seeped into all my joints. The twitching in my biceps subsided. "Miss A. said we might have to hire additional employees if the business takes off as she hopes. Maybe I could grow up and be a supervisor or a buyer."

"What did you do today?"

I chewed and swallowed. The lack of protein created a brain void. Fast-food chicken Caesar salad could only go so far. I summarized for Jenny the software planning system and the unpacking of the gowns. "Tons. Literally, those things weigh a ton— well, maybe more like ten pounds. I did see a possibility for Tracey, though. A sleek number with long, sheer sleeves and a V in the back which dips to the waist. Perfect for her figure."

"You know your mother will get ideas—"

"She better not, especially when no Mr. Right is in sight—"

"—about Allan."

Pulling aside the curtain just a fraction, I glared at a

mental image of my friend through the wooden portal.

Jenny laughed. "I'm messing with your head."

I dropped the curtain's edge to locate a squishy sponge. I squeezed soapy water along my arm. "But you're right. Mom'll get ideas."

"It's a given."

Notions about hunky Mr. Wellborn came to my mind. I'd like to see him wearing a tight white T-shirt and low-slung jeans. His six pack. The short sleeves tightened around his biceps. The broad shoulders. And the jeans dropped low enough to reveal skin and a trail from his bellybutton to more interesting regions—

"Speaking of the hunk, Allan stopped by," Jenny said.

"Oh?" My thoughts raced at the idea of "what does he want." "Too bad I missed him."

Nothing.

"Okay. I'll bite. What did he want?"

"He said, 'Hey.'"

Without a doubt, Jenny believed she was hilarious. "Aren't you special?"

"You sounded like the church ladies. He asked if you wanted a ride to the studio."

*The man knew how to punch all my buttons. Irritating.* I smacked the water, sending drops flying. "Allan doesn't understand N period O period very well."

"You deserve happiness, Hattie. We all do. He's the guy, The One. Take my advice—chase Allan, tie him to the bed, and you do the voodoo on him."

I dropped the sponge and depressed the toe-pop plug to open. "Lord, how I've tried."

"Failure's not a choice. Try again, and if that

doesn't work, again. Are you a quitter?"

"No." *Until I resembled an idiot.* I snagged the towel to wrap my torso, feeling indignation root in my tummy. Standing, I adjusted the ends under my armpits and maneuvered the curtain to one side to step over the rim. I opened the hall door. "If only his cell phone wouldn't interrupt us." I smiled. "He would probably like the binding part."

With a grin, Jenny bounced her brows. "I hear police handcuffs are the way to go."

I laughed. "Funny. What else did he want other than the ride offer?"

"Here." She plucked my phone from the counter next to the toothpaste tube and a glass jar filled with cotton swabs. "Push one."

I stared at my phone, utterly amazed. "You assigned a number...on speed dial...on my phone? Without telling me? When did you do this?"

Jenny shrugged. "Long time ago. Seemed prudent."

Sometimes, her efficiency left me...speechless.

I rubbed my forehead. *Do I want to talk to Allan?*

Chapter Five

I hovered a thumb over speed dial button one. Phoning Allan brought uncertainties in the end. We would get together, and oops, his cell would invariably intrude. Or he would say, "Gotta go," and leave. Or both.

After hearing his "gotta go" phrase way too many times, I decided I didn't like it. In fact, I loathed it. His words caused me to wonder where I stood with him. I certainly didn't feel important—although he told me differently.

Knifings and shootings interspersing our brief encounters left me scared to death. Through all the gory stuff, somehow, I developed stronger emotions, most likely love. The flutterings in my heart were a good indicator. Right now, I couldn't admit anything to anyone and especially, not to Allan. Yet, deep down, I knew:

—Stating I loved him would make me feel vulnerable.

—Mother would be happy with the love part.

Allan made it plain when he yelled through the door the other day. For him to stop by should be deemed major importance. However, the monkey on my back told me to make a move. With a long sigh, I punched one.

"Hi, sweetheart," he said.

Caller ID could be scary. His voice sounded cinnamon bun sticky sweet and warm, too. "Howdy. Jenny said you made a pitstop?"

"Yep. Somebody dumped a huge problem on me, and you get to help."

I transferred *huge* to an image of enlarged man-parts. I squeaked. "Problem? How, er, huge?"

He chuckled. "Not the problem you're thinking of, sweetheart, although I am up—ha-ha—for whatever whenever."

Strange how we shared brainwaves. And maybe a "huge problem." However, *why try?* His cellphone would buzz, a version of coitus interruptus.

"What's up?" I cringed. What a terrible line and not the best one to say right now.

Allan laughed and laughed.

The deep breath I blew ruffled a few eye-level hair strands. "Can't we discuss your problem at tonight's tango lesson? I'm dripping and shivering."

"Fresh out of the tub? Which equals naked."

Of course, he knew naked. All men claimed to like "naked."

"How about phone sex?"

"Smartass." I cradled the cellphone between my shoulder and cheek while I re-tucked the towel.

"Phone sex will have to wait, sweetheart. I'm not kidding. I have an enormous challenge. I don't want to talk about it in front of Tracey and Stuart."

I checked my hair in the mirror. *Passable.* "Okay. Enlighten me."

"Stuart's mom threw the rehearsal dinner my way, I mean, *our* way—"

"She what?" As I straightened, the phone slipped. I

grappled for the device. "As the M-I-L, she plans the rehearsal." *Some people.* "You're a cop. Don't let his mom manipulate you. Handle it, big boy." *Aren't I supportive?*

"No kidding." Allan blew a long sigh. "I don't know what to do. I felt sorry for Mrs. Steems. I got to thinking—"

"I can't wait to hear—"

"You can help me."

*I am so not believing her…and him.* I set my makeup box on the vanity and touched up my eye shadow. "How's that?"

"You work for a bridal salon."

"What's your point?" *I've been on the bridal job for two days, and already the whole world thinks I know what I'm doing.* Makeup done, I shuffled to my bedroom, where I dropped the towel. "I'm no freakin' expert."

"You have lots of experience—"

"I do not—"

"You have lots of friends and cousins—"

"Only one is married—"

"And girls know what to do—"

"I do not—"

"You have a new job at the bridal shop—"

"So?"

He drew a breath.

I hit Speaker on the phone and dropped it on my bed. I pulled on my undies and bra then shoved my arms through sweater sleeves.

"Hattie? Are you there?" he said.

"I'm here." Quickly, I stuck the device to my ear. "I didn't help with Corrine's wedding, and my job at

Wonderland began the other day."

"Way more experience than me. Please. You owe me."

Turning on the Speaker feature again, I dropped the phone a second time. "I owe you a big fat nothing. Not. A. Thing." I flopped across the end of the bed and pulled on my jeans, wiggling them into place. My belly flattened enough to enable me to zip them. After I jumped to my feet, I snatched the phone to my ear. "I paid my dues by baby-sitting Lucky."

"In your dreams. Remember the engagement dinner you asked me to go to with you?"

"Same song, second verse, maestro." Only crickets followed my statement. I was over the moon when Allan escorted me to the engagement dinner, a "dream come true" date. We danced intimately, kissed, and attempted almost wild, almost sex.

In my Book of Debts, I didn't owe him one iota. However, I could hear my mother in my ear, trotting out a page from the "Right Thing to Do" lecture. What Stuart's mom did broke all wedding protocol, and Allan doing his saintly thing told her he would help, which translated meant he desperately needed somebody else's help.

"Fine. I'm in, but you owe me more, like a date to the"—I grasped on the first thing that popped in my head—"opera."

"Opera? Since when do you like opera?"

I held back a grin. "Since yesterday."

Allan blew a huge sigh. "Done." He paused. "Opera?"

I terminated the call. Something-something-something smacked me wrong because he agreed too quickly. I didn't want to go to the opera. He hated opera. I did, too. Nothing good would come out of this arrangement.

"Three minutes 'til," Jenny yelled. "Step on it."

"Allan will need lots and lots of help." I shoved my feet into driving mocs and grabbed my trench coat. I revisited my conversation with him as Jenny and I dodged drops to her car. We scrambled into the four-door sedan, and I informed her what was what.

"Stuart's mom is just like him." Jenny checked her rearview mirror before changing lanes. "Always full of surprises."

"Wait until I tell you about the opera."

"Opera?" She canted her gaze toward me very briefly. "You hate the opera unless Bugs Bunny's singing."

Jenny knew me too well. Didn't everybody think *The Barber of Seville* was the best opera evah?

****

After I entered the studio, I paused to note the expanse of the hardwood floor and the spicy dance music. I blew a disgusted snort. *A couple of lessons to go—my ass.* My shoulders drooped. *Is it horrible to wish for a sprained ankle to get out of this mess?*

My conscience didn't agree, reiterating "for my sister, for my sister" in my head. I dumped my coat and handbag on a chair and turned to face the room with my arms crossed over my boobs.

Jenny did the same except for the "crossing the arms" part.

Ms. Yolanda paired us with the same partners, and of course, Allan did a repeat as mine.

Stuart and Tracey stood at the other end, holding

hands, their gazes never leaving each other's faces. An ecstasy bubble entombed this bride and groom-to-be.

Right now, I thought them rather self-centered to act so ooey-gooey. I swore to God their constant smiles were tattooed on them, and the overwhelming impulse to smack 'em consumed me.

Allan's expression resembled the cat caught face-planting in a bowl full of cream. He took my hand and set his other to my waist.

I positioned mine in the designated spot on his shoulder. Heat inched into my palm and spread along my arm, my neck, and fanned across my cheeks.

With a smirk, he tugged me closer, letting our bellies rub together. So close, his irresistible pine scent teased my nose. *Oh boy.*

"Let's see if we do better this time," I gritted through clenched teeth.

His devouring-you grin made me twist my mouth. I rolled my eyes. "Stop leering like-like the Big Bad Wolf."

"Just practicing my tango expression." He relaxed his hold, and a soupçon of distance crept between our tummies. "The story implies the Big Bad Wolf lusted after Little Red Riding Hood."

*Great.*

Ms. Yolanda clapped. "Anda one, anda two..."

Allan and I slid sideways. "I don't have a red cape," I said.

"Buy one. We can indulge in fantasy role-playing."

*Role-playing?* "Whatever." Two to three minutes of silence encompassed us as I concentrated on my steps. "How about we change the subject? Exactly what do you have in mind for the rehearsal dinner?"

"I've never planned a rehearsal dinner before. I've been to a few, but only as a member of the party-hearty gang." He crinkled his nose. "Any suggestions?"

Arcing my arm over my head, I tilted back and studied the ceiling. Everyone believes the position looks romantic; however, one's back could go wonky. On the fourth count, I dropped my arm and realigned. "What about a picnic at Sommerville Lake, you know, the spot—"

"On the hill with the best view of downtown. Nice. Very nice." He stopped moving and took my hands. "What about rain?"

I bent my leg around his calf. "You could rent the Waterworks building on the other side of the lake. If the weatherman predicts sunny weather—yipee. The patio would be ideal. If rain comes, go inside. Or both, depending on how many guests you invite."

"Class, lunge," Miss Yolanda said.

I lunged to my left, and Allan did the same toward his right.

"Good. Straighten and lift your arms over your head," said Ms. Yolanda. "Lunge again. Ladies, point your toes. Wrap your leg around his front calf. Whip away your leg. Wrap a second time."

I looked at my foot. Toe pointed and wrapped my leg around his calf.

"Faster," she said.

I whipped faster and kicked his ankle.

Allan hopped on one leg as he kneaded the sore spot on the other.

Ms. Yolanda glanced over her shoulder.

After he shook his leg loose, he straightened. "Back to the dinner… Chairs and tables inside and outside seem redundant."

*Redundant. Spoken like a reformed accountant.* I pursed my lips. "How about setting bales of hay outside for a casual farmhouse feel? Festive and different. Can be recycled for mulch afterward."

"Another good idea," Allan said.

*Reading Mom's decorating magazines is paying off.*

He flicked a glance at Stuart. "Your future brother-in-law doesn't look like a farm boy."

"Hardy har-har. Tracey likes the farmhouse look. Dress the bales in burlap. We—"

"*We* sounds hopeful." Allan dropped his arms.

Sliding my arms to my side, I prayed to the one above to find the best response. I ticked off my left hand. "Checkered napkins, fried chicken, mashed potatoes, hot buttery biscuits with homemade strawberry jam. A good ol' grandmotherly-style meal sounds yummy and not very expensive."

Allan made a slow, easy smile. "Fried chicken's one of my favorite foods."

"See? Easy peasy, too. And a buffet is ideal."

"Now, you're talking."

I inclined my head. "Is Stuart's mom helping with the moola end?"

"Mrs. Steems said she would pay. She's out of town and didn't know what or how to host a rehearsal dinner. As if I would know." He scrubbed his palms. "What about dessert?"

"I'm glad you mentioned dessert—my specialty." I thumbed my chest. "How about Texas chocolate sheet cake topped with pecan fudge frosting or peach cobbler and vanilla bean ice cream. Or both. I'd eat both."

"You do have a sweet tooth. I vote for you to make the food arrangements. I'll reserve the Waterworks Building and buy—"

*Golly, his white toothy grin makes him even more attractive.*

"—the hay. I'll order balloons in their wedding colors— By the way, what are their colors?"

"Colors?" I wrinkled my nose. "Balloons? What for?"

"All celebrations require balloons." Allan's face took on a solemn and serious expression. "Lots and lots of them."

Which explained why every time he gave me a gift bag, he tied on a balloon.

"Tracey's colors are blue-ish green or greenish-blue, like sea foam, and peony pink. I'll work on an invitation list, too." I rubbed the side of my nose. "Who do you want to ask to the reception besides the wedding party and family? You can invite out-of-towners, but you don't have to."

Allan pulled me tight into his arms. "Grandparents."

"Anda one, anda two," Ms. Yolanda instructed with dips and sways to urge the class.

I resumed my hold. "Perfect. We can send e-vites."

"I'll lick the stamps."

I followed his lead. "Those don't need stamps, silly. However, you do have a point about paper invitations. Very classy. I can get the guest list from my mom."

"Can I lick the stamps?"

"No licking stamps anymore. Just stick-ons." I tilted my head, wondering about his stamp fixation.

"Are you being deliberately obtuse?"

"Maybe."

I snorted. "You can address the invites, too."

"Your handwriting's better."

Allan grazed his cheek along my jaw—on purpose. The rasp from his five o'clock shadow caused funny sensations to revolve in my chest. I relished the feeling and whispered, "You're welcome."

He drew back and stared long and hard.

The moment suspended everything as we stared into each other's eyes. Had he said, "I love you?"

Ms. Yolanda's clap broke my romantic notions. "Let's go over the steps again, and then we'll combine them with what you learned in lesson one. Look at your partner. Anda one, anda two…"

Jolted from our feelings, my partner and I took forward steps and paused. I extended my leg with pointy toes. Joining hands, we lifted our arms.

"Glorious, best man and maid of honor." Ms. Yolanda bestowed on us a beaming smile. "Simply glorious."

*Glorious—my ass.* Off to the side, I noted Jenny collapsing with laughter. I sure hope we don't have to show off again so the others could study our moves.

I pushed a finger against my thudding temple. *Does tango stuff give everyone a migraine?*

Chapter Six

The following morning dawned bright and clear, the way most days did in Sommerville. Our rainy moments came in the fall and spring and sometimes, with incredible and violent thunderstorms. Today—I drew a deep inhaling breath—felt exceptional.

My workday began in Wedding Wonderland's gown room, finishing what Miss A. and I had started the day before—unpacking wedding dresses and toting new goods to their respective places. With the phone tucked under my chin, I listened to my mom float ideas for Tracey's big day. Once she glommed onto my new job and the possible perks I might have, she was all about saving money.

"I'm telling you Tracey needs our advice," Mom said.

My sister should be paying me big bucks for her defense.

"Mom, come on. Whatever Tracey wants, she should have."

"Whatever she wants?" Mom asked. "You know what she'll do."

*God, her nasal tone of voice is annoying.* "What?"

"She'll get what she wants—thanks to you."

I slit open a box. "Tracey's your only hope."

"Looks like she is."

I could only wish. What Mom categorically

implied, she believed me hopeless in the marriage department.

"First, you don't marry college boy—"

*Not again. Not this diatribe for the million trillionth time.* "Mom."

"Then Tracey eloped to Vegas with her first husband, that-that…salesman. She must have been desperate. We've despised him since forever."

I tried to interrupt. "Mom."

"Then, they divorced. I still hate him."

Only an act of God could stop her train. I raised my voice a fraction. "Mom."

"Harriet Lee Cooks, you don't have to yell."

I didn't and wouldn't after she screamed my full name, which would never be music to anyone's ears. "Sorry. I wanted to remind you. You were okay with my turning down college boy." Standing in front of a rod, I shoved aside a gown with my shoulder and hung a dress.

"I'm sorry. Caught up in the moment. You did the right thing about your college boyfriend. You didn't love him enough, not the way you love Allan."

Knowing my mother spoke the truth about my feelings worried me. She could just be saying I loved Allan because of her desire to match us. However, lately, with being paired for the tango lessons, Allan and I shared an intimate space and really looked and touched each other. Nevertheless, commenting would only get me in more trouble.

I heard Mom inhale.

"I want Tracey and Stuart's wedding to be perfect, unlike her first one. Eloping to Las Vegas embarrassed the whole family."

*Most likely, her over everyone else.*

"Let's make a good memory to supersede the bad one."

"I didn't know Tracey carried a bad memory. She said she purged everything—you know—when the Funsisters and I burned the piñata which resembled him—"

"Piñata? You burned a-a piñata—without me? Where did you get a piñata? Why didn't I get invited to hang out?"

*Because the piñata was purchased for a girls' night out, which explicitly meant no mothers.* "Mom, I had the piñata made. Then we knocked back tequila shots and a baseball bat was involved. Instead of filling the piñata with poo, like he is, I put in lots of chocolate. We ate and ate, and later, we torched the trashy remains."

"Sounds a bit violent. I wish you'd asked me, though. I know how to use a baseball bat. A few swipes would've been gratifying. Jonson Leggett the Third has no place on planet Earth. I also prefer to drink my tequila in margaritas."

*Because margaritas are more civilized?*

"Of course, Tracey has some memories," Mom said. "How that nasty man treated her would haunt anyone."

I carried a voodoo doll resembling Jonson Leggett the Third for a long time. While waiting in horrible traffic, I pulled the toy from my car's console and gouged a three-inch upholstery pin two or twenty times into the body, limbs, and head. How many depended on how long the light stayed red and cars didn't move.

"Well, no worries now," Mom said. "Tracey's

happy with her beau."

I tugged my skirt into place. "While we're talking about Tracy and Stuart, I have good news. I found the perfect gown for her. I've already phoned Trace, put the dress on hold, and she said she'll come in for a fitting. Okay?"

"I hoped—wished—"

Did I hear wistfulness in Mom's voice? Being sentimental? "Wished what?"

"No way she would wear…mine?"

Before now, Mom had never said she wanted her daughters to wear her wedding gown. The style was so dated. I knew Tracey wasn't into hers. As gently as possible, I asked, "Tracey know how you feel?"

"Not exactly. I've not asked if wearing my dress interested Tracey, maybe more like hinted. Maybe she already considered mine as an option. I discarded the idea when she didn't say anything. Kinda makes me sad no one will ever wear my dress again."

"I'm sorry. Here's an online idea"—hurrah for Pinterest—"repurpose wedding dresses into christening gowns."

"Really? Sounds fabulous. Then my dress won't be wasted. I can have two made, one for her and one for you—"

*One for me???*

"—anyway, I wanted to be at your store when she tries on the dress—"

When Tracey and I discussed having a trying-on-a-dress party and including our mom, she nixed the idea. A big woo-hoo would never be her style. She and I agreed Mom would critique everything which could possibly make the event less shiny and joyous. The only way to minimize her involvement and our sanity was not to include her. Harsh.

"Mother, she can try on gowns on her own. I'll be there, and Miss A. knows a thing or two. Most likely, she'll pick a few she likes best. We'll take pictures, and then she'll ask you to help her decide. Okay?"

Mom sighed. "I read the trend seems to be a big blow-out with the mom, mother of the groom, and the besties—"

*Mom said* besties? *Crazy.*

"—and champagne when trying on dresses. An event she'll remember for the rest of her life. I didn't get to help the first time, and I really want to for this wedding. She *is* my daughter."

*Well, rats.* I tried. Mom played the mother-daughter-tugging-my-heart card. Maybe something disastrous like a typhoon would prevent her from coming.

*Lordy!* The store bell chimed the tune "Here Comes the Bride," signaling a new customer's arrival. "Work calls, Mom. Gotta go."

With a smile on my face, I quickly disconnected, only to see strolling toward my desk the most despicable person I knew, the slimiest of slimes my mom and I had just discussed—my ex-brother-in-law, Jonson Leggett the Third. Tracey's first husband and soon-to-be new hubby to Barbie Fenster.

My disposition soured.

I remembered my sister's marriage to Jonson lasted one year. One. Miserable. Hellish. Year. Tracey was young, fresh from college. They met at a happy hour, and Jonson easily swept her off her feet. The swarmy, blankety-blank-blank pool salesman sweet-talked my sissie, and they eloped to Vegas one bright spring weekend four years ago, which almost broke Mom's heart.

What happened afterward did break Tracey's.

During the honeymoon, Tracey discovered him doing the nasty with a floozy he picked up while playing craps. My sister hid in the walk-in closet while they banged away—horrible for her.

I only wish Tracey had videoed the twosome so I could have shared his raunchy sex with all humankind.

His shenanigans didn't end in Las Vegas. Hell no. Back at home, he nailed his assistant, then a client, then—Well, everyone got the picture. Unbeknownst to my sissie, I ascertained through friends of friends he'd taken the marital plunge before my sister.

While Tracey stumbled and bumbled her way through their short union, I minded my own business, held her hand, and listened to the never-ending sobbing. I relished the idea of telling everyone how vile he was. But I didn't. He would have taken revenge on my sister. I couldn't let that happen.

His betrayal and indiscretions shattered Tracey's heart, and after the divorce, and lots of time, she eventually healed to ultimately blossom when she fell for Stuart.

Staring hard Jonson's way, I remembered how I didn't like him from the moment I met him. Detested. Abhorred. Loathed. Despised. He looked the same— tall, thin, light brown hair, and hazel eyes. He carried an air of savoir-faire. But I knew better. Egocentric. A know-it-all.

Rage scorched through my body. No way did I trust him.

If only he would burn in hell.

Probably hell would chuck him back.

*So how come he's here at Miss Anastasia's Wedding Wonderland?* Then, click. When I interviewed for this job, Miss A. mentioned high-profile clients coming to the store. Undoubtedly, she meant Jonson and Barbie.

My attention focused on the giggling and glowing gal hanging onto his arm. Barbie Fenster was a cute, average height, dark-eyed, and dark-haired honey with Ms. Sommerville Automotive Parts written all over her. She left her tiara and sash at home. Not hard to imagine them in place, though.

I straightened the white work jacket Miss A. gave me when I arrived this morning. She'd embroidered my name in pink. Composed, totally neutral, I fingered a button before speaking. "Welcome to Wedding Wonderland. How may I help you?"

Jonson's gaze didn't leave Gushing Giggly Girl's face. "Jonson Leggett and Barbie Fenster have a two o'clock with Miss Anastasia to plan our wedding." He pecked the tip of his fiancée's nose.

*Ick.*

Barbie cooed. Seriously…like a dove.

She buzzed his lips.

Thankfully, no tongues were involved.

"Please have a seat." I indicated the reception area where they dropped into the chairs, still holding hands and staring into each other's eyes. "I'll inform Miss A. you're here."

Returning to the desk, I grabbed the phone receiver and pressed Miss A.'s number. It took everything I possessed to not run to her office and to tell her Jonson embodied the underbelly of patrons.

Miss A. picked up after two rings.

"Miss A.? Mr., ah, Leggett, and Miss Fenster are here for their consultation."

Upon hearing her reply, I nodded. I returned the handset to the phone base. "Miss A. will join you momentarily."

I shouldn't have bothered to inform them. So engrossed with each other, my comment didn't compute.

Their hands roved over their upper arms and shoulders. He glided his index finger across her jaw in a sensual caress. She flicked her tongue along his earlobe.

*Gag. A. Maggot.* Turning my head, I covered my mouth with my hand to suppress the urge to puke.

Within a few moments, Miss A. emerged from her office, garbed in her crisply ironed Wedding Wonderland jacket, and joined the couple in the reception area.

Amazingly, Jonson stood and bowed over Miss A's hand. With clasped hands to her chest, Barbie looked at her prospective groom with loving adoration.

At Wedding Wonderland, Miss A. gave each client a white notebook containing a checklist to help them track the wedding plans and also included images of the items ordered through us—the whole enchilada for arranging the greatest day in a couple's lifetime. For the most part, the information matched the software program. Giving the client the book caused The Day to feel more special, which made the bride feel more special.

Miss A. waved the duo to the chairs and set a personalized tome on the table in front of Barbie, who riffled through the pages.

Finally, Barbie backtracked and landed on the title page. Her excitement visibly showed in her waving arms and antsy demeanor as she pointed out her name and Jonson's entwined in a whimsical calligraphy. "See, dear? Our names. Don't they look sweet?"

"Oh, my darling one," Jonson said. "You're the sweetest."

"No, darling, you are."

"No," he said. "You are."

*Ick. Ick. Ick.* I rubbed my tummy.

As they discussed items, Miss A. flipped through the book, noting specific details.

Barbie listened intently and nodded.

I had a hard time believing Barbie truly absorbed everything she heard.

Jonson's attention focused on Miss A. and Barbie, but I wondered for how long. He could be rather fidgety, like "out of control little kid who needed medication" fidgety.

From under my eyelashes, I discreetly observed Miss A. work with the gruesome twosome. Mostly, Barbie answered her questions. My employer made notations on the software form she opened on her tablet. After Miss A. completed the consultation, I would review the questionnaire for any possible mistakes and omissions while the client, in this case, Barbie, tried on wedding dresses.

Miss A. pressed Barbie's forearm. "Now, Ms. Fenster—"

"Please, call me Barbie." She smiled, bumping her shoulder with Jonson.

He blinked out of his stupor and looked at his

darling one.

"Everyone does. Don't they, my love?"

Barbie turned her head to look at Jonson with a longing, which caused my stomach to churn and burn.

Jonson pressed a kiss on her forehead. "Yes, but I call you my darling."

I cringed over the "darling" part. He used the same endearment for Tracey. In my mind, I called him "asshole."

"Of course, er, Barbie," Miss A. said. "We've finalized the paperwork. Why don't I escort you to the gown room to select some dresses?" She glanced up. "And Mr. Leggett—"

He gave her his toothy grin. "Call me Jonson."

Too bad I hadn't pursued a career in dentistry as my vocation. I would drill his root canal without anesthetic.

"My pleasure," Miss A. said. "Jonson, please wait here."

Jonson pouted and took a few steps after them. "I want to be with Barbie. She'll need my advice."

Miss A. tick-tocked a finger and pointed to the chair where he had sat. "Would you want bad luck because you caught sight of the bride in her dress before the wedding?"

Jonson's eyes widened. His gaze shifted for one moment to his right, then returned to Barbie.

Miss A. laughed at his expression. "An old saying. I'm teasing you. However, I wouldn't want to buck tradition, would you?"

Maybe he'd seen wife No. 1 and No. 2 in their gowns beforehand, which would explain why those marriages curdled like expired milk. But seeing the girls in their finery wasn't the primary reason why. His "little johnson" didn't like being contained. *His way* or *no way*. More yuck.

I had seen his tantrums in action. He hated when someone over-rode his wishes and loved making people squirm. For once, he checked his anger, probably to please Barbie.

With a small laugh, Jonson half-assed joined Miss A.'s joke as he slunk back to his chair. He picked up the bridal magazine sitting on the small glass table between the chairs.

I didn't bother to inform the loser of the difficulties of reading upside down.

I trailed my gaze to Barbie, who chatted and pranced her way with Miss A. to the gown room as if following the golden trail to the fabled emerald city.

After a few blinks, Jonson comprehended he wasn't reading.

He rotated the magazine to the correct position. But he must have had little attention for the article because he dropped the magazine back on the table and flipped through the invitation sample book.

I downloaded the consultation program. I tap-tap-tapped on the keyboard, reviewing the data Ms. A. entered. Discreetly, I looked from the corner of my eye to see him glance my way. My tapping must have diverted his concentration toward me.

His expression vanished, and his color faded to flour-paste white.

I stole a longer look, secretly reveling at his shocked face. I laid my hand across my heart. "Why, Jonson Leggett the Third," I drawled, using my best girly-girl gush. "Oh my, oh my, it *is* you."

*He-he-he, here's where my mean streak flowed forth.* "I haven't seen you in ages, like at least three or maybe four years. Your loss. What on earth are you doin' here?"

He crossed his arms and nodded once. "Hattie."

Surprisingly, Jonson said my name and didn't choke. No excitement, no interest in his greeting, mostly indifference—a reaction I knew well. Jonson hated me, but I hated him more.

"What a looonng time," I said. "Surely, you've found greener pastures." *Like under a rock. In a grave. In the frigid regions of the North Pole—no. Too close to Santa Claus. Wouldn't want the jolly fellow contaminated.*

"You're looking so-soooo…you. I presume you're getting married again?"

Chapter Seven

"None of your business." He buried his face in the invitation book.

*Sourpuss*. Jonson didn't want to talk to me. Like he could dissuade moi. I personified the persistence of a dog digging for a buried bone when needling him. "Oh, but the wedding business *is* my business."

One eye appeared over the top of the book.

"As you can see"—I emphasized my point with a sweeping arm motion, taking in the whole store. Standing, I twirled about to model the newly embroidered jacket—"I'm an employee of Wedding Wonderland. Tee-hee-hee."

I stepped closer, circling the back of his chair to the far side.

His head jerked from left to right.

"How exciting for you, planning—what? Your third or fourth trip down the aisle?" I pressed a finger to my jaw. "No, no, no. I had it right the first time—your third visit to the altar—that I know of. My, my, my. This will be your *third* marriage, not your *second*, not your *fourth*. Your *third*. I bet Ms. Fenster believes she's a lucky gal. Wouldn't she love to hear war stories about your prior nuptials?"

I scrubbed my palms in a deliciously wicked way and, for a fun effect, swiveled toward Miss A. and his fiancée.

"Stay. Away. From Barbie. Bitch."

I spun about. *Bitch—me?* I squinched my eyes and glared. Jonson hadn't seen anything—yet. Like most women, I could channel my inner bitchiness if I wanted, and, oh, how I wanted to. I rubbed his skin raw, but I always had. We never-never, ever-ever liked each other. From our first meeting, something intuitively inside me recognized how he embodied a snake oil salesman. Totally untrustworthy.

He knew I knew.

I knew he knew I knew.

Scowling, Jonson re-crossed his long, khaki-clad legs, adjusting the "freshly starched by the cleaner's creases" at his knees. From the side table, he picked up the water bottle Miss A. gave him and, ever-so-casually, drank.

"I have no problem telling the owner about you and insist she fire your ass," Jonson said. "If she doesn't, I'm happy to take my business elsewhere."

Of course, he delighted in playing dirty, but his hold-Hattie-hostage scare tactics didn't worry me. I wished for a cattle prod so I could zap the monster multiple times in his most vulnerable spot. To hear him squeal like a suckling pig would bring me great joy.

I probably sounded perverted.

But doing so wouldn't be fair to Miss A. and the success of Wedding Wonderland. I could contain my antagonism. Softly, I said, "Does Barbie know about your…extracurricular activities?"

"Like I already said, you"—Jonson pointed—"stay away from Barbie."

"No problem," I said with joy but didn't mean.

I caught Miss A. squinting our way. Worry molded

her mouth, just a downward turn to the corners.

She led newly gowned Barbie onto the viewing platform.

"Hattie," she asked. "Would you like to join us?"

"Delighted to, Miss A." I walked away, then remembered the hog in the room and paused. Over my shoulder, I said with a sweetness I didn't mean, "So unlovely to talk with you, Jonson."

While chugging more water, he cut me a hard scowl.

*Squirm, you worm.* With my most beatific smile, I threw back my shoulders and sallied on, conveying how little control Jonson's "get you fired" comment swayed me.

As I drew closer to the other women, I clapped my hands and mustered cheerfulness in my voice. "Oh, Barbie." A huge sigh. "You look…amazing."

Miss A. and I oohed and aahed over Barbie. In the end, she picked a traditionally styled, long-sleeved, solid lace, stark white, full-skirted ball gown with a deep U in the back. Tiny, tiny pearl buttons had been fastened at the waistline. Swarovski crystals and more pearls were sewn onto the lace bodice, and when she turned and struck her Miss Somerville Automotive Parts pose, sparkles glinted and flashed, doubly emphasized in the mirrors.

Miss A. located on a display shelf a glittery tiara—after all, Barbie had been crowned a beauty queen multiple times—and a veil not trimmed along the edge with the matching lace, but with a row of the same crystals.

After noting any fitting issues, Miss A. escorted Barbie to the changing room to help her undress. She stowed the gown in her office for her alterations friend. She brought the tag to the check-out counter, where she entered a whopping amount in the computer.

From over Miss A's shoulder, I watched her complete the transaction.

Jonson stepped forward and inserted a debit card in the reader.

My mouth twisted to one side as I wondered *will his card bounce?* When married to my sister, he acted like he never had any dough. He frequently lost at poker, but Tracey said he never won much when he did win. Right before she announced her divorce intention, he cleaned out their joint bank account. One could surmise he did the same for No. 1 wife.

*I'm betting Barbie's dad, the one loaded with beaucoup de Benjamins, funds him.*

The idea crossed my mind—*should I inform Barbie what Jonson would do to her and her family?*

But I didn't.

Couldn't.

Not the right place or time.

Every day, I read the "Aunt Sally" advice column in the *Sommerville Express*. She counseled countless readers to button their lips. I should heed her guidance. Besides, who would want to be Ms. Spoilsport, ruining Barbie's happy day?

Hopefully, she would see Jonson's true colors before the monstrous event and boot him to the curb.

Miss A. returned Jonson's card and placed the receipt in a white leather folder embossed with the store's name. She handed it along with a pen to him for his signature. "Here you go. If you will sign on this line…"

He scrawled his name, adding a flourish to the III. Clearly, a financial institution offered him credit.

"Thank you so much, Miss A., for all your help. I look forward to our planning sessions." Barbie tilted her head and smiled.

Once Barbie's additional purchases were bagged, she gathered the sacks and, in the fashion of a rock star's entourage, swept Jonson out the door. She chattered the entire way to the high-priced, German sport utility vehicle he drove.

Miss A. and I stood in the doorway and called "bye-bye" like flight attendants watching passengers deplane. Only I didn't mean what I thought in a nice way. More like in a "good riddance" manner.

Miss A. returned to the desk.

Slowly, I followed her. Revenge ideas churned in my head. Nothing would be better than to conjure up a sabotaging scheme. Jonson belonged to the slimiest lizard category like the "disturbing, flesh-eating Komodo Dragon with flicking tongue and sharp talons" kind. The creepiness of the mental image infiltrated my brain, causing my shoulders to auto-shimmy.

Miss A. rounded the desk to pick up Jonson's half-drunk water bottle and tossed it in the trash can. All the while, she prattled on about how "incredibly thrilled" their upcoming nuptials were.

I wanted to scream.

"You know," she said. "Barbie's parents are outstanding in the Sommerville community. Her mother is on the Sommerville Library Board—"

*With my mother.*

"Her father chairs one for the Sommerville Performance Hall—"

*With my father and Mrs. Wellborn.*

"Mr. Fenster owns the local lumberyard, although the business grew to be more than that. What a grand coup to get his help."

I hated to say Jonson's standing was never built on a good foundation.

"Hopefully, when their big day hits the newspapers," Miss A. said, "Wedding Wonderland is mentioned. The store will get lots of word-of-mouth referrals. Barbie and Jonson's influence will go a long way in discoverability."

Scrolling the mouse, she reviewed the appointment, information, and selections.

Then, a niggle of puzzlement crowded her eyes, as if she remembered something.

"Hattie, as a long-time resident of Sommerville, you know a lot of people—"

"I do."

"How well do you know Jonson Leggett?"

Tainting her opinion didn't sound like a good idea. Before answering, I hem-hawed while stacking paperwork in neat piles, avoiding eye contact. I didn't know how to tell her and implement being tactful at the same time. I adjusted the stapler. Then tweaked the pen jar.

"Dearie, I think you do know him. How?" Miss A. took off her bifocals. "Dare I ask, did you date him?"

For the third time, I controlled the urge to upchuck. "No way. He's a loser." *Oops, I probably shouldn't have used my pet name for him in front of my new employer.* I had a way of stating the unexpected brutally honest truth at inappropriate moments.

Miss A.'s eyes rounded to the size of cereal bowls.

Her mouth dropped slightly open. "I apologize if I upset you. You aren't friends?"

*Fix her mistaken belief quick, Hattie, or risk termination.* "I'm sorry for being rude, Miss A." I touched a finger to my lips before continuing. "No, you didn't upset me. I do know him, but we aren't friends. We won't ever be."

"How are you acquainted—if you don't mind my asking a personal question?"

I always found being honest the best way to go. However, sometimes, reality needed to be manipulated in a delicate and subtle fashion. I placed my hands on top of the monitor. "He's a slime ball. A creep."

My social graces regarding Jonson Leggett the Third evaporated. Non. Ex. Is. Tent.

Her eyes widened as she cupped her throat. "Creep. Loser. Slime ball—why would you call him these names?"

"Miss A."—I set my fists to my hips and looked over the store, wondering where to launch my story— "what I have to say is…unsettling."

She nodded. "Take your time."

I inhaled deeply. "Long before you moved here, Jonson Leggett the Third was married to my sister, Tracey, for one year. A horrid scandal followed. She divorced him. Front page gossip in big, bold headlines in the *Sommerville Express* for the entire universe to read. My mother nearly fainted."

"Married? For only one year?"

At my nod, Miss A. tugged on her bifocals, letting them dangle from the chain on her chest.

"Oh my, not very long. You say the marriage took place before I came to Sommerville?"

"Yes, ma'am."

Clasping her hands in front of her sternum, she looked from her left to the right before pinning her bright blue eyes on me.

"I'm guessing a story is in there somewhere. Can you say what happened?"

Biting my lip, I crossed my arms. Tracey wouldn't mind me telling her side if doing so helped someone. I rubbed the space between my eyebrows. "Jonson talked my sister into eloping to Vegas. While they were on their honeymoon, he, er, engaged in a one-night stand. He came home and had another...and another—"

Miss A.'s mouth shaped an OhmyGod "O." "Why that's...that's...disgusting."

"Disgustingly true." I bobbed my head. "Jonson Leggett the Third is not a nice person. Luckily, my sister uncovered his true colors before children entered the picture."

Miss A. stood with rigid arms. Her fists balled tightly, outrage evident on her face. "He messed around while... Oh"—she fluttered her hand in front of her face—"now, he's a client. Oh. Oh. Oh. Poor Barbie. I feel so sorry for her. What is she getting herself into?" The color drained from her face as if she would collapse any moment.

I didn't handle hysterical people well. Taking her by the elbow, I guided her to a reception chair and assisted her in sitting. I raced to the mini-fridge for a water bottle, which I thrust in her hands.

Miss A. drank greedily. "I had high hopes Barbie and Jonson's event would launch Wedding Wonderland as a premier shop to visit for all wedding needs. Won't happen with them now." She took a deep breath, and once calm, she finished the bottle. She struggled to gasp. "How horrible. How despicable."

"Yes, ma'am. Later, I found out he was married before Tracey."

"Your-your sister… She didn't know?"

"No, ma'am."

"He should have told her. It's the honorable thing to do."

"Yes, ma'am, but Jonson and honorable are incompatible."

"Marriage is based on love—yes, but also, on values we admire like truth and honesty, not lies and deceit. Someone should have said something to your sister." Miss A.'s fist pounded the chair's arm.

"You'd think. People in love do silly things." Dropping into the matching armchair, I slumped against the comfy pillow back and lengthened my legs, flexing and unflexing my toes. "Blame the whirlwind courtship. He was divorced for three months. The bastard charmed Tracey off her feet and swept her to Sin City on a friend's private jet for a quickie marriage. For the total sum of a few hours, my sister experienced utter happiness.

"Jonson had a chance encounter with a floozy he met at the bar who interested him more. Tracey went to their suite to change clothes before dinner, opened the door, and heard the unmistakable sounds of laughter—his laughter and another woman's. She stayed in the closet, while they did the, um, nasty.

"After they left, she found a red lacy thong in the bed but never said a word to Jonson. Just asked room service to change the sheets and dispose of the leftover lingerie. While they did, she stood in the hallway and phoned me. I had never heard my sister cry rivers of tears. My heart ached for her. I begged her to take the first flight home, but she wanted to iron out everything with him."

Miss A. lifted her hand and shrugged. "People make mistakes."

"Not him. He's irredeemable. I swore I would have revenge someday."

"Be careful with the revenge notion, Hattie. Revenge is bad for everyone involved. Trust me on this."

"So I've heard." I returned to a proper seated position with my hands in my lap. "He's worse than a snake in the grass, a jerk, creep, slime ball, and a whole lot of other nasty words my mama told me never to say combined."

"I can understand how you feel. My ex and Jonson share comparable characteristics." Miss A. pressed a finger to the tip of her nose. "I also understand if you don't want to help Barbie and him with planning their wedding—"

I shook my head. "I need to help. I can handle myself like the professional I am. I promise to be agreeable. And nice. Very nice. You don't have to worry about anything." To confirm my oath, I shaped three of my fingers in the Boy Scout symbol. "On my honor."

She cocked her head. "If you're sure, Hattie."

All her glittery self had faded. Her immaculate white coat suddenly appeared less shiny, tarnished, like exhaustion dimmed her persona.

"I am." I bobbed my head. "I can't imagine Jonson coming back here anyhoo. Definitely, not his style."

Chapter Eight

Over the next few days, Miss A. and I worked fast and furious in preparation for the grand opening of Miss Anastasia's Wedding Wonderland. On the day of, the shop buoyed with festivity. Moms, soon-to-be brides, chummy girlfriends, friends, and an assortment of odd-ball relatives filled the store with their high-pitched squees.

Miss A. and I poured champagne and sparkling cider and passed tiny petit fours, flourished on top with a blue, daisy-like flower, especially procured from bakeries the store recommended. My mom bought goodies for mahjong from one of them.

I booked appointments for girls to try on gowns, handed out drawing slips for three one-hundred-fifty-dollar gift certificates, passed out trinkets, and answered a myriad of questions. The loud chatter and laughter had me nearly covering my ears; however, an infectious babble surrounded everyone and caused me to smile too much. My cheeks hurt.

In her element, Miss A.'s enthusiasm could be heard throughout the store. She flitted from group to group, depositing a welcoming word here and there, comporting herself as the most gracious hostess of all time.

At four, I checked my watch, happily noting only three more hours 'til closing. I eased off my right heel, rubbing the toes and the ball of my right foot across the top of my left. I wished I'd planned better and booked a slot at the new reflexology studio four doors down from Wedding Wonderland for a foot massage because of death by sassy shoes.

Instead, I popped two ibuprofen and soldiered on.

Returning my water bottle to the credenza, I turned to observe the customers. When I looked to the entry, I gasped. *Please, dear Lord, tell me it ain't so.*

But it was true.

Jonson Leggett and Barbie Fenster were about to enter the store.

Nothing, nothing I could do.

Uncharacteristically, he exhibited extreme politeness when he held the door open for the former Miss Sommerville Automotive Parts. Barbie's countenance cornered the market on wedded bliss and floated beyond glowing to starry-eyed stellar as she set on Jonson a look which promised "under the sheets" music as she passed through. Jonson looked—boy, I hated to admit—okay. He didn't deserve any more credit.

Jonson and Barbie dodged brides and groups to the desk where I stood.

He paused at a display long enough to snatch up a ten percent-off store card. When he reached the check-out desk, he thrust the discount in my face. "Apply the discount to our purchase."

Even though I detested speaking with him, I took the time to rotate the card to pretend to study the advertising copy, although I already memorized what Miss A. had printed. After a lengthy scrutiny, I shook my head. "Sorry, sir. You made your purchase before the designated date." I pointed to the last line.

Jonson rapped his knuckles on the desk. "Quit harassing me, Hattie. Clear it with Miss A., your boss, in case you need a refresher course. Now. Or you'll be sorry."

His antagonistic 'tude nearly caused me to yell. I counted to ten, took a deep breath, clamped my lips, and gave him a hard eye. "No need to consult anyone," I said firmly as I pushed the card toward his belly. "The ad is perfectly clear."

He braced his hands on the table and leaned.

A fetid whiskey stench soured Jonson's breath. I wrinkled my nose and turned my head to my right. Lightly, I cupped the left side of my face to take a fresh breath. Wanting to fumigate the room with lavender spray just topped my Hit Parade.

"You have always been a hard-ass," he said. "Just do it."

"Jonson." Barbie pulled on his arm. "Please. Lower your voice. Be respectable. People are staring."

He shook his arm from her grasp. "Back off, Barbie. You're irritating me again."

I gasped. *Irritating? Again?* Not all sounded hunky-dory in their paradise.

"But Jonson"—Barbie glanced at the customers, their attention snagged by his outburst—"You're embarrassing me."

His eyes flattened into a squinch. "I don't care. She's a bitch."

"Jonson, stop. Please. Don't talk so…ugly." She tugged on his sleeve. "Pretty please. For me?"

"Why?" Jonson jerked his arm away. "I don't care if the truth hurts anyone, especially her."

*Wow,* his snarl sounded like a rabid dog's. I pinched my thigh to keep from whacking him.

The front door opened. My sister wiggled her way through the blissful throng toward the desk. Similar to when Prince Charming found his love, Cinderella, Tracey's whole being radiated happiness.

*Crap.* Had I eaten a hallucinogenic mushroom because my worst nightmare became a reality?

I swiveled my head from Barbie and Jonson back to Tracey. I rubbed my forehead, unable to decide *what to do, what to do.* With these two, anything could happen. Beads of sweat dribbled along my spine.

"Hi, Hattie." Slanting across the desk, Tracey blew me an air kiss and dropped her handbag at her feet. "Mother declared Corrinne's three-year-old daughter should be the flower girl-slash-ring bearer. I see disaster written all over my plans and my wedding. You have to help me—"

Jonson pushed in front of Barbie. "I'm here first."

*Creep.* He didn't even utter an "excuse me" or "please" or anything nice.

"Sir, you..." Tracey turned to face Jonson. In a flash, recognition fanned over her face. Her eyes bugged. "Y-Y-You!" Her spittle flew, landing on Jonson and Barbie's shoulder.

I extended a tissue box toward them.

If Jonson could have murdered my sister right then, he would have. Every facial feature of his morphed into an ugly shade of reddish-purple. His pupils darkened in a more beady and dangerous way. He bared his teeth like a snarling wolf.

"Back. Off. Tracey. We're first," he said.

Barbie plucked a tissue and crumpled it against her

mouth. She stared at Jonson and stared and stared.

Had Barbie not seen this side of her fiancé before, the monstrous scary one my family and I knew of?

Barbie looked at Tracey, then Jonson. "Jonson"—she set her hand on his wrist—"let's go, darling. We can come back another day."

For the second time, he shook her off.

Her clasp on his arm tightened. "Hon, you're a tad overwrought. Come on."

Disrupting the merriment of the store opening—unacceptable. I wanted to stand back and watch Jonson explode but not exactly a professional stance. I needed to defuse the situation before it climaxed into something butt-ugly, and knowing him, would be gorilla hairy and butt-ugly.

I pointed to Miss A.'s office. "Tracey, would you go over there—"

"Go to hell, Hattie," Jonson said.

Fury festered inside me, climbing and ratcheting to a detonation point like Mt. Etna. *Enough is enough.* I balled my hands into fists. "Look, buster, you can't tell me what to do—"

"You're such a bitch—"

Tracey leaned across Barbie. "You sick womanizer. You can't talk to my sister like—"

"Jonson"—Barbie cocked her head in a questioning tilt—"who's…Tracey, and why is she callin' you a womanizer? And why is Hattie a bitch?"

Looking at Jonson, I grasped Barbie had no clue about his adulterous past and wondered how she missed it. But now, *now* I had the perfect moment to tell all. The whole mess. The whole enchilada. The whole sordid sickness. Miss A. might not—would not—be thrilled with the results, but I bet a fracas in her store would be less welcomed.

I had to do what I had to do—unzip my big mouth and spill all. I waved my hand toward my sibling. "Barbie, let me introduce you to Jonson's ex-wife No. two, my sister, Tracey—"

"Ex-wife? Number two? What ex-wife?" Barbie took one step back. Then another.

Shock would be a good word to describe the look on her face. Beyond shocked would be better. Her gaze took in Tracey, who clenched her hands and nodded "yes" toward Jonson, who most likely wanted to strangle all of us. A curtain of rage spread over his face.

"No." Barbie slowly raised her hands to curve around each side of her jaws. She shook her head. "No. No. No."

Nobody verbalized anything. Barbie pointed at Tracey. "You never told me anything about being married before, Jonson. Why she's...ugly."

*Unbelievable.* I had never known anyone could be as shallow as Jonson. Wrongly, I'd supposed Barbie didn't deserve him. Now, she rivaled him.

I looked at Tracey, my precious sister, whose eyes welled with tears. The overflow dribbled down her cheeks.

Seeing my sister's heart bleed intensified the tension in my chest. If I could have, I would have decked Barbie for her outrageously rude comment. Incredibly insensitive.

"I'm not ugly." Tracey straightened her spine. Her eyes blinked machine-gun quick. "You're stupid for being involved with this piece of trash."

"I told you to butt out, Hattie." Jonson closed in on

Barbie, his arm circling her shoulder. "Darling," he said in a soft sweet voice, "don't pay any attention to these-these—"

Barbie jerked back. Her body went rigid. "Jonson, you told me you were never married. You practically swore on a Bible."

If the argument hadn't been so volatile, I would have laughed at her comment. How on earth had she missed seeing *Sommerville Express's* front-page announcements of his divorces? If Barbie married Jonson now—what a rude awakening. His lies could fill an ocean liner.

Tracey brushed away the teardrops. "Th-that's what he told me, too."

Barbie stilled. "Hattie said you were number two wife. Was he married before you?"

Tracey made a small nod. "Yes."

"Don't you read the papers?" I asked.

Barbie covered her mouth with her hands, her head ticking in another no-no-no. After a long moment of examining her fiancé and us, she dropped her arms and firmed her lips. "One thing I abhor is lying. A couple should have no secrets. Never-never, ever-ever. Why did you lie, Jonson? To me?"

From the corner of my eye, I caught Miss A. observing the hellish scenario. Eyebrows tilted. Her lips compacted together like clamshells. With a generous smile at the women she helped, she excused herself and made fast tracks to the reception area.

Before she reached us, I gave the slime ball a hard look. "I think you should leave, Jonson. I don't want to call the police."

"You would love to, wouldn't you?" he asked.

"Your family would love to see me squirm."

Jonson's sneer reminded me of the ones on the faces of gangsters in the movies from the forties. I stretched my hand to the phone. "Want to find out?"

"Um," Tracey said.

I pointed and gave her a stern look. "Don't."

Jonson fixed on my sister and me the worst of the best livid looks he possessed. If humanly possible, steam vented from his ears. I harbored a concern he would punch either of us. I grappled for Tracey's hand, pulling her around the desk and behind my body.

In the nick of time, Miss A. swooped into the fray and wrapped her arms over Barbie's and Jonson's shoulders. In a sparkly voice, she said, "Barbie. Jonson. So lovely to see you today. Something you needed help with?" She raised her eyebrows. "Miss Hattie, what can we do for our star couple?"

Seeing the question in her expression, I gave the smallest of shrugs. "The gentleman"—I suppressed a choke while handing her the promo card he'd presented—"demanded today's only ten percent discount. I told him his purchase didn't qualify because they made theirs several days ago."

"Very true." Miss A. reviewed the promotional card. "However, Miss Hattie is correct, Jonson. For today only, we're giving away special promotions for Wedding Wonderland's opening. I gave you and Barbie discounts when you bought her gown." She placed the handout on the desk.

Jonson barely paid it any notice.

Miss A. smiled again. "Now, what else can I do for you?"

He jerked his head in my direction. "Why don't

you fire your bitch of an employee?"

Miss A. flinched. "Excuse me? Fire Hattie? But—"

"You heard me. Come, Barbie. We're leaving this shithole and taking our business elsewhere," Jonson said. "You owe us a huge refund. Just because we're high in society doesn't mean you can swindle a customer. My lawyer will be in contact."

He fast-paced to the door, leaving his fiancée in the proverbial dust.

With a powerless plea, Barbie looked at Miss A., then to Jonson's retreating figure. She ran after him.

Barbie looked as if she finally comprehended her influence with him didn't exist, and she needed more help than anyone could give her.

When the front door slammed behind them, Miss A. cringed.

Her mouth dropped into a large circle resembling a freshly landed, gasping-for-air trout. Fortunately, the music and the chatter masked the entire tirade.

Tracey's shoulder bumped mine.

Without uttering a word, I understood the cold expression covering her face. Jonson had done many unspeakable things. A narcissist—what I diagnosed him long ago—swung to his own tune. Even though Barbie made an awful comment about Tracey, maybe she could escape his clutches now the truth was told.

I slipped an arm over my sister's shoulders, holding her tight. "I'm sorry Barbie said horrible things about you. They aren't true."

"Ugly? Unbelievable. Unoriginal." Tracey snorted. "Real ugly will be her living with him and his sick fun and games."

Through the picture windows, I couldn't help but

see Barbie struggling to reason with him.

He clicked the sports utility vehicle's key fob to open it.

I could swear on a stack of Bibles he said, "Barbie, get the hell in the car. Now."

She did.

After backing out of the parking space, he drove away fast, clipping the island curbing, running over the purple and yellow pansies, and smashing them into paper pulp.

Miss A., Tracey, and I stared at each other. I couldn't believe what I'd seen, and most likely, the others had the same notions. After long-held breaths, the strain following Barbie's and Jonson's departure eventually dissipated. I patted Tracey's hand. "She's a mean girl and said mean things."

"She didn't know. Her words spewed out without thought." Tracey bobbed her head. "I know Sommerville is a small town, yet I haven't seen him since before our divorce, and I don't want to again."

Miss A. placed her hand on her chest. As it dropped away, she moved closer and bent her head. "Tell me quickly what took place."

"I'm so sorry. My fault," Tracey said. "Not Hattie's."

Miss A. swallowed, tweaking her jacket into place. "You're Hattie's sister, the one who is marrying soon?"

"Yes, ma'am. Tracey Cooks. I'm so sorry about the…fuss."

Miss A.'s gaze took in the room, as did mine. All the other customers' merriment continued as if nothing had transpired—*thank God.*

"Everything looks good, girls. Just tell me what

happened."

"I—"

"Let me, Trace." I faced Miss A. "From the get-go, Jonson walked in the store in an unpleasant mood, compounded by his drinking. He practically dragged Barbie inside. He demanded a discount on their previous purchases—"

Miss A. shook her head. "No way. I gave them a generous discount based on using their images in our materials and on social media when Barbie registered."

"Jonson didn't care. He assumed he could bully me into something different—you know—just because. That's the way he operates. Then Tracey waltzed in. Jonson recognized her, and choice words were exchanged. Barbie asked about Tracey, and I shared the truth. The end." I gave my shoulder a bare lift.

Miss A.'s normally poufy pouty lips thinned. "I see."

"I'm sorry, Miss A." I paused. "Probably, their marriage was doomed from the beginning."

She bobbed her head. "I'm beginning to think so, too."

With a from-the-heart sigh, I uttered the words I didn't want to say but had to—the very ones which might set me job hunting again. "I didn't act professionally. If you want to let me go—"

She set her hand on top of mine.

"No, dearie. You are staying. I will never understand how people do not embrace the sanctity of marriage. It is forever and ever, not for the moment."

"Jonson doesn't comprehend the concept. Not with a small part"—with a mischievous grin, I crooked my little finger—"like his."

Behind her hand, Tracey snickered for a moment, then grew somber. "And how would you know his man part size, sister dear?"

"Why, sister dear, you told me."

"So I did."

The corners of Miss A's lips pulled in a silly smile. "I'll gladly refund his money. Anything to disassociate me and the store from him. He *is not* the kind of customer we want representing Wedding Wonderland."

"I've been thinking all his dough comes from her rich daddy," I said.

"I wouldn't be surprised." Miss A.'s exhale puffed her chest. "Now, let's get back to work. Circulate with the champagne, Hattie. Tracey"—she twined her arm with my sister's—"let's look at wedding gowns. I believe Hattie set aside a special one just for you. I can't wait to see you try it on."

With an energized set to her mouth, she sailed forth, towing my sissie to the gown section.

Miss A. had shown another characteristic I admired. A force to be reckoned with. Unflappable.

Chapter Nine

Dead dog tired, I questioned whether my BFF was Jenny or not because I found myself dragged to the rehearsal studio for another tango session after Wedding Wonderland closed for the day. The grand-opening event seemed never-ending, and my feet hurt more than possible, making dancing lessons unappealing. A good meal would have relieved my fatigue—if I had found time to eat something other than the petit fours we passed out at Wedding Wonderland.

Regretfully, I eyed the front entry as I walked the concrete path to the studio. *Only two more lessons to go. Praise the Lord.*

I stepped inside tentatively, noting the nearly dim lighting. I settled my gaze on Ms. Yolanda, garbed in another from her crazy caftan collection. I bet she crammed her closet with one in every color.

Stuart and Tracey stood by the chairs lining one wall, having a heated discussion. Expressive arms flew everywhere. Fingers stabbed near the eyes. Very unlike my sister to be animated, and I'd never seen Stuart flail his arms. Mainly, he personified quirky tics and bad clothing choices.

Something had turned South in paradise. After a few minutes, Stuart's expression changed from his usual puppy dog self to one of drawn eyebrows and a downturned mouth.

My sister repeatedly pressed a tissue to the corners of her eyes, her mouth scrunched in a frown.

*Were they discussing what happened at the shop with slime butt? And does Stuart know about Tracey's past marriage?*

Tracey's gaze traveled past her fiancé and settled on me. I lifted one shoulder and raised my palms.

She shook her head.

*Fine.* Tracey didn't need my help, and I lacked anything to offer except to corroborate her story of the "close encounter of the lizard ex" kind.

I didn't want to be pulled into their hullabaloo. No way because today, I'd had enough. If their chat grew lively again, I would station myself on the opposite side of the room and prepare for a Great Escape. I pressed my back into the wall, and when I determined no one paid any attention, I inched my way to the farthest corner.

I stopped when I spied Mr. Migh-tee Fine Allan leaning against the wall opposite me. He studied Stuart and Tracey like paradise between them faded with the setting sun, and, if true, wondering if he would be off the hook as best man.

Allan dragged his index finger along the curve of his jaw.

I couldn't focus on anything except his luscious mouth, which made mine water with memories of his soul-deep kisses.

With nothing else to do or no one to talk with, I limply tossed my hands, crossed the room, and inserted myself in a space next to his right side. Instantly, a snap and crackle ignited just by my body being in the proximity of him. I swallowed hard and closed my eyes to control my feelings, so hoping they weren't transparent. Now was not the time for anything "us."

Allan said, without looking my way, "Something's different."

"Oh?"

"Stuart and Tracey aren't happy."

"Wow. You must have special powers to determine that."

He cut me his squinty eye look. "I do. Special cop powers."

Even the stupid lopsided tilt to his eyes was hot.

"What happened?" he asked.

I shook my head and shrugged. "I know nothing."

"Wrong answer. You share everything with Tracey."

*Not everything everything.* "Perhaps, not a Cadillac kind of day at Wedding Wonderland."

"Not surprised. Trouble follows you at your so-called jobs."

"Stop being judgmental. I didn't do anything"—I took in his "not believing you" look—"well, okay, not much."

Allan shifted and sighed. "I can't wait to hear."

I crossed my arms, bumping my backside against the mirrored wall. "Today, we experienced a teeny tiny kerfuffle between Jonson Leggett number three and Tracey."

"Kerfuffle? My, Grandma, what big words you know."

"Thank you. I'm sure my eighth-grade English teacher appreciates you noticing."

"Smart aleck."

"Just a teensy-weensy disagreement."

"With Jonson? The blowhard? Hardly." Allan snorted. "He graduated with my class in high school. Didn't have many friends. An ass-wipe back then."

He slanted his head and locked on me the "tell me everything" look. "Rumor says he's getting married."

Allan's expression made me uneasy. I squirmed. "Yup. To poor, little rich girl Barbie Fenster of the lumberyard family. But maybe not after today."

"The suspense is killing me."

"Leave it alone, Allan. The drama—awful. Just awful." I shook my head. "Look at Stuart. When is he ever so animated? Aren't accountants supposed to be rather…contained?"

"A huge misconception amplified by television portraying accountants as nerds. Back to the original subject—what if I'm called on to be a supportive best man?"

"You know how all couples have their moments?"

Allan dipped his chin. "Enlighten me. What moments?"

"This is one of them."

He squinched a look. "And you're an expert on couples—how?"

Allan always ruffled my proverbial feathers. "I've been part of a couple before."

"So tell me, exactly how long ago did you date college boy?"

I flexed my fingers to ball my fist to sock his bicep. He was saved when Ms. Yolanda stepped to the center of the room, and the plastic coin trim on her caftan, which she most likely bought vast yards of, clicked.

She clapped. Undoubtedly, Ms. Yolanda stored more tango torture tricks in her sleeves.

The students formed a circle around her—a little too eagerly, in my opinion.

Allan dropped a groan before he pushed off to join the group.

I surrendered and stood by his side.

She lifted her hands. "Class, let's practice what we've learned so far. Find your partner."

No one dared to move.

"Come on," Ms. Yolanda said, with summoning hands. "Or I'll add fifteen more minutes to the set."

Instantly, the group scattered like a bug bomb tossed on an intrusion of roaches.

Rotating to face Allan, I set my hand in his. His attention locked on me. A tingling increased to a burning flame through my palm and up to my neck. I sensed my head going hot, and undoubtedly, my face turned the color in the fire-engine red category. I managed to place my other hand on his shoulder.

"Closer." He curled his fingers around mine.

My heart beat hard. My breath caught.

"I won't bite."

I shuffled my feet. "All talk. No action."

"Well, maybe just a nibble."

However, the twinkle in his eye and the one playing with his smile betrayed his "almost" pledge. Maybe one tiny love bite would be okay. I snorted. "So you say."

I half shut my eyes and shifted into the intimacy range—becoming all too aware of his bigger body, remembering the last time we were naked, remembering how extraordinary he felt on top of mine. Good. Really, really good—

*Snap out of it, Hattie.*

After the rest of the students assembled, Ms. Yolanda clapped. "Anda one, anda two…"

Allan guided us in one direction, paused, posed. I skimmed my right leg in a half circle while Allan sharply swept my left arm in an arc over our heads. My gaze connected with his. Challenge, lust, and all man were discernible. In an odd way, something inside me switched to…excitably scared. The back of his hand slipped along the side of my arm to just above my wrist.

With each stroke, goose bumps pimpled my skin.

Ms. Yolanda aimed her remote at the music system. Notes faded away. "Class. A moment, please."

Quickly, I released my hold with Allan. But I couldn't tear away my gaze. So intently, I stared at him, and he stared at me, I sensed something like our souls merging.

"We're leaving." He grabbed my hand, my handbag, my coat, and dragged me to the door.

I felt my friends' stares bore into my spine as they watched him rush me to his truck. When I glanced back, all of their mouths shaped an "O" like a perfect donut—except for Jenny's.

Her mouth quirked upward as her fingers fluttered bon voyage.

Outside the studio, I found myself stumbling and bumbling across the parking lot to the 4-Runner.

Allan pounced a button on his key fob and jerked wide the passenger door. He shoved me inside with my handbag and coat dumped at my feet.

I didn't like the rough stuff he exhibited, and when he opened his door and slid inside, I said, "Now, wait a minute, Buster—"

He pointed his finger at my face. "Shut up."

"Shut up?" *He raised his voice and told me to shut up?* I couldn't believe he spoke to ME like that.

The engine cranked on, and he shifted the SUV into gear. He concentrated on exiting the parking lot and turning onto Boston Avenue.

I crossed my arms. My mother never allowed us to use the phrase "shut up." She said those words were akin to cursing. I bet a shiny quarter Mrs. Wellborn didn't permit the use of those two little words at their home either.

"You cannot tell me to shut up. Not now. Not ever. Pull over, Allan. Now. I'd rather walk than ride with you."

"Even in the cold?"

"Even in the cold." I would thaw…someday.

"No." He slid a sideways look my way. "Relax. Nothing bad will happen. Sorry about the rough stuff."

*So you say.* I arranged my coat over my legs. "When the Mothers Always Know Network gets wind of our encounter—which they will because they always do—and convenes tomorrow at Super Saver grocery store over vegetables—maybe cauliflower'll be out of stock—you'll be in deep doo-doo for saying shut up. Trust me; I'll make sure you are."

Allan glanced my way for a nanosecond then refocused on the road. "Why? I haven't done anything wrong. We haven't done anything wrong."

"You manhandled me and said a naughty word."

"Manhandled? Funny." He chuckled. "And yes, I might have naughty ideas."

Despite his snatch-and-grab routine, nothing would happen. Mr. On-His-Way-to-Sainthood wouldn't violate me. But I didn't like the approach he used right now.

I stared at the passing scenery. Nothing great. This time of year, nighttime crept in early, right about drive time. The leaves had fallen off the trees, leaving bare black limbs piercing the sky. The grass's texture resembled straw. The days grew cooler and cooler. Soon, the holiday season would be upon us.

I shifted a "from under my lashes" look his way. "Nothing has happened between us."

Even in the truck's dark cab lit by the dashboard lights, an attractive glint glowed in his eyes.

"Aw, there's hope."

*In his dreams. Well, maybe in mine, too, without all the rough stuff.*

Allan turned into the shopping center, which housed Mama's & Papa's Italian Bistro. He slotted his car, killed the engine, and cracked his door. "Come on."

My mouth watered just by staring at the restaurant storefront. His idea involved food. Better yet, Italian food. *A most excellent plan, and I could almost forgive him for the near kidnapping.*

Out of the blue, my tummy gurgled. I laid a palm over my abdomen, hoping he hadn't heard the noise while I pretended nothing transpired. Feeling pleased, I opened the truck's door and stepped out, tossing the coat around my shoulders.

His hand extended behind him in my direction. "Come, Hattie. Please, have dinner with me."

Hunger overruled anger. I folded my hand with his. We walked to our favorite Italian restaurant. He held wide the glass entry door and let me pass through first. My senses were overpowered by the most fabulous scents ever—spicy garlic, sweet tomato, yeasty bread, and sharp onions.

I loved Mama's & Papa's Italian Bistro, a place my parents frequented with Tracey and me since elementary school. The same Tuscan prints decorated the golden faux-finished walls. The same Tony Bennett and Frank Sinatra tunes oozed from the sound system.

I breathed in deeply then looked at Allan, overwhelmed in gratitude. "Nirvana."

He crinkled his eyes. "Forgiven?"

Not sure which time I should forgive him for—when he'd eaten dinner here with Blonde Bimbo and broke my heart or for dragging me tonight. "I'm starving. So, you're forgiven. By the way, did I say thanks for rescuing me from tango lessons?"

"My pleasure." He touched the tip of my nose.

"This is way more fun."

The hostess led us to a booth.

He waved to the table. "Would you sit next to me?"

Oh God, the intimacy—thigh to thigh, arm to arm, shoulder to shoulder. I didn't know if I could handle the closeness. "S-Sure."

After we wiggled into place on the banquette and the menus were passed around, I verified my favorite entrée and smiled. I closed the menu. "Lasagna."

The waitress' pencil hovered over her pad. "Comes with a dinner salad."

"Perfect. With house dressing on the side."

Allan returned his menu. "Same. And two glasses of Pinot Grigio? Okay for you?"

"Yes." I ducked my chin. *How well he knows me.* After she left, a lull descended between us.

He tapped the red-checked cloth. "Want to talk about Stuart and Tracey now?"

The waitress placed filled wine glasses on the table, a breadboard with a small hot loaf, and a container of whipped butter.

Allan lifted his glass. "Cheers."

I touched my rim to his. "Cheers." I took a few swallows, letting the full-bodied citrus taste roll over my tongue. I set my glass on top of four red-and-white squares.

He set a buttered slice on my bread plate.

"Thank you." I chewed contemplatively. "Jonson and Barbie visited the store today. He demanded the ten percent discount Wedding Wonderland offered to new customers. He pitched a royal fit after I told him his purchase didn't qualify because they bought her dress and stuff earlier before the Grand Opening promotion. Then Tracey came in, not noticing him at first. But when they did see each other, ordnance exploded—the kind like an atomic bomb, all stink and smoke, mushrooming skyward with toxic vitriol.

"Maybe I didn't use my best behavior, especially when he lit into his fiancée. But then, Barbie didn't act so nice either. She had the gall to call Tracey ugly."

"Let me guess. You said something not-so-nice in return." He sipped his wine.

"You bet your sweet tushy—"

"My tushy is sweet? Cool."

I put a second slice on my plate, adding a dollop of whipped butter on the side. "No one talks to my baby sister like Barbie did." I chewed three, maybe four, bites.

"Hattie?" He tapped the tabletop with his finger. "Tell all."

"Fine." I set my butter knife on the plate and wiped

my hands on the napkin. "But I say justifiable. I told Ms. Smarty Pants Barbie, Tracey was Jonson's No. 2 wife because nobody—and I mean nobody—messes with my sister, especially him." I took my fork and punctuated the air like I stabbed Jonson Leggett the Third in his heart.

Allan nearly choked on his drink. He set his glass on the table, swiped his mouth with his lap cloth, and coughed. "S-Second ex-wife?"

I nodded and bit into the bread.

"I'm missing something. Are you saying Jonson was married before Tracey?"

"Duh, didn't you read the papers? Didn't your mother tell you?"

"Okay, sometimes, I skip the paper when I'm super busy and"—his brow narrowed—"don't you dare repeat this. I can tune out my mom."

"No way." Shocking it was.

"If you ever say a word, I'll deny everything." He grinned.

Why did Allan have to smile in such a sexy lazy way? He was way too suggestive. I cleared my throat.

"What did Barbie do?"

"At first, she looked sad, her face all droopy like she would cry. Then, as if smacked with a divine revelation, she leaped all over Jonson like fleas on a homeless mongrel. She had no idea he was married two times before and wanted to know why he implied otherwise. My take—he lied."

His left brow lifted. "Jonson, my friend—not—lied by omission."

"Big time. A big fat whopper." I slid my wineglass along a row of checks. "Maybe he's a borderline sociopath."

"Hmm. Most people disclose their marriage background when they begin dating."

"Guess Jonson wanted to avoid anything which could impinge his reputation and prevent him from dipping into the Fenster family wallet."

"Surely, someone said something before now."

"You'd think."

Allan recrossed his legs. "He has a charming way as narcissists do. Anyway, she's better off knowing before the wedding instead of later when he divorces her."

"How do you know he'll divorce her?"

He made a "huh" face and shrugged. "He's got a pattern. He's a serial divorcer—"

"Serial divorcer—what a funny word."

"It fits."

"Miss A., my boss, would agree with you. We discussed the sanctity of marriage." I frowned. "She looked unbelievably…appalled when I told her about Jonson's prior vows. She has hard and fast opinions about the sanctity of marriage."

"Speaking of"—he put a slice of bread on his plate—"what are your beliefs on, uh, marriage?"

My face grew hot. I had a hard time looking at Allan. I stared into the depths of my wineglass. "At first, looks attract two people to each other. They like what they see and feel, and lust comes into the picture."

"Kinda like us."

I rolled my eyes. "But to stay together, two people must have values they respect and a willingness to compromise and work together. But most of all, no lying. Ever."

The waitress set the garden salad in front of us. Not very imaginative, but fresh, not bagged, assorted lettuce, a few curls of carrots, a token tomato slice, and garnished with one black olive. After a liberal dose of ground black pepper and light zing of salad dressing, but no extra cheese, I picked up my fork and took a bite, relishing the zesty tang.

Allan stabbed his tomato. "Very wise assessment."

"Some people say commonalities, too. Like us—"

He raised one brow. "As far as I know, no us."

His serious eye-look wasn't working on me. I pointed my lettuce-loaded fork his way. "Just for an example, say we're together. We both like movies."

He speared his fork in the mixed greens, giving it a go-over before eating. "I tolerated your romantic comedies."

I rolled my eyes a second time. "One time. *One time* we watched something I preferred. I don't savor the blood-and-guts police dramas you favor. Sarcasm in case you were wondering."

Allan set his utensil on his plate and wrapped his fingers on the glass' stem. "I think we were teenagers when we watched one cop show. If I recollect correctly, your mother called, and you hid the remote."

I giggled. "My plan all along. No channel surfing."

"It worked."

Our lasagna arrived. Setting my hands on either side of my plate, I stared at the hot yumminess, ignoring our marriage conversation for the important stuff—eating. I inhaled all the tomatoey, garlicky goodness and dived in. No talking, just appreciating.

I saved half a portion for dinner the following night, because everyone knew pasta tasted better the next day and because I needed tummy room for dessert.

Allan and I negotiated and shared a good-sized wedge of chocolate cherry cake with a fudge-y frosting.

I polished off the last swallow of the white wine with a shoulder lift. "Mmm. I feel better. No hostilities toward you."

"Then, my job's done." He set his empty glass next to the dirty dishes. "Anything else?"

"No."

"I'm shocked. You ate like a horse."

"Ooh, a compliment from the sainted one."

"Cut that out. You know I'm not 'saintly' anything."

"Your mom and my mom think so."

Allan frowned and switched to drinking water.

I should quit harassing him. "Thank you for saving me from Ms. Yolanda." I folded my napkin. "You didn't have to be so rough."

"You know, I'm sick of how every time we do those stupid dance lessons, everyone stares. I've never seen so many eyeballs, except fake ones in the Halloween punch."

"Please." I snorted. "You know why."

He canted his head.

"Allan, you're no dimwit."

His foot grazed my ankle.

I jiggled. "What—"

He did it again only harder.

"Hey, stop." I narrowed my eyes into viper slits. "What's going on?"

"Just trying to get your attention." He bounced his brow. "So, who's the dimwit now?"

Right. *He's playing Mr. Non-Nonchalant.* I drank

some water, then folded my napkin. "It's possible, you're *trying* too hard, bud. You had me at ravenous."

Standing, he tossed money on the table. "We're wasting time, sweetheart."

*Oh boy.* A twinkle in the eye plus footsie under the table equaled romp in a bed. I asked coyly, "Where to?"

"How 'bout your place? It's…closer."

*My favorite plan.* A small, secretive smile shaped my lips. I looped my handbag over my arm.

Like a perfect gentleman, he aided me in scooting from the banquette, then covered my shoulders with my coat.

As I found my way to the front door, his hand glided across my lower spine and rested, sending my heart into palpitations. Girly giggly bubbles burst inside me. *Now? Now? Now?*

Outside, an old-fashioned streetlamp lighted our way to his truck. At the passenger side, I paused only a moment, and in the small space of time, I moved within his arms and brushed a light peck across his jaw, sensing stubble rough my lips. I liked what he offered and wanted—desired—craved more.

After his arms wrapped around me, he tilted his head. "Try messing with me again, young lady, and I won't be responsible."

Mighty pleasing invitation.

He asked, "So straight to your place or your car first?"

*Oh boy, his idea sounded better and better.* I stepped in his truck.

He rounded the front end and climbed in, too.

"Would you mind"—I gave him a sideways smile—"if we picked up my car first? Otherwise, we might get silly texts from friends."

He chuckled. "No problem."

I grinned back. After starting the car, he reversed out the lot, shifted into gear, and drove back to Ms. Yolanda's. Not long later, he slotted his 4-Runner next to my Jeep in the studio's parking lot.

Someone took pity on Jenny and gave her a ride home because I didn't see her standing on the curb, tapping her foot in an "about to blow my top" manner. Before I exited, my gaze met his.

His hand covered mine and squeezed.

Whatever magic dancing in his eyes had me bending his way and kissing him. He cradled my body against his chest, his hand cupping the back of my head before drifting along the column of my neck and to my shoulder. He pulled me tighter. Our long, luscious, and lovely kiss promised everything—everything a man and woman wanted from each other.

Him. Only him.

And sex. Like, sex without Allan's phone interrupting.

Our kiss deepened with intensity and responded with meaning and depth to sear my heart.

Allan threaded his hands through my hair.

I tipped back my head, and small moans escaped my throat. Swirls occupied my brain. My girl parts thrummed.

"I can't believe," he said, his breathing heavy, "I let you talk me…into dropping you off…first."

His fingers toyed with a hair strand at my temple and followed the length to the ends. God, his touch brought incredible intimacy.

I extricated myself from his arms. The corners of

my mouth quirked, even though he most likely couldn't see my expression in the low lights. I exited the truck and walked to the Jeep's passenger door, where I powered open the locks. "Won't be long. I promise. I'll be right behind you."

Something white lodged under my windshield wiper blade caught my eye. I tugged and unfolded the paper: *Told you so.*

*Jenny.* I laughed and flapped the missive at Allan. Inside my car, I turned the engine over, adjusting the temperature knob. With longing and anticipation in my heart, I looked his way only to see him slap his phone to his ear.

*Holy crap.* A sinking bottomed in my belly. *So not good.*

A nanosecond later, he mouthed, "Sorry."

*Duty. His goddamn duty called.* In a flash, everything—every emotion, every sensation, every feeling—circled down the drain to pool in my feet. I pounded the steering wheel. *No. No. NO!*

Disgust, coupled with disappointment, filled my throat. I wanted to curse like a sailor and, certainly, ram his truck with mine. But not really. I wouldn't want to injure my Jeep baby.

He shifted his vehicle into Drive. He barely looked at me as he drove away.

Nobody would be surprised. When work summoned, Allan was Johnny-on-the-spot.

And I was Josephine-in-the-dump.

*Damn.* I flopped against my seat and fanned my face. *Would sex with Allan ever happen?*

I shifted my car into gear and pointed her home. "Sorry," he'd said.

117

A kernel of gloom and doom rooted in my belly. Yes, indeedy, I was sorry. He was sorry. The whole universe was sorry. *Are we ill-fated romantically?*

Chapter Ten

The next day at Wedding Wonderland, I carried a load of cleaning supplies to the front entry. My cell buzzed. I fumbled for my phone in my coat pocket. A fast glance at caller ID told me who phoned—ma mère. Like I wanted to talk with her right now. However, ignoring her would be futile.

*With all the wedding stuff, she'll never leave me alone. Never.*

With a sigh, I dropped the roll of paper towels and window spray at my feet. I connected, shoving my phone under my chin. "Just a minute."

I grasped the bottle of window cleaner and tore off a few towels. I spritzed the door's glass inset. "What, Mom?"

"You don't have to be so rude," she said.

I polished the entry door window to a streak-free shine, just like the product claimed. "Mom. I'm working. You've got to stop calling me about Tracey and Stuart's wedding."

"You're so contrary. We have important things to do."

Mom's "contrary" remark ruffled my feathers, but I wouldn't engage her. "For example?"

"I have a question."

"Only one question?" She undoubtedly had drafted a long, long, looong list to consult.

No reply.

*Lordy.* "Fire away." While she chatted on and on and on, I admired my work and shifted to pretty-up the glass in the second door. As I wiped, I saw a truck slotting into a spot next to the handicap sign positioned in front of the store. I stared harder and grimaced. Not an ordinary vehicle, in fact, a Toyota 4-Runner in granite driven by the man I didn't have a rendezvous with last night, thanks to his almighty cellphone. My non-sex bedtime whatever—Allan.

I straightened my spine. *The dirty rotten rat.* This morning, Allan sent an early stupid text with one solitary word—"*Sorry.*" The man needed better communication skills. "Sorry" sounded so lame, like lame with a capital "L." He better have stashed an apology up his sleeve. A big fat one. And flowers. And an expensive handbag would be welcomed, too.

Because his device wasn't available for my use, I squashed the compulsion to run over mine with my car. Doing so would require buying a new one with money I couldn't waste. *Am I trending toward violent tendencies because of him?*

He exited his vehicle, looking past his truck to the street. He wore a navy suit, red tie, and black Oxfords.

Adding his car plus good looker plus business clothes, I didn't have a hard time determining Detective Allan Wellborn hadn't come for a social call. No sir-ree, "business" was written all over him.

I opened the right door and sprayed a cleaning product on the outside glass. Mom's "Hattie" in my ear shifted my focus back to our conversation. Dumping her could be difficult. In my whole life, she left conversations when *she* wanted to. Considering the subject—Tracey—and the upcoming tying of the knot, she would be hard to shake.

"Hey," I mouthed, pointing my finger as he stepped to the sidewalk in front of the store. I paused long enough to take a little sidelong look at Allan, pointing to my phone. "Mom."

He nodded and walked away.

I slanted an under-the-eyelash look. Getting no nookie required major punishment, and tormenting Allan would be very satisfying, like playing a wicked game of Twister. I said, "No, Mother. I won't try on wedding gowns for you." I slid another sideways peek.

Instantly, his eyes morphed into lizard-like slits. The smallest tightening to his jaw indicated what I said had unnerved him. *Ha.* I loved watching him squirm.

After a long pause, he relaxed and pretended not to listen while fingering the reproduction limestone façade surrounding the next-door store's windows.

*Serves him right after all the things he's done to me, the biggest one being the lack of a stupendous orgasm.*

I gave my sport another "go." "Yes, Mother, I agree. A good style for my figure. I like the lace over the see-through underwear look. All my valuable body parts would show through. Very sexy."

Mom screamed loud enough for the entire universe to cover their ears. "Hattie, what are you saying? Are you and—"

Allan couldn't ignore our conversation. His eyes widened, and his jaw dropped, nearly slamming into the concrete under his feet. Undoubtedly, he heard more than he wanted and advanced closer to the men's shop, probably easing his way to the parking lot.

"Mom, candlelight satin will be a better match for my skin tone. White is just too-too...white. Not everyone can pull it off. I'm sure Allan will be happy with whatever I pick."

A grim, flat-lipped look slowly replaced the stunned one on his face.

I choked back all so I wouldn't laugh. I turned sideways to add, "Okay, I'll find something soon, and remember, pink is my favorite color."

I dropped my phone in my white Wedding Wonderland jacket pocket. I so didn't have anything to say. We pretty much covered all over tango lessons and dinner. Well, except for the playdate part.

He bent closer to the haberdashery window. A beat or two later, he looked at me.

I glared at him with my hands on my waist and my foot tapping.

Straightening, he broadened his shoulders, and with determination, he returned to Wedding Wonderland, halting in front of my toes.

Somehow, I managed not to do an about-face and ride out of town. I focused on Allan's shoes. Shiny, highly polished, expensive black oxfords. Eventually, I roved my gaze over his legs in his "authoritative" spread stance to the black belt with the silver buckle circling his waist, to the knot of his blood-red tie, and finally, landed on his face, trying to determine why he came to call.

*Yup.* His stare read "Detective" and "Detective" meant business.

"Hattie."

"Allan."

"Nice coat, Miss Hattie." He ran his finger across

my name embroidered in pink on the left shoulder of the jacket. "You look…professional."

"The general idea." I jerked the front placket into place, making his arm fall to his side. "What's cookin'?"

He bobbed his head. "I need to speak with you."

"About business or about no pleasure?" Rising to my toes, I pretended to peer behind his back, then rocked to my heels. "You didn't bring a box of chocolates or a bouquet; therefore, business." I lifted my brow. "Am I right?"

"What you are is a smart ass."

His finger returned, skating a long, very slow trail over my jaw. I suppressed the urge to moan like a woman in heat.

"It's important, sweetheart."

"Oookaaay, saintly one—"

"Knock it off."

*Touchy, touchy.* "Sorry. Out here or inside?"

He looked through the window into the store. "Anyone else here?"

"Not right now. Miss A., the owner, drove to the hardware store, but she'll be back shortly. We need light bulbs and a few other things. Pretty funny how she's always misplacing the hammer."

He said, "Let's go in."

"Fine. But don't call me sweetheart."

He barely curled the corner of his mouth. "Yes, sweetheart."

Rolling my eyes, I pulled open the door and paused to collect the cleaning supplies. Allan hadn't been in the store before now, which gave me another opportunity to torment him. *He-he-he.* "Dying to see Wedding

Wonderland?"

He skirted me in the calm and cool manner of James Bond and stepped further inside.

"Top of my bucket list."

After locking the door, I circumvented him to walk to the transaction desk, where I placed the cleaning bucket on the floor next to the table leg. When I pivoted, I found him staring slack-jawed at the whole wedding enchilada. Chandelier, mirrors, flowers, crystals—all floored him. His swallow betrayed his normally unflappable countenance, the one cops perfected for pulling over speeders and writing a nasty citation.

Not surprising. Bridal shops and their glory were intentionally decorated to catch the customer's eye. In the few days of my employment at Wedding Wonderland, I'd seen a boatload of out-of-their-depth fiancés. Just entering the shop humbled the most confident of men. Allan Wellborn looked to be no exception. He acted exactly like every other regular Joe who didn't know what he had gotten himself into.

He refocused on me and said evenly, "This p-place is...different. Not exactly Dollar Bonanza."

"Wow. What a gourmet shopper you are."

"They have good prices on cat food—"

"And plastic cutlery."

"If you say so."

Our inane conversation drove me batty. "And how is my furry friend Lucky?"

"He could use some company." Again, he looked over the store.

I teased, "First time in any bridal salon?"

"No comment."

That meant yes.

He flashed his badge with picture ID. "Official police business."

I squeezed my forehead into a "V" as I bent closer to study Allan's identification picture. His photo looked more like a mug shot—as if I had any experience with mug shots except what the news showed on television. The side-to-side views of the criminals weren't so bad, but the frontal one with a towel covering the bad dudes' shoulders, and a big bad hair day? *Ick.*

My passport photo looked better than his license one. Could anything be so awful? I pursed my lips and tweaked my mouth sideways. "Not your best effort. Sorta geeky like an accountant."

He shoved the ID in his navy suit coat's breast pocket.

Numbers coursed through Allan Wellborn's blood and in his family. His dad worked as an accountant, and I was pretty sure his sister said something about his grandfather had punched numbers as well. After a few years of calculators and creating Excel spreadsheets, Allan abandoned his career for the excitement in police work.

I stabbed my finger in the area where he stashed the ID. "Where's the pocket protector and pens? Oh-oh-oh, we can't forget the yellow highlighter."

I got the "go to hell" face policemen excelled at bestowing, part of their training along with the deadpan "not saying anything" look.

He pointed to the reception chairs. "May I?"

"Sure. Want a bottle of water?"

He shook his head. "No, thanks. I'm good for now."

I removed a bottle from the mini-fridge and sat opposite him, smoothing my black knit skirt along my thighs. Over and over, I rubbed while wondering what legitimate business brought him to the store. I frowned. "Do you want to talk about the rehearsal dinner? That's not official business. I arranged everything on my part. Did you—"

"The rehearsal is not official business. But I'm making headway on my end." His big body took over the chair with a creak. He shifted delicately, and when the sound squeaked again, he bent and checked the legs. "Sure this won't collapse on me? It seems…fragile."

"Positive. What do you want?" I slanted my head.

"Oh, I know. Let's get back to the discussion about you abandoning your date in a parking lot like a superhero bent on a mission to save the world from some evil crime lord descended from another realm. At least, the guy kissed the girl passionately before racing off."

I slid back in my chair and took a long drink. *Do I sound a little bitter? Probably.*

One brow arched. "Funny."

I lifted my water bottle. "You aren't."

"I know you're mad, and I apologize. The job comes—"

"First. Don't I know. Yet, I still come back for more. I must be a masochist."

Allan looked at me from the corner of his eye while removing a notebook and pen from his coat pocket. He thumbed through and stopped after about twenty pages. "Yesterday, in the parking lot of Super Saver Grocery, a store cart retriever found Jonson Leggett the Third dead in his car."

I set aside the bottle and stood. I clapped more than

vigorously. I clapped and clapped until my palms stung. "Well done. Well done. Who did it? I want to thank him-slash-her?"

His whistle reverberated low and long. "Pretty disrespectful. I should be stunned."

"I'm not, nor have I ever been a fan." Dropping back in the chair, I flipped my hand dismissively. "Someone did the world a ginormous favor. Ask anyone in Sommerville. They'll agree with me."

"Wow. Don't hold back."

My sister's pickle with Jonson had made the front page of the *Sommerville Express*, captioned with a "Jilted Wife" headline. The accompanying photo of Tracey with scary witchy hair and raccoon eyes didn't help. The town added two plus two and grasped the sordid story.

"Yup. Cold-blooded." Allan rolled his pen through his fingers. "Don't you feel bad for his family?"

I pendulum-ed my finger. "Aren't Jonson's parents the ones who instilled crappy values?"

His head bobbed. "You have a point."

He sure spent a lot of time on Jonson and his death. *Why?* "So, why are you here?"

"We've notified Ms. Barbie Fenster, his fiancée, who informed us Mr. Leggett and Ms. Fenster have been planning their wedding through the shop"—he consulted his notebook—"Miss Anastasia's Wedding Wonderland."

I nodded my affirmation. "Until recently—"

"Recently?"

"Yes. Don't you remember what I told you last night over dinner? Until he fired us."

"Right." He fumbled through some more pages.

"I'm here because Ms. Fenster said something about an altercation. To interview you and a Miss Anastasia Fernholly, the owner."

"Okay." Miss A.'s errand to Super Saver resurrected. "As I said, my boss should return soon."

"When?"

I consulted my watch. "Any minute. She had to stop several places before work."

"In the meantime, let's chat." He crossed his leg, resting his notepad on his thigh.

Yep, the same muscular one which failed to wrap around my hip. Parts of me went squirmy and boiling. I coughed. "Why?"

"You know—your sister, Tracey. And the argument with Jonson. You heard it, and I need to know in great detail what transpired."

I teethed my lower lip. *Is Allan investigating Tracey as a possible murderer?* I swallowed hard and deep, feeling a greasy sickness swilling in my belly. *What if he wants to arrest Tracey? But what for? She didn't do anything.* I ran my finger over and over the length of my nose while I considered how to proceed.

Slowly, I drew myself upright and stared at The Great Detective, not trusting him. Fury raced through my head. I didn't know what to think or believe, and I certainly didn't want to get Tracey in trouble. No way in hell would he get any information from me. *The turd. I'll keep my mouth shut tight.*

"Leave." I exploded to my feet faster than fast and pointed to the door. I stalked toward the entry as quick as I could and yanked open the door. "Leave. Leave. Right now."

On my heels, Allan followed, but he didn't go

anywhere. Instead, his hand rested on top of mine.

I sensed the heave of his chest against my shoulders. His warm breath bathed my hairline right below my ear, a very vulnerable spot sending sizzles over my neck. An ache for more, the same as when I anticipated a round of almost wild, almost sex, rooted in my heart.

With a deep breath, I composed myself and said, "No, Allan. Go."

"Nope. Come on."

He took my hand and pulled me back to the reception area.

I was not a happy camper. Resisting, I stood firm. Immovable. But with one glance, my stubbornness threatened to wilt, and I dumped myself in the chair.

He said, "Sorry. I can't say so enough."

I pinned on him a firm glare, the despicable evil-eye kind which could make an ordinary person flinch, but not him. Maybe because he'd seen mine on multiple occasions. "Possibly, time to find a new phrase."

"Ouch."

I stared and stared, waiting for the words to gush from his mouth, while the wrath entrenched in my soul threatened to erupt again. "How could you, Allan? Seriously. How could you come here and accuse my sister of something foul? You should have blamed me instead of Tracey. She doesn't have a mean bone in her body. For gosh sakes, she doesn't kill bugs. She sets them free."

Allan gave a double-take. Raising his palms, he made a minute shrug. "You know the drill. It's my job. I have to ask."

"Your job," I spat. "Not such a good family friend,

are you?" Cynicism seeped into every single word.

"I guess not, at least, not this time." He crooked the right side of his mouth. "I'll probably hear from my mom. She doesn't like me bothering you."

"I'll hear from mine." *With the option he could be struck from the potential son-in-law list.*

"I'll steer clear of yours."

*Me, too, because Mom's lecture on Mr. Saintliness's pluses ran too long.*

Allan slanted his head. "At what point does their shtick end?"

*How funny.* A small curve tweaked the corners of my mouth. But my sensibility reigned, and I recovered. "Never"—I crossed my arms and squeezed—"ever. Mothers, especially the kind like ours, will always inject themselves in their children's lives. Part of their DNA makes them."

He snorted and lifted one eyebrow. "Did you inherit the gene?"

I matched his brow lift with one of my own. I raised my bottle of water close to my lips and said before taking a drink, "Wouldn't you like to know?"

"I would, sweetheart."

Allan's answer surprised me, making my hands quake. I knocked back some water. He had an odd way of saying he cared to unearth the tiniest thing about me. "Don't call me sweetheart."

Neither of us said anything for a bit. I gave in first with a sigh. "What do you want to know?"

Chapter Eleven

Allan pulled a recorder from his coat pocket, pressed a button, then stated my name, Harriet Lee Cooks, the date, the time, his name, and credentials. "Are you acquainted with Jonson Leggett the Third?"

I didn't want to divulge my sister's private affairs because Tracey should tell the story, not me. Besides, I more than hated Jonson—my mouth would get me into trouble—and could be accused of dispatching his body like I wanted to on multiple occasions. However, when the scandal broke, the public saw my sister's past based on the vast spread in the paper. "God, yes. My sister was married to Jonson Leggett the Third for one year."

"What?"

Not often had I startled him.

He recovered his police professionalism. "I mean, would you repeat that?"

"Everyone knows. Jonson Leggett the Third eloped with my sister, Tracey, to Vegas four years ago. The marriage was dissolved within twelve months."

"I didn't know all the details. You know how our mothers gossip. I don't listen. Go on." Allan scribbled. "Tell me what you know."

He trotted out his "tell me" phrase to obtain information from people in a gentle, folksy manner, probably part of his detective training. I'd been on the receiving end several times. The first was when he found out I worked at the insurance company where he investigated stolen car parts and a related murder. The second time was when the Blonde Bimbo picked off guys in the accounting office—the same male co-workers I'd been friendly with.

I told Allan, "Jonson and Barbie arranged a consultation with Miss A. to begin the wedding planning process. Preliminary information was inputted via a form on the store tablet and auto-forwarded to our laptops. Barbie tried on several gowns and headpieces and purchased a selection. She looked stunning.

"While Miss A. helped Barbie, Jonson sat in the reception area—in the same chair you're sitting in now—and thumbed idly through the invitation book, the one on top of the table." I pointed to the tome by his side.

He glanced at it.

"Yes, that one. When bored, Jonson finally looked in my direction and recognized me. I pretended to be glad to be reacquainted with him. Pretend is the operative word. He disgusted me."

I relayed all the gory details, the same ones I passed on to Miss A. the afternoon after Jonson and Barbie's first visit.

Detective Wellborn listened to the whole story. "Anything else?"

"No. On the day of the grand opening of Wedding Wonderland, he rammed his way into the store and insisted, I mean, insisted-insisted on a ten percent discount."

Again, his eyebrow arched. "And you said—"

"No."

"Because—"

I shifted to one hip. "I said no because they purchased Barbie's gown before the opening. In exchange for their help in promo materials, Miss A. prepared a package that reduced their costs significantly. The discount he tried to use became effective on the day of the grand opening, not before."

"And what did Mr. Leggett do?"

I rubbed the length of my nose. "Jonson made incredibly rude comments. He cursed, called me names, and shoved Barbie. Rather abusive. Probably verbally abusive. Tracey walked in the store, all happy and care-free. I had pre-selected a few gowns for her to try on. At first, she didn't see Jonson, who stood on the other side of Barbie. But when he interrupted Tracey's chat with me, everything changed. My sister was not happy. I was not happy. Barbie was not happy. He said ugly things to Tracey, too. He said ugly things to all three of us. So fed up with his nonsense, I informed Barbie about his marriage to Tracey."

"Yikes. Sounds"—Allan worked his mouth—"combustible. How did Barbie take it?"

"Poor thing. She just about burst into tears. She begged Jonson to tell her the truth. He didn't pay her any attention."

"What happened next? Did Tracey threaten Jonson?"

"Fuck no."

He tick-tocked his finger. "Language, sweetheart."

I set a finger to my lower lip, letting the endearment pass by. "Sorry. That would be a plain, ol'-fashioned...no. Tracey would never, and I repeat, never-ever hurt anyone."

The store door banged open as Miss A. shoved her

way inside. The bags and laptop she carried nearly made it impossible for her to walk.

Being the polite gentleman, Allan set his notepad and pen on the tabletop and stood to assist her.

"Hi, Miss A." I rose as well, waving my hand at Allan. "May I introduce you to Detective Allan Wellborn from the Sommerville Police Department?"

Miss A. surrendered her packages to him, and after he set them on the desk, she dropped her handbag and shook his hand. "So nice to make your acquaintance, Detective. Are you a special friend"—she shot me a playful, inquisitive look which had me roll my eyes—"of Hattie's?"

"Our mothers are good friends," he said. "And my sister's Hattie's best friend."

"Uh, Miss A..." Summoning the right words wouldn't be easy. I firmed my lips.

"Yes, dearie?"

"Detective Wellborn is here to interview both of us."

Her brows notched together. "Interview? Why?"

"I don't know how to say..." I shot him a look. "Do you want to tell her, or shall I?"

He nodded his head. "Go ahead."

"I'm afraid it's not good news. I'm sorry."

Miss A. gripped the back of a chair. Her fingers curled into the wood. White creases striped her knuckles.

I inhaled deeply. "Someone found Jonson Leggett in his car in Super Saver's parking lot. He's dead."

"Dead?"

Miss A. looked from Detective Wellborn to me and back again. Her face dissolved of all color to sickly white. She stumbled backward.

I shot a hand her way to grasp her elbow before she crashed.

"I-I don't believe it," she spluttered.

"I'm sorry."

She stared at Allan.

He nodded. "Yes, ma'am, it's true." He filled her in on all the gruesome details.

"How surreal," Miss A. said.

My employer shifted again in a wobbly way. Concerns for her well-being took precedence. "Do you need to sit, Miss A.?" I asked.

"I believe I will, my dear. Shopping—what a nightmare. And the awful news on top…" She touched her forehead. "I think I'll go to my office."

Allan said, "I need to conduct a one-on-one interview with you, Miss A. Can we have a private chat?"

"Of course. Hattie, can you manage?"

Comprehending what Miss A. hadn't said, I smoothed my hand over her arm, feeling the crisp white fabric of her store jacket. "I can. You're just a phone call away. No worries."

"I'll carry your packages." After Allan stuffed his pen, notebook, and recorder in his suit pocket, he picked up her purchases.

Miss A. led the way to the office in the back, closing the door behind them.

Approximately thirty minutes later, Detective Wellborn and Miss A. emerged.

I looked their way, noting she looked less pale, undoubtedly due to the never-ending pot of coffee she brewed in her office. She gave a brief tour of the premises and, with a wave, also gave Allan an abbreviated version on how the wedding business operated.

While they talked and strolled about the store, I did data entry work on the computer—Misses Jacobs, Watson, and Wilson would be notified by email of upcoming decisions regarding flowers; however, I kept one eye on the twosome. And sharpened my hearing, too. I didn't want to miss any details, although I believed Miss A. would fill me in later.

Their excursion ended at the transaction desk.

I stopped typing and launched myself to my feet.

"Anything else you need, Detective Wellborn?" Miss A. looked from him to me as a small cagy smile rippled her mouth.

"No, ma'am," he said, shoving his notebook in his jacket pocket. "I appreciate your cooperation."

"Absolutely." She held out her hand. "Please let me know if I can do anything for you and the Sommerville Police Department. Anything. Anytime."

He shook hers. "Yes, ma'am. Thank you for your help."

She peeled away, pausing to tidy the leaves on the artificial flower arrangement by the dais. She returned to the office, where she shut the door.

Allan shifted his focus. "She seems like a nice lady."

"She's a pro. I'm fortunate to be learning from her," I said. "I remembered something you'll be interested in…about Jonson."

He lifted his right brow. "Tell me."

"Well, my sister said something long ago in passing—"

"Which is—"

"He liked to play poker."

Allan snorted. "Most guys play some."

"Ha. More than some. He played a lot. High stakes. Which would explain why he had money issues."

"Okay." Allan removed his pad and scribbled. "And this is relevant to his murder…how?"

I shrugged and dragged a finger in a phantom line across the desktop. "I don't know for sure. Maybe Jonson lost a lot of money or borrowed a lot of money from some kind of mafia guy—"

"You've been reading mystery-thriller books again." He snapped shut his notebook.

I stomped my foot. "Be serious."

"Fine. I'll check. Poker-playing mafia guys. It's worth a shot."

While stowing his pen and pad, he glanced my way. "Good to see you."

*Good to see you?* Could he have used better words for more than a friend? *I'm thinking stupid.* I suppressed the urge to roll my eyes. "Bye."

When he reached the door, he stopped long enough to rock his hand in the "I'll phone you" signal.

*Seemed destined to talk.* I trailed Allan and glared at his truck as he drove away. When I couldn't see him anymore, I turned my attention to Miss A. She had looked distraught over the news about Jonson's departure from the earthly realm to the underworld. I should feel some remorse as well. I mean, murder was gruesome and all. But I didn't. I couldn't say or think enough of what an asshole Jonson was. The big wide world should be greatly rejoicing because he couldn't dupe any more young women to the altar.

As I made my way to the back office, I plucked blue puffballs of lint off the carpet. I knocked on her office door. "Miss A.? May I come in?"

"Of course, dearie," she called.

I opened the office door and stepped inside, depositing the balls of carpet lint in the trash can. I brushed my hands. "You seemed distraught about, er, what happened to Jonson. Maybe you might want to talk about it?"

"Oh, Hattie," Miss A. rubbed the space between her eyes. "I feel so sad for Barbie."

She mopped her tears with an old-fashioned hankie trimmed with yellow and purple crocheted pansies, the kind my grandmother had crafted.

"I'm incredibly disappointed. I hoped Barbie and Jonson's nuptials would be a good launch for the shop and give us publicity," she said. "I hoped Sommerville's poshest clientele would follow their lead."

"I know. It's just awful." I circled her desk and patted her shoulder. "Don't worry, Miss A. We'll think of some other plan for Wedding Wonderland. It'll be good, I promise. For certain, I'll hook my mom and her mahjong buds into telling everyone they know about the store."

"I appreciate anything anyone can do, Hattie. I feel so low right now. I left everything behind." She looked in my direction through water-filled eyes. "Can you imagine?"

"No, I can't." Although I nearly could. When my life didn't work out like I wanted, I considered relocating to New York for a coveted buyer's position with a prominent department store. But final decision time came, and I said no. In my heart, leaving my family and friends was not an option I could bear. Ultimately, leaving Allan and the unknown gray void between us—I just couldn't. I had to know if "he and I" would become "we."

I gave her another comforting shoulder massage. "I admire how it takes a lot of chutzpah to make a new start in a new town."

Miss A. didn't say anything except to press the cotton square to the drops trickling down her cheeks. Once under control, she squeaked, "Yes, it does. But I *had* to make a life change. Nothing—"

"Change can be good. Change means a new life adventure, doesn't it?"

She nodded.

"Now, don't you worry." I sounded just like my mom. A section from her pep talk on "Consolation" sprang forth. "We can do it. Everything'll be just fine. You'll see."

Miss A. glanced my way. "Are you a special friend of Detective Wellborn? I felt something like"—she shook her head—"vibes, maybe more than vibes. Maybe electricity. The unmistakable chemistry kind linking a man and woman. Whatever I sensed, it danced in the air."

My body still vibrated just from being near him. I tilted my head from side to side. Something popped in my neck. "Sorta."

"Sorta?"

"Allan Wellborn and I have tried to date. We ate dinner together the other night."

"I see." Miss A. dipped her head. "Tried to date? I would try harder. He's extremely handsome."

"Yep. Migh-tee fine." I sketched an outline of his physique in the air, which I followed with a thumbs up. "Our mothers have planned our wedding for years, like since the Wellborn family moved to Sommerville when their kids were toddlers, but lately, it's…he's… Everything's hopeless." I lifted then dropped my hands.

"Surely not hopeless, dearie."

Miss A. looked clueless. Telling all would take a freakin' eternity. Time to find out what Allan had discussed with her. Nonchalantly, I rubbed my finger over my pursed mouth. "Did he say anything important?"

She sighed. "Detective Wellborn asked about Barbie and Jonson's appointment. I explained how you visited with him more than I did—sorry if I threw you under the bus—and how I helped Barbie try on gowns. How we've been emailing and phoning Barbie about the planning after Jonson's squabble here. That's all."

With nothing else to occupy my hands, I selected a yellow sticky note pad and ripped off a sheet. I creased it into a perfect square. "I didn't kill Jonson, Miss A."

"No, dearie, you didn't. I bet my life on it." Miss A. stood, stuffing her fists in her jacket pockets. She sniffed. "Barbie's account should be on hold. I'll phone her. Maybe a family member will answer and can help."

"I'll get her cell number." Returning to the reception desk, I ripped off a new sheet from the sticky pad. I typed Barbie's name in the database and retrieved the information. I ferried what Miss A. needed to her. "Here you go."

"Thanks, dearie." Setting her hand on the handset, she studied the paper.

Her pause worried me. "Miss A.?"

"Hmm, dearie?"

"Anything else you need?"

"No." She tweaked her mouth to one side. "I hate to disturb Barbie in her time of grief. Maybe I should leave a message, asking her to call when convenient."

"Your plan is very considerate." After I backed out of her office, I quietly closed the door.

Returning to the reception desk, I plopped in the chair, setting it to swivel from side to side. I propped my chin on my tented fingers and reflected on what transpired this morning. Not every day a cop visited and informed one about the murder of someone you hated. I had no idea Miss A. put a lot of promo eggs in the Jonson and Barbie basket. Her plan not working out? Devastating.

I stilled the chair, selected a pen, and rat-a-tat-tatted a silly beat on the desk. I would have to rely on the adage Mom shared: time will pass, and all will be better. One day. Not today, nor tomorrow. But eventually.

Miss A. and I could think of something new. I resumed swiveling and tapping, fixing a drawn-out look on her closed door. What Miss A. did in her office—I hadn't a clue.

Did I want to know everything?

Chapter Twelve

True to his hand signal, Allan called me later in the evening. "I need to locate Tracey."

*This did not sound good. I didn't get to answer with a "howdy" before being blasted with his demand.* "Tracey? As in my sister Tracey?"

"You're not a dimwit, Hattie. Your sister."

"Why?" As if he would tell.

"Stop playing games, sweetheart. Give me her number. It's important."

*Hmm. Definitely not liking the sounds of his "important."* "Like police important?"

"You have to be the most frustrating woman on earth."

*Deal with this, moron.* I hung up. My phone rang right away. I looked at the screen. Allan again. *Not surprising.* "Yes?"

"I apologize."

"Hard to say?"

Nothing but grumbles.

"I'm sorry, I didn't understand you through your complaining. I'm guessing we have a bad connection." I stabbed the "off" button again.

The phone rang. "Please, Hattie. Will you *please* give me Tracey's phone number? Please."

Lots of "pleases" in his ask. Yanking his chain? Tons of fun. I grinned. "I'm thinking."

"Can you think faster?"

"Maybe you could try the white pages." Again, nothing. "So, why do you want her number?"

Allan let out a long sigh. "Jonson Leggett's murder—remember?"

I froze like an icicle. The importance of *why* Detective Wellborn wanted to speak with Tracey dawned on me with crystal clear clarity—my sissie became numero uno at the top of his suspect list, especially after the near argument with Jonson at the store.

Before I would dish any info, I required confirmation. "We discussed the sister topic this morning when you came by Wonderland. Let me reiterate, Tracey didn't do anything."

"Hattie."

Allan paused a long time, which he seemed to do a lot when he talked to me, like I frustrated him. Right now, he frustrated me.

"You know how it works," he said. "The police interview any and every person relevant to a case. Every piece of information. Everything."

The sternness in his voice annoyed me. "Allan, Tracey didn't do it. She didn't kill Jonson Leggett the Third. *I* would kill him for what he did to *my* sister."

"Don't say stuff like that to a policeman, Hattie. You could get into serious trouble."

*Fine. Be a butthead.* I hung up a third time and went straight to the computer. *Allan might be right, but he could get Tracey's phone number elsewhere, like the phone directory, or from his mother, or the police database. I don't care where, but not from me. I would never be a traitor, especially to my sister.*

I teethed my lower lip. *And if Allan thinks badgering me for my sister's number so he can interrogate her is how to get a girlfriend—he's dumb.*

Settling my fingers on the keyboard, I typed. I would email my family and the other Funsisters to let them know about Detective Wellborn's game plan. No way in hell would he get any information from us. We would form a corral around Tracey, making a fortress so impenetrable, broken bones from trying to break through would be his hugest problem.

Funsisters protected each other. Our code.

****

During my prime sleepy time, Jenny stumbled in my room and laid my cell phone on the side of my face.

Instantly, I sat straighter, my phone dropping to my lap, letting out an earth-shattering "intruder alert, intruder alert" screech.

I set my hand to my heaving chest when Jenny came into focus. "What is it? Are you okay?"

She pointed to my cellphone buried in my comforter. "Your phone…has been ringing…a lot."

I hadn't heard a thing; however, I left mine recharging on the credenza in the living room. "Didn't hear it."

"Someone wants you badly." She yawned. "You might adjust the ringer."

"Sorry." I groped amongst the covers to locate my cell and placed it against my ear. My eyes closed. "Hello?"

"Hattie. Hattie. Answer me."

An exceedingly familiar sharpness in the voice penetrated my sleepy state. I forced open one eyelid. "Mom?"

"Wake up."

"Sorta…am…now." I stared at my alarm clock—two A.M.—and my phone—still two A.M. "It's two freakin' early in the morning, Mom. What do you want?"

"I wouldn't call you unless important," she said. "Very important. An emergency. A family emergency."

I brushed the hair from my eyes. "This better be good."

"You're not sounding one bit respectful, young lady. I know I taught you better."

She had, but phoning at two A.M. didn't seem respectful either. "I apologize. What's the emergency?"

"The police questioned your sister."

"Tracey?" I threw off my bedcoverings. "Questioned? Police? Really? When?"

"Really. Allan hauled her to the station. I bet everyone in Sommerville knows."

And warranted a two A.M. call. I ruffled my hair. "Allan told me he needed to talk to Tracey and asked for her phone number. I declined to give it. Didn't you see my email?"

"The one discouraging him?" Mom asked. "I did. I'm guessing his mother gave him Tracey's number. I'll be having a huge talk with Shirley tomorrow at Super Saver. Radishes are on special."

*Radishes?* I shook my head. Mom? Unstoppable.

"Tracey said Allan pressed her to come to the police station to conduct an interview. He just about accused her of murdering Jonson," Mom said.

Every pore in my core seethed with red-hot anger over what Allan did. I gripped my cellphone tighter. "The rat. Allan tossed his regulation policeman crap

145

spiel my way. I told him not to bother Tracey, but did he listen? Nooo. Everyone knows she wouldn't hurt a fly. She wouldn't murder anybody. I'll give him a piece of my mind right now. Bye—"

"Wait. Hattie."

My mom didn't sound like her usual unflappable self. I said, "I'm guessing something did happen."

"Well, your darling sister might…have done…something."

"Like what constitutes something?"

"Like maybe she left…fingerprints on Jonson's car something."

"Fingerprints? On Jonson's car?" *Lord, help us.* I shut my eyes to blot out what Mom disclosed and pressed my palm to my forehead. A few seconds passed before I squeezed my eyes open. "I don't get it. Are you saying Tracey bumped into Jonson at Super Saver?"

"She said so when Dad and I picked her up at that-that horrid place," Mom said. "Honestly, I don't know what to think, Hattie. Things are…are scaring me. Scaring all of us. I'm so worried."

Now, the desperation in Mom's voice really-really-really shocked me. Never, ever frantic, Mom epitomized the kind of woman with every curl in place. And all lacquered with super freeze-y hairspray in case of a possible tornado. Furthermore, all I's were dotted. All T's crossed.

I covered my lips with my fingers. "Oh. My. God."

"Tracey wouldn't tell me when and why she talked to Jonson. I expect pig-headedness from you. Not her."

I set my lips and slung my legs over the side of the bed, then stood. I crossed to the chair where I'd tossed a pair of jeans and a white T-shirt. I pulled on the pants. I stuck my arms in the shirt sleeves and wriggled my head through the opening while juggling the phone. "Your darling daughter is a brat."

"God. Tracey has to tell somebody the truth," Mom said. "Come now. We can't do anything until she does. Hurry. Please."

"Tracey will be talking plenty when I'm through with her."

\*\*\*\*

I broke land speed records to get to Mom and Dad's house, but then, not a whole lot of cars were on the road—or cops. Usually, they seemed to home in on me like bees on pollen. Upon entering my parents' house, the atmosphere of a funeral parlor—dead quiet—enveloped everything, everyone, everywhere.

I'd never seen my mother's house look so messy. Used tissues and coffee cups lay on top of the kitchen counters in piles. Trash spilled from the overflowing receptacle and littered the floor. Ordinarily, Mom would be plucking the tissues with tongs and tossing them away.

A small sob came from the dining room. I cut through the kitchen to the formal dining room, where I found Tracey sitting in a Duncan-Phyfe styled chair at the head of great-grandmother's table. Black mascara streaked her cheeks. Her regular stuck-out hairdo climbed to Empire State Building height.

On each side of the table, Mom and Dad paced, not uttering a word, and worry painting their faces. The only difference between them—Mom twisted her hands over and over and over.

I crouched at Tracey's left side, set one hand on her arm, and put the other on her knee. I took her hand, and her fingers curled with mine as she blankly focused on me. I said, "Hey, Trace."

My younger sister peeked at me through her wet lashes.

"Mom phoned. She explained what she could."

"I-I know."

"She said the police interrogated you."

Tracey pursed her lips and gave a half shrug. "Yes."

I reset my crouch. "You have to tell us what happened."

With angry swipes, she yanked her hand from mine and dried her eyes. "Isn't anyone listening? I. Didn't. Do. Anything."

Her hysterics rivaled a prime-time soap opera.

"Okay?"

"Calm down. Yelling won't help. I'm on your side, Sissie, we all are. But something happened, and you need our help."

Rising, I shifted a chair to face her and sat, resting my forearms on my thighs. "Allan bugged me for your number, and when I wouldn't give him the time of day, he asked his mom or went to the police databases. I think he thinks you spoke to Jonson—which must be true because the police found your fingerprints on his car. Why, sister dear?"

"It's so stupid." Tracey pressed a tissue to each corner of her eyes. "Your boyfriend—"

"Not."

"—implied he would arrest me if I didn't come in for a chat."

"Doesn't seem like a lot of evidence if you ask me," Mom said.

*Me neither.* "Allan has to resolve everything by making a timeline."

"Doesn't he need DNA?" Mom asked.

"They'll get statements, eyewitnesses, fingerprints, videos. Trace, can you please tell us? Nothing leaves this room." I crossed my heart with my finger. "I promise."

Mom and Dad crossed their hearts, too.

My sister blew her nose. She pinched the used tissue with her thumb and forefinger just like a seven-year-old.

Mom passed her a napkin.

Dropping the tissue, Tracey pressed her gooky fingers to the napkin.

"I went to Super Saver to get Yummy Gummy's new pistachio and cherry flavored ice cream for Stuart. When I walked through the parking lot toward the entrance, I passed Jonson's car. Only I didn't recognize his drive. Not the old beat-up truck I knew. Some big European boxy thing." She stared. "Looked brand new."

I still wanted to know where Jonson got the money for an expensive ride, like over one-hundred-thousand dollars ride. *Maybe from Barbie's family. Maybe she has a big trust fund. Or maybe winnings from the poker-playing mafia.*

*Wait a minute. Could Jonson have been a hit?* I should follow up with Allan again. "Ice cream for Stuart. Got it. Jonson's new ride. Got it. Go on."

"Just minding my own business." Tracey squinted. "Happy…you know?"

I nodded. The whole solar system knew cloud nine had nothing on Tracey and her happy-ever-after.

"I weaved between a truck—a red one, I think—and a mini-van toward the store's entrance. About the time I passed Jonson's driver's side, a hand—*his hand*—shot out in front of me. For a sec, the idea some stalker, murderer, or rapist scoped me out and scared me." She pouted. "He's just as evil."

"I would have been frightened, too." I plucked a new tissue from the box Mom passed me and handed it over to Tracey. "What next?"

"Then he said in a long slow deep drawl, 'Traaaceeee.' He would say my name like that when he tried to sound sexy. He could be charming but rarely was. Ick." Her shoulders shimmied. "My creep-o-meter rose to danger-danger. I ducked his arm. In a flash, he grabbed my bicep and pulled me next to his vehicle. I set my hands on the door to push away, but I couldn't.

"My white jacket"—she face-palmed me like a traffic cop—"I know what you'll say about wearing white after Labor Day, but don't—was smudged across my chest and tummy with car grunge."

"Hmm. I can't imagine Jonson letting an expensive car be dirty."

"Me neither." Tracey plucked the dingy undershirt, one which had been through multiple washings, she now wore. "Huh. I forgot the police took my clothing. Something about evidence." Her look of puzzlement shifted to remembering. "Yes, that's why, and why I'm wearing"—she plucked the front of the T-shirt—"whatever this is instead of my suit."

I tilted my head. "The white designer suit you found at the consignment store?"

"Yes. I couldn't believe the price—"

"A good value—"

"Girls." Dad's fist slammed the table, causing us to jump. "Stay on track. I'm pretty sure Allan didn't take Tracey to the station to talk about women's clothing."

"You're right, Dad. Allan never talks about fashion." *Except, on occasion, he said something about removing my clothing.* I set my hand on Tracey's. "Please, continue."

She bit into her lower lip. "Jonson said, 'Hey, darlin', how ya doin'?' I nearly vomited, especially after how he treated me in Wedding Wonderland the other day, you know, when we argued."

"What argument?" Mom asked. "You never said anything about an argument with Jonson."

"Give Tracey a sec, Mom. Jonson's main goal was to cause trouble." I rubbed my sister's shoulder in my best sisterly fashion. "He makes me sick, too. You should have christened his car's interior. I know I would have."

"Now, I wish I had, but as we all are aware, I'm an anti-vomit person. I held it in. The ol' swallow and breathe through the nose trick." Tracey gave an appreciative baby smile. "I only wish I'd keyed the driver's door just like you and I did after the divorce from hell."

Tracey smacked her hand over her mouth and looked at our parents, whose mouths dropped to the floor. "Oops."

Dad stood and walked around the table. "You keyed Jonson's car?"

"It's nothing, Dad. No worries," Tracey said.

"Doesn't sound like nothing to me," he said.

Tracey shrugged. "I couldn't help myself."

I stood, lacing my fingers, stretching my arms over

my head, and stretching from my right to my left. "Like Tracey said, Dad, nothing, just a teeny tiny insignificant nothing. Really. Jonson deserved more plus."

"Sounds like…revenge." Dad shoved his hand through his hair. "Nothing good comes from it."

"You remember his piece of doo-doo truck." I dropped my arms. "The ancient pale gold and white one with the tailgate which flopped open spontaneously? Kinda funny."

"Somebody should have declared his truck a deathtrap," Tracey added. "He probably didn't notice the damage."

"Girls." Dad compressed his lips. "Your mother and I taught you to respect others' property."

They did, especially Mom with her "Respect, Respect, Respect" lecture. Must be the one time her talk didn't stick.

I lifted my palms. "Don't be mad at Tracey. A light bulb idea whacked me. I could say sorry, but considering whose car we'd violated, not really."

"We raised you better."

"You did. I blame the wine."

His lips flattened to near white. "You were drinking and driving?"

"A bottle of Moët." I shrugged. "We celebrated Tracey's divorce. What better way?"

"I don't want to hear any more about his car." Mom posed her hands prayerfully against her chest. "Tracey, please finish."

"Yes, ma'am." Tracey inhaled. "Jonson and I were face to face. I could smell the cheap whiskey on his breath—"

"He smelled like booze when he and Barbie were

in the store," I said.

"Not surprised. Wish I had known Jonson could throw back a drink like a fish." She frowned. "Anyway, I wanted to get away and tried but couldn't. I have a couple of bruises."

She unfolded her arm. Sure enough, three oval-shaped imprints left by his fingers discolored her forearm.

Mom gasped. "That's not an ordinary grab. It's…brutal."

Dad inspected the bruise, too. "I wish he'd resurrect so I could kick his ass."

All three of us stared at my father, who rarely said anything, letting Mom do most of the talking most of the time.

"It's horrible." I dug for my phone stuck in my hip pocket. "Tracey, did the cops take pictures of your arm?"

"A woman cop watched me undress and took pictures." She shook her head. "I don't think they know. I didn't know."

"Not even when you changed clothes?"

"No, I didn't notice until later." Tracey slid her left hand over the owie, blanketing the hurt with warmth from her body.

"You should have told them. Heads up." I hit the camera app on my phone and took several photos of her arm and face, explicitly including a close-up shot. I would forward the photo to Mr. Perfect Policeman Allan.

"Why did you give them your clothing?" I asked.

"I don't know. I felt discombobulated. The other detective asked, and I agreed. A policewoman escorted me to a room." She lifted her right shoulder.

*Lordy, this sounds so scary.* "So, go on. Tell us everything that happened."

Tracey swallowed deeply. "Jonson held my arm. I pressed my hands against the window frame—where the police found my fingerprints. I don't know how I managed a calm voice. When I asked him about his upcoming marriage, I choked on my words. He gave me one of those twinkly, revolting looks and said, 'You know, Traceee, we always were good together. How about a last quickie before my big day?' "

Chapter Thirteen

Tracey pushed her hand over her forehead and sighed. "I think I'm might be sick."

Dad gulped.

Mom gasped and ran for a bowl. She pressed one in Tracey's arms. Tracey cradled it tightly.

I popped my eyes wide as I balled my hands into fists. Jonson Leggett the Third—creep extraordinaire—propositioned my sister—*my sister*—while engaged to Barbie Fenster, poor girl. Barbie had no idea about Jonson and his horrible demeanor. None at all.

The epithets tornadoing through my head were positively not PG-rated, more like Triple X. With my heart and soul, I ached to punch Jonson, but now, I couldn't, seeing how he was already dead. "Sissie, I-I don't know what to say."

"Oh, I have tales to curl your hair and more. It's sick." Tracey nodded. "Jonson sent flowers a while back. And emailed."

"He what? He emailed…you?" A smashed, moldy green-pea sickness rooted in my tummy. Eyeing the bowl Tracey held, I rubbed a circle around my belly button. "Why didn't you tell me?"

"Or us?" Dad asked.

*My parents must be in their own unspecial hell now knowing what Tracey went through.*

Tracey hung her head, her hand passing over her

face and dragging her skin in a grotesque way, conveying how exhaustion took over her. She put the bowl on the table. "No one could have been more disgusting than Jonson. I wanted to be as far away from him as possible. I wanted to tell you, but I couldn't." She pointed toward Mom and Dad.

Tracey aimed a finger at my chest. "And I know you. *You* would have more than keyed his car."

I pressed my finger to my chin. "You are right, sister dear. I'm thinking slashed tires—"

"Hattie," Dad said.

Dad's warning tone said he wasn't pleased with what Tracey and I did long ago. And usually, I wouldn't have done anything remotely resembling the destruction of private property. "Sorry—again. But not really—again." I scrunched my nose and tilted with a shrug.

"I trashed those sucky thoughts PDQ. Besides"— Tracey pressed her back to the chair—"I had happier plans to think about, like my wedding to Stuart. I couldn't let Jonson's vileness take Stuart from me."

Dad laid his hand on her head as a parent would to a small child. My heart melted.

"What happened next?" he asked.

Tracey glanced up. "My blood boiled. It brewed and bubbled, and a fierce red took over. No way in hell would I sleep or do anything with the moron. When he wouldn't let go of my right arm, I socked him with my left, right between the eyes. His head cracked back. His grip loosened."

She shook her left hand as if still feeling the impact of hand to face.

"I ran away—"

"Did you tell Allan?" I asked.

Tracey shook her head. "No."

I threw my hands in the air. "God, Trace. You left out the important stuff."

"She didn't say anything to anyone on purpose," Dad said.

"Not a word," Tracey said. "I didn't want to get in trouble."

"Yet, you gave the police your clothes." Shaking my head, I set my hand to my temple.

"What?" Dad asked.

"Nothing. I promise it's nothing. Continue, Tracey." I pointed at her.

"When his grip loosened, I ran like the devil to my car. My hands were shaking"—she extended her arms—"see? They're trembling while I'm telling you. Jonson epitomized the Devil."

Tracey set her hand on her heaving bosom. "Once inside my car, I locked the doors. I could hardly start the engine fast enough. I kept poking the key everywhere, missing the ignition.

"But I finally did and rolled on two wheels out of the lot to the street. Someone honked, I think." Tracey passed her hand over her mouth. "I probably swerved in front of them."

"I'd have done the same thing." I shrugged. Getting far away from Jonson was a superb idea.

Her frown deepened. "I didn't get Stuart's ice cream."

"I promise you he'll live."

"But he wanted this flavor." Tracey's face crumpled into the "little lost lamb" expression.

Very pitiful.

"Why does crap happen?"

Behind her back, Mom and Dad shared a concerned expression, one which came with years of marriage. Just a solemn look at each other, but everything conveyed through their connection. None of us said a word.

Tracey being safe mattered more than anything.

I tapped the table. "Now, you know why I insisted you take the self-defense class with the Funsisters."

"Yes, Ms. Bossypants. Your persistence paid off." Tracey leveled her lips. "I don't want anyone to find out, you know, how the jerk propositioned me. I couldn't take the humiliation." She buried her face in her hands.

Mom scrambled to Tracey's other side. She tucked a strand of her hair behind one ear. "We won't say anything, darling. Not a word."

But one entity *had* to be told. "Sorry, Mom. You're wrong. The police need to know." I tapped the tabletop. "More than likely, someone will blab to the press."

"Why?" Mom rocked back on her heels and stood. "Tracey didn't kill him. She hit him."

"I'm positive his murder is of supreme interest to the public. He was set for life when he married a Fenster," I said.

"I'd still punch him like I wanted to do to the newspaper photographer."

"What photographer?" I asked.

Dad grimaced. "The one hanging outside the station. Most likely waiting for some big scoop. Tracey shielded her face with her handbag."

"See?" I shoved Tracey's shoulder. "You can thank me later for suggesting the big purse, too."

She made a crinkly nose face. "Told you so."

"Well, I did."

"You did."

"The photo will be on the front page or in the Metro section forever. All of Sommerville will see it." Mom crossed her arms with a "humpf."

Dad cupped Mom's shoulder. "You know how it is nowadays. A politician will say or do something stupid, and newer news will take its place."

Mom covered his hand with hers. "We could only be so lucky."

I rose, paced a bit, dragging my hand across the top of the chairs as I went. "I have an idea."

Tracey snorted. "I hope it's a brilliant one 'cause brilliant is what I need."

"I can't believe you two are bickering." Squinting, Mom drew back slightly.

"We're not." I glared at my sister. "I'm betting Super Saver has security cameras. We need to check their footage. If Tracey didn't kill him, someone else did, and I think the store's cameras might have captured the bad guy or gal. We ask for a copy, and then we'll know for sure." I curled my fingers in a gimme. "Let's see your hand."

Tracey rested her extended left arm on the kitchen tabletop.

"Make a fist," I said.

Tracey showed me her fisted hand.

I saw three swollen knuckles, and from the forming scabs, some abraded skin. I put the phone's camera into action again on her fist and then on her flattened hand. "Done."

"So how did Jonson die?" Dad asked.

Everyone looked at each other.

I tossed my phone to the table. Then our gazes turned to Tracey.

"What?" Tracey asked, palms lifted. "I've said it over and over. I don't know. What I do know is I Didn't. Do. It."

"If Tracey didn't, then who did?" Raising her brow, Mom looked at Dad then me.

"Maybe his first ex-wife? What's her name?" I asked.

They shook their heads.

"I don't remember her name. I heard someone in Australia offered her a job," Tracey said.

"Not far enough away, IMHO," I said. "Someone would be doing the world a favor if Jonson was launched to Mars with no clothes so his willy would freeze off."

Tracey shook her head. "He wouldn't leave his milk train."

"No. Whoever that is. Allan didn't say anything about anything?" I asked.

They shook their heads again.

"Elaine?" Dad asked.

"I know nothing." Mom raised her hands.

"Shirley know something?"

Mom turned aside her head and pressed a fresh tissue to her nose. She gave a brief rub. "I've been too embarrassed to call, and now is kinda early."

"She's your best friend, Elaine," Dad said.

"I know."

*My poor mother. She was not dealing well with Tracey's mess.* I massaged her shoulder. "Sorry, Mom. Mrs. Wellborn *is* your best friend. If anyone will have your back, it's her."

"You're right, dear."

"You sound redundant," I said. "Let's review a sec. Detective Wellborn questioned Tracey solely because of her fingerprints."

"And because she was previously married to Jonson," Dad said.

I looked at him. "Allan says he doesn't know all of Tracey's story. By the way, how did the police get her fingerprints matched?"

"Tracey, your mom, and I attended a program at the station where you get fingerprinted," Dad said. "When did we go, Elaine? Like five years ago?"

"I think so," Mom said. "Took forever to de-ink."

"They called them elimination prints," Dad said. "Just in case."

*Wow, I'm glad I missed their field trip.*

Slowly, the color drained from Tracey's face as her hand slid over her mouth.

"Trace, what is it?" I asked.

Mom launched to her feet.

Dad touched my sister's shoulder. "Tracey?"

With her mouth covered, Tracey shook her head. "Wh-what if my punch caused Jonson to have a brain injury or an aneurysm, and I really did kill him?"

I veed my brow. "I don't think that can happen. Are you super strong? I didn't think you were, but maybe you beefed up with the defense training."

"Hattie, not funny." Dad shook his head. "We can ask a doctor."

"Let's go with a no for now, Sissie," I said.

"Okay." Tracey's hand fell away. "I know I didn't confess to anything. Not. A. Word. That's what the crime shows say—do nothing. I said nothing."

*Television, the great educator—not. Except for the guy in the British detective series. He needed water to dilute his sarcasm.* "They didn't read you your rights and stick you in the pokey. I say you're okay."

"For now." Mom collapsed in an armchair in the adjoining family room. "I will talk with Shirley Wellborn. Most likely, I'll reconsider having Allan Wellborn as a son-in-law."

Shocked and amazed, I turned to stare at her. *What in the wide world of sports is she talking about, especially at a time like this?*

With a "never mind" in my head, I circled the room, scrubbing the back of my neck and hearing the scratchy sound of dried hairspray. I thought about Tracey's predicament. What Allan hadn't done and didn't know. Who else would want to murder Jonson Leggett the Third?

None of us knew how Jonson died. No one knew what kind of evidence the police uncovered. The police might have lifted Tracey's fingerprints from his car, but maybe others were deposited, and did the cops identify them? *Does Super Saver Grocery have a security camera?* Nowadays, most businesses did, placing them strategically in the parking lot. Surely, Super Saver's video would exonerate her.

"Hattie."

Mom touched my hand as I passed her.

"You'll have to talk to Allan."

I grabbed handfuls of my hair. "Impossible. You try."

"Allan responds to you."

*Maybe sexually he does.* I overlapped my arms.

"He never tells me anything when he's working a big case—remember?"

Mom tilted her head. "Perhaps... Never mind."

*Yikes.* "Lay it on me." *God only knows what she is thinking.*

She leaned closer. "Perhaps, well, perhaps your approach is wrong."

*Lordy. Her innuendo. Now, I get it and pretty ballsy of her.* I rolled my eyes ceilingward. "What approach? The one where I ask politely? Or how about the one where I take off my clothes and seduce him? Which scenario do you prefer, Mother dearest?"

"Hattie, you crossed a line," Dad growled.

"Me? I crossed a line? Sorry, Dad. She did first." I pointed at my madre. My mother had some nerve. "Unbelievable."

"Whatever it takes—"

"Elaine," he said.

All of us stared at Mom—me harder than them. Mom jumped overboard, like off-a-giant-cliff overboard.

"Somehow, Mother, your brilliant idea sounds like Jonson's—me propositioning Allan the same way Jonson propositioned Tracey." I stabbed my chest with my finger. "I. Am. Not a hooker."

Tracey cupped the side of her mouth. "Even if Allan looks like sex on a stick and as if sex with him would be stupendous."

*Please, God, stop the madness.* I jostled her with my hip.

Her shoulder butted back.

"Elaine. Hattie. I've heard enough squabbling." Dad looked toward the kitchen for a moment. He then returned his gaze to my sister. "Trace, will you see Stuart anytime soon?"

I checked my phone, not giving Tracey a chance to answer. "Tomorrow. Another dreaded tango lesson."

Tracey stumbled to her feet with her arms wheeling so she wouldn't crash and burn. My sissie's voice fractured like a dropped Ritz cracker. "Thanks for your support, sister dear. We wanted our wedding to be u-u-unique."

She whipped her gaze from Mom to Dad to me. With wide eyes, she palmed her cheeks. "Oh My God. Oh My God. Wh-What about St-Stuart? He won't want to marrrry meeee."

Tracey's sobbing escalated to Noah and the Ark proportions. She whirled about, the chair crashing on the floor. She ran down the hallway to her childhood room.

When the door slammed, I flinched.

Mom shot Dad and me the see-what-you've-done glare, an over-the-shoulder, squinty-eyed one.

She loped after Tracey.

Dad and I gaped at each other.

He lifted and dropped a hand. "Your mother didn't mean...you know...you should seduce Allan." Briefly, he glanced toward the kitchen again. "God, I can't believe I said that to my daughter."

I snorted. "You could have fooled me. Maybe Mom's watching too much TV."

"I suppose. Maybe too much of the feuding housewives," he said.

"No kidding," I said.

Rubbing his finger lengthwise across his mouth, Dad didn't say anything more.

I teethed my lower lip. I had nothing either. Not for a long while. Guilt hung in the air. Bizarre colored the whole situation.

I couldn't take the unexpressed pressure anymore. I flung my hands toward the ceiling. "Okay, fine. I'll chat with Stuart—"

"Don't forget Allan."

"Fine," I snarled. "Allan, too."

"Thank you." Dad uprighted the chair Tracey overturned, then squeezed my shoulder, and kissed the top of my head. "You're our only hope."

*Wow.* "Only hope" like a famous sci-fi action hero. *Very scary.*

Chapter Fourteen

After the sun rose and headed to the west, to be the supportive sister I claimed to be, I shook my head and drove to Miss Yolanda's studio. Only one student made an appearance beside me—Allan.

Tracey and Stuart didn't cancel the tango lesson; yet, they didn't show either. Probably due to Tracey's hysteria over being questioned by the police, and quite possibly, she could still be sobbing in her bedroom over Stuart like a two-year-old told to eat her peas. Beginning to feel as if doomsday was plastered all over their wedding, I couldn't blame her.

I squinted at the gorgeous specimen. *Unbelievable.* Didn't he have other duties to fulfill? Like finding who killed Jonson, not hurling accusations at my sister, and almost arresting her. On the other side of the coin, I could try Mom's "plan" of seducing and quizzing. He did look might-ee fine in his sport coat, navy slacks, and a red tie perfect for binding one's wrists.

*Binding wrists?* I can't believe I had BDSM notions. *Lordy.*

With his right palm on the glass, Allan gazed out the bank of windows overlooking the parking lot, which undoubtedly, flooded the room with blazing sunlight during daylight hours.

Now, nothing could be seen but inky darkness polka-dotted with stars and silhouettes of gaunt branches which occasionally scratched the glass in an eerie horror fashion.

Allan didn't move toward me. Just stared with a look which almost dared me to say something.

He shifted back his khaki jacket with his hand. "I don't want to talk about it."

Message received and duly noted—not the perfect time to chat. Or seduce. *Prick.*

He checked the time on his watch, and he turned his gaze to the entry. "Where are the other tortured tango-ers? They're late."

The Funsisters's grapevine plan to shun him worked fast. I raised my index finger. "One…Jenny has a sick headache." False. "Two…Corrine's in Bayston." True. "Three…Tracey's still crying." True. "Four…Maybe Stuart's on an out-of-town audit—"

Allan flashed his palm. "I get it. The gang's mad. So, why are you here?"

"I didn't want to come, but Mom persuaded me." I twisted my lips. "For Tracey. I would do almost *anything* for my family."

His lips firmed. "I know."

*Did he know?* I lengthened my spine in a stretchy yoga pose. "You interrogated my sister."

Slowly, he turned his head to look. Nothing said. Nothing more.

I locked gazes with Alan for a long while. Finally, my anger festered to boiling. "I'm guessing the rest of the party doesn't want to be near you because, you know, you might arrest them, too."

"I see fingers all over this." He bit into his lower lip. "Mostly yours, telling them I'm a rat and to stay away."

I shrugged. "Could be."

"I know you. I'm not surprised."

I trailed a finger along the wall as I paced six feet away, and when I turned around, changed to the other hand. "All of us hated Jonson, except for Stuart. I'm not sure if Stuart knows about Tracey's first marriage. I suppose we could have conspired to plot the dastardly deed à la Murder on the Orient Express-style."

"Funny," the saintly detective said.

I wiggled my phone. "I know something you don't know."

"Oh, joy."

"I bet you didn't know Tracey has bruises from where Jonson hurt her arm."

Allan squeezed his lips in a tight flat line. "I didn't know."

"Guessing the police didn't do a thorough job."

"You did." Setting his hands on his hips, he tilted closer. "You took pictures?"

I rotated my phone. "I did. Wanna see?"

He curled his fingers. "Show me."

After scrolling to the photos I took the previous night, I passed my cell. "Go ahead. Look. They are disgusting."

As he examined the images, his mouth drooped in a frown. "What's this?" He pushed the device in front of my eyes.

"Oh. Tracey's fist—the one she socked him with."

"Now, we're getting somewhere."

"Not so fast, geek-boy—"

Allan raised one brow. "You're calling me geek-boy?"

"Sorry, a holdover from your high school days of

pocket protector *and* trombone."

"The trombone you make fun of paid my way through college."

While I considered, I pushed my bottom lip forward. Hadn't his parents ponied up his tuition? "I didn't know."

"I don't know how you forgot me being in the marching band."

"Ooh. Ooh. I remember, and oh my eyes." I blocked my eyes.

"So, I've always been geeky?"

I uncovered one eye.

Allan squinted. "You know the saying—"

I uncovered my face and sketched an imaginary arc. "The entire universe knows the saying: Geeks rule."

"And don't forget it, sweetheart."

"If I need a reminder, I'll check your senior photo. Stop calling me sweetheart."

"The picture captured my…manly essence." He stroked his forefinger along his chin. "Some women think I'm…studly."

*Essence? Studly?* Lordy. Crazy. I shimmied my shoulders. "Back to Jonson… He said some crude and rude things. Tracey was pissed, which resulted in a left hook to his face. I'm confident when the medical examiner inspects the creep's body—"

"Hold on." He flashed his palm.

"Yes?"

"You're way too familiar with police procedures. Possibly bad. Very bad."

"Funny." I grinned. "You'll find the proof."

Allan returned my phone. "Interfering in my case

isn't a good idea, Hattie—"

I stamped my foot. "I'm only protecting my family. You'd do the same—"

"'Fraid to say it?"

Who would argue over geekiness in anyone? Not me. But the twinkle in his eyes looked mighty compelling. "Geek-boy."

Miss Yolanda, wearing a silky maroon caftan trimmed with a fringe of gold coins the size of dimes, sashayed in our direction. "Hello, dancers. Only the two of you tonight?"

I bobbed my head. "Yes, Ms. Yolanda."

"I'm très désolée."

She shrugged with a "whatever" frown, arranged us next to each other, and patted our limbs.

"Doesn't matter. Besides Stuart and his fiancée, you're the best dancers. All eyes will be on you. Now, young man, take your partner in your arms."

Neither of us made the first move.

The last thing I wanted at Stuart and Tracey's wedding was to have "all eyes on me." I should man-up for my sister's big day. Through my lashes, I glared at Allan.

Hard steel in his black eyes fixed tight flashed back.

His jaw gritted.

My *first* move would be to kick him in the shins and launch a major assault, but Mother wouldn't like the fighting part. Lifting my chin, I gave him my best you're-gonna-suffer expression.

Allan snorted. The tenseness in his shoulders subsided. He quirked the right corner of his mouth.

Taking my hand, he raised one in the "ready"

position and set his other at my waist. I settled into the proper posture.

"Feel the music embody your spirits. Become *one* with your soul. Become one with your partner." Miss Yolanda turned on the music and clapped. "Anda one. Anda two…"

Allan and I glided two steps, paused, whipped about, and then repeated in the opposite direction.

"Good. Do the sequence over." Ms. Yolanda rolled her hand.

Clueless about what "sequence" she talked about, I followed Allan's lead and let him have his way.

Ms. Yolanda stopped the music.

She handed me a red rose.

I took it gingerly and discovered she'd stripped off the thorns.

"Set the stem between your teeth," she said. "Repeat the steps you just performed. Pause. And you, young man, will bend close, and with your teeth, you'll take the rose from her lips."

Ms. Yolanda swooped her hands. "Go on."

*Oh Lord, Allan would be within kissing range. This is too-too much.* Even though he excelled at kissing, I couldn't do any smooching after the grilling he gave Tracey. I pinched the stem between my fingers and glared.

His eyes held a challenge-you glint.

My insides screamed "retreat." But I wouldn't. I couldn't. Obtaining more intel so I could find something to exonerate my sister hit the top of my mental to-do list. Permanently.

I clenched the stem between my teeth. A green sap oozed on my tongue. The taste? Beyond icky.

"Class. Ready?" Ms. Yolanda looked at each of us, her brows lifted. She pointed her remote at the sound system. The music resumed. "Anda one. Anda two."

Allan and I glided and turned. Glided and turned. Paused.

"So, Jonson is dead." Thanks to self-taught ventriloquist lessons, I mumbled barely coherent words around the stem.

"Yup."

Pausing, I spat out the blasted flower, smacking my tongue. The residue in my mouth made me sound stupid and silly. I fought the urge to spit. "The Sommerville Live at Five news ran a story." The program broadcasted a story about the murder as I dressed for work. "Good ol' press shares the scandalous stuff every time."

"I've said nothing." Allan shifted and brushed his hand through his hair. "You know how it is in Sommerville. News travels fast in a small town."

I shot him a hard look. "Is the Sommerville Police Department giving Tracey's case special treatment because the whole town thought Jonson a—quote—a pillar of society—unquote?" I couldn't help coating my words with scorn. "A man amongst men. Known and loved by all—"

Miss Yolanda returned.

At the lift of her hand, I again put the flower in my mouth.

She stepped away and motioned for the dancing to continue. She retreated to prop her shoulders against a wall and check her phone for messages.

Before Allan and I resumed dancing, he bent closer.

So close, his breath fanned over my cheek.

"And as you stated, the deceased was hated by your family."

*Guess the whole world was aware of the Cooks's position on all things related to Jonson Leggett the Third.* I struggled to swallow. "Er, maybe."

As Allan straightened, his gaze bored into mine. "Hate can cause people's behavior to change. They do despicable things, like murder."

I yanked the flower out of my mouth. "The Super Saver's video recording must be confirming evidence for you to focus on my sister."

He stopped and let go. His eyes narrowed. "How…did…you—"

Ms. Yolanda moved between us. "Problem?"

*Yes.* I bet he thought so, too.

"No," I said.

"No," he said.

Then the bane of my existence rang.

Allan dug his cell phone from his pocket. In long strides, he reached the studio's door. "Wellborn."

Twirling, the rose's stem in my fingers, I skimmed one pointed foot in a half-circle across the floor and then the other as I tried to eavesdrop on his conversation in case Tracey's difficulty came up.

"Yes, sir," he said multiple times.

Which told me one big fat nothing.

"Immediately." He shut off his phone and flicked a look. "Gotta go."

"Not surprised." I squished my eyes into slits and twirled the rose, watching Mr. Dutifully Bound exit.

He paused by the door and looked back.

I blew him a pissed-off kiss.

His brow wrinkled.

I tilted my head and lifted my chin. *So there.*

"That one"—Ms. Yolanda pointed her finger at Allan's retreating form—"he's always in a hurry."

"Yes, ma'am, he certainly is." I jerked my fists toward the floor, breaking the flower's stem. After I inhaled and exhaled a few times, I felt my heart rate slow down and calmness overtook my mind. I scooped the flower pieces from the floor and walked over to the exit, chucking the scraps inside a trash can. Through the windows overlooking the parking lot, I heard Allan fire up the truck's engine and wheel out to the street.

*Rats.* Almost had Allan clenched in my hand. *I must find another way to get the answers I need.*

\*\*\*\*

Back at my apartment, Jenny pounced on me the moment I entered. All Vegas gamblers could have bet mucho dough on her wanting to know about my efforts to question Allan about Tracey's predicament.

I shook my head and shook off her arm. "Not now." I headed to the bathroom for a meditative purging soak. After the tub filled with grapefruit-scented hot water, I piled my hair in a clasp on top of my head and slipped into the steaming bathwater to soothe away the worries.

After a few minutes, I took my newest paperback romance, *The Virginity of Arabella,* sitting on the toilet seat conveniently located next to the tub. The lurid cover of a shirtless, dark-headed man with more muscles than brains, clasping a young woman by her upper arms, her curly blonde hair cascading down her bare back, and her pale rose evening gown slipping from her shoulders made me pause. *Still, someone, even*

174

*fictional, is getting more sex than me.*

Flipping to my marked page, I read:

*The act captivated her, yet her mind still wandered. What happened to the magician's diminutive assistant she fell in love with at the magic show? Just this morning, the Las Vegas FBI agents interviewed her about the pit boss found dead behind the Castle Casino. Someone had sawed him in half.*

Depleted of energy, I could barely stay engaged in reading. Work. Tracey. Allan. Tracey. Tango. Allan. Cushioning my head on the side of the tub, I succumbed to the hot water and its relief. I closed my eyes and slipped deeper into dreamland. I sensed the book drop on the bath rug. Somewhere out there, the doorbell rang. *Not now. Sleep.*

"Hattie, wake up," a voice called.

I must be dreaming because no one with a sexy deep voice would be in my bathroom. I flipped a lame wave to signal "go away" and sank deeper in the sudsy depths.

"Sweetheart," the voice said. "Wake up. We need to talk."

"Sweetheart" registered. Allan called me the endearment many times—despite me asking him not to. I reluctantly batted my eyes once…twice…three times before I could squeeze one orb wide open.

Allan leaned against my bathroom doorway, blatantly observing me floating in the tub—well, naked. For the time being, bubbles covered my strategic parts.

Bubbles popped. *Oops.*

In a flash, I pressed my boobs against the side of the tub. I grabbed the towel I'd tossed on the rug. With my free hand, I flipped shut the book. I would be more than embarrassed if he discovered my love for romance, even if his sister lent me the book. "Get out," I said in my most threatening voice.

"I don't think so—"

Allan bobbed his head in a confident taking-in-the-whole-room way.

"—looks pretty good."

*Why the dirty rotten, no-good scoundrel.* I compacted my lips and squeezed my eyes into lizard-like slashes. "Leave. Now. Or—"

"Or what, sweetheart?"

*Hmm.* "I'll call…call—"

"The police? Ha. The police are already here."

So he was. Then an "aha" hit my head. "I'll do worse. I'll call your mother."

Allan wagged his finger. "You don't play fair."

"She's darn scary, and if anyone can wrangle you, it's Shirley Wellborn." I lifted the book, eyeballed the throwing distance to the door. "Going?"

He raised his hands, palms out. "No need to get violent."

Violent? My yelling equaled violent? He didn't know what violent was. I hurled *Arabella* in his direction.

He dodged left as the book thunked against the wall by his ear. "That's playing nasty, girlfriend."

Gripping the towel, I gritted my teeth so hard, they hurt. "I'm. Not. Your. Girlfriend."

"Okay, sweetheart."

"I'm not your sweetheart, either."

He shook his head. "Sadly, you're not."

"You are…mean." *Stupid word.* Nothing else

entered my mind.

Allan bounced his eyebrows. "I would be glad to show you how mean I am."

Sexiness seeped sweetly like a toasted, oh-so-gooey marshmallow in a fresh-from-the-fire s'more. I knew what he meant.

"Besides, if I remember right"—he cupped his hand and examined his fingernails—"I've seen you naked a couple of times."

And I'd seen him naked, too, but he didn't have free rein to watch me whenever he pleased. I glared the nastiest look I possessed, one sure to scare small children and white mice. "Leave. I mean it."

He smiled.

"N-period. O-period. W-period, Allan. I don't want you to show me how mean you are. I don't want to talk about you seeing me naked before. I don't want anything to do with you—"

"Why not?"

"Why not?" I raised my hand and dropped it in the bubbles, splashing soap across my cheek. Then I remembered the naked part and went chest-to-tub again. "Because you're on my hit list, buster, because of my sister. You dashed from tango lessons before we could discuss her situation like adults."

Allan leaned his six-foot-plus body against the doorframe and crossed his arms. "Had to—"

"Had to? *Had to?*" A blood vessel in my temple throbbed to popping point.

"Had to. Office called."

"You say the 'had to' phrase all the time, and it makes me sick. Your 'had to' 'tude better be good. My mom's pretty angry with you."

Slowly, he ran his thumb over his jaw. "My mom came close to disowning me."

"Fat chance. Shirley Wellborn wouldn't disown her adored, holier-than-thou, on-the-way-to-sainthood son. Your mom's scary, though." All my grade school friends believed Mrs. Wellborn was scary. Her flying monkey expression intimidated Navy SEALs.

I grappled the towel into place and pointed with my free hand. "Go."

Allan just ignored me.

Watching. Waiting. The hint of a smile curled one corner of his mouth.

"You look good, Hattie."

*Most naked chicks look good to most men.* "I swear you have hearing issues."

Nothing. Nothing but a big, wide, making-you-uncomfortable-and-I-love-every-minute-of-it grin.

*Brat.* I flushed with more embarrassment. Maybe pleading with him would work. "Come on, Allan. Give me a break. Please. I'll get out of the tub as soon as you leave." A slip of my feet caused a splash. "Pretty please. The water's cold. I'm shivering." I shook for good measure.

Allan stood as immovable as Mount Rushmore. As Pikes Peak. As Mount Fuji.

Forming a new plan, I struggled from the water and stood, wrapping the damp towel around my torso. The soggy covering outlined my jiggly bits. I very cautiously stepped over the rim and walked to where Allan stood in the doorway. He stared like a fat cat lapping a bowl of cream. *Time to move on.* In a flash, the towel fell to the floor. I gave him one giant drippy shove, which pushed him against the hallway wall. I slammed the door behind him.

"Hey, you got my coat wet."

Pressing my ear to the closed door, I heard Allan grumble with a few expletives. *Tee-hee-hee.*

"I still have a good imagination," he shouted. "Very good imagination. Like what cold water does to your nipples."

I rolled my eyes. *Ya, put your imagination to work and see where it takes you.*

Snagging a clean towel, I dried and dressed in Plain Jane undies, black sweatpants, and a ratty Jeep T-shirt, arranged my hair in a ponytail, and swiped on a teensy bit of mascara. Leaning closer to the mirror, I dabbed on a colored lip gloss and smacked my lips in approval. *"What we women go through to look good."*

I opened the bathroom door to my bedroom and found Allan lounging on his side on my bed, and his coat flopped open. Casually, he flipped through *Arabella*. I held my breath and prayed he hadn't read anything...embarrassing. The romance contained racy passages with long, incredibly descriptive sex scenes, not to be shared with someone of the male species. However, some guys could take lessons from those passages.

Setting hands on my hips, I watched him turn several pages. "Learn anything...interesting?" I got the policeman look, which said "squat."

"What's interesting is you used the word 'learn.'" Allan said, "The guy has nothing on me."

"As you know, I don't know."

"I'll borrow it when you're finished. The diminutive person passage you earmarked sounded fascinating."

*Damn.* Allan looked migh-tee fine in navy slacks and white shirt. I sat beside him on the bed. He let me tug the book from his hands.

Allan and I stared at each other for a while. Bucket loads of energy pulsed between us. If he made the right overtures, I'd hop on top of him, despite what I said earlier.

"Um," I said, "I'll take a page from one of Mom's lectures and be polite."

He grinned.

Mom's infamous little talks spilled over the Wellborn family, too.

"How about the 'Be Nice to the Uninvited Guest' one?" he asked.

"I'm being nice." I extended my hand. "Soda?"

He laced his fingers with mine. "No nookie?"

"Nookie?" I arched one eyebrow. "What century are you from?"

"This one."

He yanked me on top of him.

"Now, I call our current situation nice *and* interesting."

Allan scanned my face as his hand tucked a stray hair strand behind my ear.

All the togetherness caused me to want, to pant, to yearn, to beg him to kiss me, kiss me, kiss me. With a slight shift, I wiggled my body. I placed my forearms on either side of his head. I toyed with his crisp hair; then, I let the same hand drop to thumb his lower lip. It felt soft, damp, lush.

He cupped the curvy part of my buttocks, pressing our pelvises together.

Leaning over, I let my cheek skim across his

temple. I felt his heart rate accelerate, and his breath grew heavier.

I paused to take in all male, all him. I connected my gaze with his. A suggestive glint burned in his eyes. Our mouths were moments away from devouring each other. An immense bulge developed on his side and pushed into my thigh. Hot swirls rose in my body, making my head scorch and the girl parts throb in the what-are-you-waiting-for way.

Allan's hands crept under my T-shirt and along my spine.

A lazy smirk shaped his face as his head dipped to the right.

"You'd better stop. You might get more than you bargained for," Allan said.

I twitched my lips as awkwardness raced over me. "Stop might not be on today's agenda."

"Hussy," Allan said. "Your mom and dad won't like you making love with a traitor."

Chapter Fifteen

His sideways grin and man-hands on my waist said a whole lot about his intentions. "Killjoy. You mentioned my parents during almost wild, almost sex." I smiled. Even with a thrumming humming throughout my body, somehow, I twisted around and pushed off the bed to stand, a bit lopsided. I held out my hand. "Come on."

Taking my hand, Allan fashioned a not-very-happy look and let me lead him to the kitchen.

I snagged two sodas from the fridge and motioned toward the table. "Popcorn?"

Allan drew a circle on the wooden tabletop. "If feeding the enemy is allowed... Sure."

I put a package in the microwave. Mr. O Gorgeous One ate a lot of popcorn over here. I could fix him a ham and cheese sandwich; however, he annoyed me in the bathroom, so *nah*.

Allan and I popped the cans' tabs. While the bag of corn circled in the microwave, I waited for his explanation regarding Tracey. He sure was trying my patience.

The kernels underwent a rush of explosions and then slowed. I listened intently because the acrid smell of burned popcorn turned off everyone. The scent lingered forever. At a *bing*, I grabbed the bag, ripped, and dumped the contents in Grammie's multi-colored bowl.

I set the popped corn and a paper napkin in front of Allan.

Dragging the bowl to his belly, he tossed back a handful of kernels and chased with a big swallow of cola. He fingered a condensation drop on the top of the can. "I had to talk to Tracey. Her fingerprints are all over Jonson Leggett's SUV's door. You know…the one he was found dead in."

Fingerprints could be damning evidence. On the crime docu-dramas, sometimes, fingerprints could be used as elimination prints, like Mom and Dad discussed last night. Maybe Tracey's would.

Allan poised his hand over the bowl. "Know how Jonson afforded his car?"

I hoped Allan, the detective, knew a good answer to his question about Jonson's finances. "I'm clueless. Barbie might know. What does his bank account say? Did her family talk to you?"

He dug his fingers in the snack. "We're working on those details now."

While watching him munch, I pulled the popcorn bowl my way and stuffed my face. "What about witnesses?"

Allan shook his head. "None, so far, except for a possible Super Saver employee." He lifted his chin. "The Cooks family is tighter than tight. I know you think you're protecting Tracey, but you aren't. What's she saying?"

No way could I tell Tracey's whole story. "She isn't saying anything for fear of incriminating herself."

With a puzzled frown and his finger rubbing along the can's lid in a circle, he stewed over my comment.

"Sooner or later, we get the truth, Hattie."

"How cliché." Then I remembered the pictures I took of her bruises. I retrieved my phone from the bathroom. "I forgot to send you the photos." I clicked on an image. "What's your email?"

"What? You don't have it memorized? I'm wounded." He pressed his palm to his heart. "Wounded."

"Whatever." I typed Allan's name, and his email address did appear. A few clicks later, I said, "Done."

I returned the bowl to the middle of the table. Allan and I snacked on the popcorn for a while, not talking, but obviously, thinking about each other. The "stirring" looks he and I shared said a whole lot more than our words did.

"Tell me from the top why you interviewed my little sister."

Allan snorted. "Give me a break. You know the drill; I'm not supposed to talk about ongoing investigations."

"You'd better." I swooped the bowl to my chest before he could get any treats.

Allan crooked his finger. "Dangerous, sweetheart."

"Threatening" was written all over his words. "Still not scared."

*He-he-he.* Being the nice person I am, I passed the popcorn.

He said, "Jonson Leggett the Third—"

"Can't anyone say his name without the third suffix?" I asked.

Allan shrugged. "Habit. Anyway, he was found dead in his car at Super Saver Grocery store on Boston—"

"I already knew that. How did he die—"

He held up his hand. "Wait a minute. We need to strike a bargain right now."

I crisscrossed my arms over my chest. "What do you have in mind?"

"What we discuss is between you and me." Allan aimed two, V-shaped fingers at my chest and back toward his.

I nodded again.

"You can't say anything, and I mean *anything*, to your family *or* mine."

*Man, Allan dragged his heels.* "I doubt you'll tell me *anything* the public doesn't already know."

"Probably not, but just in case. Don't tell Jenny. Not your Funsisters. Not my sister. Not your parents. Deal?" He scrunched his brow.

*God, he is so serious.* "Deal." I bumped my fist against his.

His chest heaved before he said, "Jonson Leggett, the Third was hit on his right temple with a blunt object."

Oh my God. I cupped my cheeks and pushed my hands into my hair. Part of me was horrified, and the other part knew Jonson was out of my sister's life forever. "How horrible."

"Yup. Someone hit him hard. Brains. Bones. Blood. You know." He took a hit from his drink. "The photos are…gory."

*Does sound rather horrendous.* "Ick. You don't know what was used?"

Allan scratched his jaw. "Not sure yet. Maybe something ordinary like a hammer or tire iron."

For a minute, I considered what he said. "Tracey

isn't known for skills with tools. I have never, ever seen her use a hammer or a tire iron, although she might have when we were kids, and Mom forced us into helping Dad fix something. Exactly where were Tracey's fingerprints?"

"On the driver's door underneath the window frame." He leveled his hand in front of his sternum. "About so high."

*Hmm.* "Exactly what Tracey said. Didn't find any of hers inside the vehicle?"

"Not so far. I've never seen anyone keep a mouth shut like Tracey." He blew a short breath and set his hands on his hips. "Not a damn word."

Allan stared at me. "You sure are pretty."

I sensed my cheeks grow hot. "Flattery will get you nowhere."

"I know what works on you." He winked.

"Stay on your side of the table, and I'll stay on mine. We're physically distancing." I sipped and then, because I had nothing else to do, wrapped my can with a napkin. "You know Tracey didn't do it."

Allan closed his eyes and shook his head slowly. Opening his eyes, he said, "Hattie, I know it. You know it. But the police don't know it."

He sighed deep and hard. "I've known you for a long time. Your parents raised you and Tracey with good morals and values. You aren't violent people. However, in my professional experience, something— one little thing—can cause people to snap and do the unthinkable."

*Like a creepy, ex-spouse propositioning and stalking could be a motive. At some point, Tracey will have to tell Allan her story, especially if doing so keeps her out of jail.* "Tracey still didn't do it."

"As I said, you know it, I know it, but the department doesn't know it." Abruptly, Allan stood and thrust his hands in his pockets, dropping his chin to his chest. "Jonson Leggett the Third, a prominent citizen from a long-time Sommerville family, well known in the community for charitable endeavors and his ground-breaking work in computer sales, yadayadayada—"

"Seriously? He worked? A first. And since when is computer sales"—I did the quote thingy— "groundbreaking. He didn't invent anything. And how did he afford his luxury SUV? Did he drive a company vehicle? I think the key to the whole enchilada is to follow the money."

Allan glanced my way. "That's a thought. As I said, I'll check on who owns the car. Probably leased. I'm thinking some muckety-muck pressured the department to get his murder settled quickly because of his community standing."

"Ha. You mean toilet standing. You're making Tracey sound like a scapegoat. How many times do I have to say she didn't do it?" I motioned for him to return the popcorn bowl.

He set down the bowl, placing his palms on the tabletop and leaning in. "You sound like a broken record, Hattie. If Tracey didn't do it, she'd have to explain where she was, who she was with, what she was doing, etc. We do know she talked to Jonson."

"Fine." Standing, I snatched the bowl and carried it to the trash. The unpopped kernels fell into the can. When I released my foot off the lid lever, the lid snapped sharply shut. "I'll get Mom and Dad to hire a lawyer, and we'll find the best solution."

He barely lifted one shoulder. "Your prerogative."

After setting the bowl in the kitchen sink, I turned to face him. "What about any witnesses?"

"I said, so far, only one was identified. The security video—"

"Ack so." I smacked my hand against the countertop. "You *admit* knowing about videos."

"You're killing me, Hattie," Allan said. "Super Saver Grocery's video. Tracey is seen standing by Jonson's car window. She rested her hands on the door frame. Just like I told you."

"She told me the same thing."

Allan nodded.

"Let me think for a minute," I said. "If Tracey's prints are only on the outside, not the inside, how did she hit him on the right side of his head?"

Allan's eyes bugged like he hadn't considered the scenario. Surely, he was a better detective than me. "If you keep studying the footage longer," I said, "you might see more, maybe someone else."

"Like what?" He gave a squint, then drank deeply.

"Just a suggestion."

"If you know something, you should say so."

I laid my hands on my hips. "I. Know. Not-a-thing."

"The video is grainy at best. You'd think Super Saver would utilize better technology."

"Here's what I think"—I rubbed the tip of my nose. The Sommerville police had weak evidence against Tracey, which gave me some hope—"you can't positively ID my sister from the video."

"I'm not admitting anything," Allan said. "An expert is working on clarifying the footage, and we'll be asking nearby businesses for their videos."

"Good move."

He stroked his chin. "We rounded up several Super Saver employees to interview, but most likely, some already left without knowing what took place. Only one reported seeing an older woman in the vicinity, which doesn't mean Tracey was with Jonson. Super Saver's a huge grocery store with a large parking lot. Many people are in and out all day long."

"Okay." I ran my finger across the tabletop. All his statements about Super Saver were true. "No one can specifically identify Tracey. And she can't be ID'd from the video?"

I swear to God the man had mastered the policeman stance—hands on hips, a narrow look off to the distance—primarily used when frustrated.

"Not yet."

More hope blossomed in my heart. "And you don't have a weapon?"

"I think I've said enough," Allan said.

I pointed. "Here's what I think. If you found the weapon, you'd test it for fingerprints and find Tracey's aren't on it."

"Like I said—"

"Right. Like you said."

Each of us was lost in our respective theories, hopefully figuring out a way to help Tracey out of her mess.

I said, "I'll get her to talk to you."

"You do that"—Allan chugged the rest of his drink, crumpling the now-empty can with his left hand—"and I want to know as soon as possible what you find out, or better yet, convince her to come to the station and tell me. Get it?"

After dropping the can in the recycling bin, he walked over to my side, and skimmed his right index finger over my cheek, off my chin, and along the column of my throat to the valley between my breasts.

I went hot. Red, hot coal, bonfire-flaming hot.

A little mysterious smile shaped his mouth as his finger traced my lower lip.

"You looked cute all messy in the tub."

Snorting, I did the "whatever" expression, combining it with the rolling of my eyes, but didn't knock away his hand. Women all over the world beat themselves silly, trying to look their best for their man, and this one liked me wet and messy. The truth? If Allan and I were meant to be together, he would have to take me with all my pimples and scars. I shuffled closer.

"I liked the bubbles," he said. "One pert little nipple peeked out."

*Golly.* "Thanks for informing me."

He slanted forward.

I had a great deal of experience with him and "leaning in." "Leaning in" suggested a whole lot more than leaning. Like boy-slash-girl things.

His nose nearly Eskimo-kissed mine. "Glad to be of service. I could do delicious things with it. Do you taste as good as you look?"

Overcoming my embarrassment, I met his gaze. "Better."

In one fast move, he pulled me to his chest and captured my mouth in body-numbing kisses.

"Oh God," I moaned and traveled my lips over to the soft spot below his ear, where a faint scent of pine bloomed. A vibration began in my girl parts and moved to my chest, where it quickened into lust between my legs. His left hand inched under my shirt, tracking a course along my ribs, toward my breast when—

*Buzz, buzz.*

Allan stopped kissing. "Sorry." He stuck his hand in his inside coat pocket for his phone and checked the screen. "Not me."

I rubbed my cheek over his jaw. "Has to be. Your phone's the personification of bad timing."

Again, he studied his device. "Sorry. Still not me."

"Must be mine. Whoever it is can leave a message."

Allan took in lip action.

His mouth sluiced across mine in a sloppy, hungry mode—God, what a red-blooded male. I wanted more and nearly scaled his body to get it, too.

But my phone didn't roll to messages. Somehow, in our grasping and grappling, we smashed the Accept button.

What I heard would never be music to anyone's ears.

"Harriet Lee Cooks, where are you? Why aren't you answering your phone? Pick up. Pick up. PICK UP."

My body altered into freeze mode. Mother. My mother. She would be the one calling right in the middle of hanky panky with Allan Wellborn.

I dropped my arms. I looked at Allan through my lashes and repeated the line he said way too many times, which I despised as much as I despised cold, canned green peas, "Gotta go."

## Chapter Sixteen

The next day, I zipped through traffic to Wedding Wonderland, cornering the turns. I hated being late, like super late, for work. Wipers swished across the windshield, giving a shoo-shoo, shoo-shoo sound, clearing the light mist. Driving like a maniac could cause an accident with all the rushing and hurrying. I swerved to miss a small, white sedan about to play bumper cars with a monster-sized, red, four-by-four pickup.

Last evening, Mom left a second message on my phone. I didn't listen because I believed it might be about Tracey, and Allan didn't need to hear anything right now. I wanted to keep anything related to Tracey private. After Allan exited my place with an unsatisfied look on his face—no first base—I proceeded to my room to return Mom's call, except little would be said on my side. She didn't answer. I left a message, saying I would speak with her later.

The hour grew late. I'd bundled myself to bed. However, sleep eluded me. The idea of making love with Allan swirled through my brain.

I rolled to my back, sticking my hands under the back of my head. My ruminations turned to Tracey and how she and my family depended on me to get information for her exoneration. Then flipped back to Allan. When forty winks finally subdued my overactive mind, I missed the alarm.

*'Nuff said.*

I turned into the retail lot and slotted my car in a spot a few rows away from the store, leaving ample space for customers to park closer to the entry so the rain wouldn't soak them. Wonderland probably wouldn't see many patrons today. Nasty weather had a way of discouraging shopping, except for the "bored-out-of-my-gourd," hardcore shoppers. Rainwater—good for the landscape. Bad for retail business.

Running to the front sidewalk, I splashed through the few puddles from the morning shower, praying I wouldn't ruin my shoes. A wiser plan would have involved bare feet. I pulled on the store's door handle and found it unlocked. *Miss A. is always on time.*

I stamped my feet on the mat and stepped inside. "Miss A.? Miss AAAAA?"

"Back here, dearie."

I tracked her voice to the office. The door stood open.

"I'm putting away the supplies I bought at the home improvement store the other day," she said.

"So glad you got the chance to go."

Miss A. shook her head. "I can't believe how disorganized I am."

"You aren't. We'll get there eventually. You've been running like a madwoman." I slid my arms in the store jacket. "Did you get a hammer or find the one you lost?"

"I never did find it, but I did purchase a new one."

She rummaged through a plastic bag and fished out the tool, displaying it for my inspection.

"Nice." I adjusted my lapels. "I'll head over to

reception and get to work."

I left Miss A. to her organizing. At the desk, I set my handbag inside a drawer in the credenza, then locked it. "I'll boot the computer, too."

"Thank you, dearie."

I heard a loud clang of something heavy hitting the floor.

"Oops. I'm okay. I'm oookay. I dropped the hammer. Missed my foot."

I smiled. *Miss A. can be funny.*

She and I immersed ourselves in our respective duties for a while. I lost track of time. Once I completed the data entry, I took a dusting cloth and brushed it over the tabletops and chairs. Satisfied, I straightened, humming the last tune playing on the oldie station—a sweet love song composed by my mom's favorite seventies rock band.

I polished the windows and the leaded glass door.

Miss A. joined me. She crooked her head to peer at the dark cumulonimbus clouds threatening to dump buckets of water.

After a long stare, she turned to me.

"Hattie, a reminder. I have a bride scheduled for one this afternoon. Her mother will be with her. But I wouldn't be surprised if they canceled with the rain and all."

She tipped her head and looked again at the clouds in various shades of gray.

"As much as we need rain, sometimes, it hinders business."

I placed my hand on her shoulder. "I understand. Though, we never want drought again."

"No, indeed. Where I come from, drought isn't a

problem. Lots of fog and mist."

"Lucky you." So, maybe Miss A. hailed from a rainy climate. "In some places, a shower falls nearly every day, like Mexico. Puerto Rico. Hawaii. Seattle. And England."

Miss A. shrugged. "Yes. Carrying an umbrella is a must."

I didn't probe for additional information. She always spoke carefully when divulging personal details. Some people kept their mouths closed until they became more comfortable with whom they were sharing. Most likely, she would tell me her story in her way.

"Oh well," Miss A. said, "we can mega clean the store."

I lifted my cloth. "Can do." Then I remembered what I vowed to accomplish today to help Tracey. "Miss A., since we're having a lull, would you mind me taking my lunch now?"

She blinked. "Lunch…now?"

I tapped my wristwatch. "It's almost noon. We've been busy."

She checked her phone. "Why it is almost noon. Surprising. They say 'time flies when you're having fun.' "

"I need to run an errand. I wouldn't ask to go now unless very, very important."

Miss A. flapped her hands in a fluttery manner. "Oh, go on, dearie. Just be back to help with the customers we're expecting in an hour."

I flew to the desk, unlocked the credenza drawer, and snatched my handbag. I jogged out the front door and dodged raindrops to my car. I started the Jeep and steered my vehicle in the direction of Super Saver Grocery store. Checking the scene of the crime seemed like a numero-uno idea. Cops weren't perfect, although *someone* might say they were.

At least, Mr. Perfect Policeman Allan Wellborn would.

**** 

I turned my car into the Super Saver lot and slotted in a space a few rows from where Jonson had left his vehicle. From Allan's interpretation of the video provided by the grocery store, Jonson parked next to a light pole. Because I knew Super Saver almost as well as my mother's little lectures, I knew exactly where to go.

With a glance out the window, I confirmed the rain continued to fall. Opening the car door, I stuck my umbrella through the crack, unfurled it, and exited. I picked my way around puddles in the asphalt until I came upon the spot where Jonson's car had been located. The crime scene investigators towed away his luxury SUV; however, the tattered tails of the yellow plastic tape emblazoned with *Crime Scene* in black lettering remained. The colored bits flapped in the cool breeze.

I pictured Jonson's window rolled down, and the silhouette of the left side of his head down to his shoulder visible.

I pictured my sister walking alongside his car, intent on going inside Super Saver for Stuart's ice cream, completely oblivious she passed Jonson's vehicle.

I pictured Jonson's arm shooting out the open window and yanking Tracey closer, the front of her white suit coat brushing the door panel, her hands resting on the door frame, trying to push away from him.

I pictured the startled look on Tracey's face when he grabbed her. His dimply grin, which captivated many but raised suspicion in others. His perfectly coiffed hair held in place by hairspray. The starched shirt sleeve monogrammed with Jonson's initials on the cuff.

My imaginings seemed so vivid, I could virtually feel Tracey's heart beat faster.

After Jonson propositioned her, Tracey's disgust morphed into terror. Recollecting his oily words, I shuddered when fury gripped my insides. My hands fisted tightly. Even dead, the creep gave me the willies.

I only wished I'd been with Tracey. Likely, Jonson wouldn't have touched her. His intimidation tactics didn't work on me, and I would have defended her. Nothing he said or did could shake me up. And he knew I knew.

Carefully, I dodged puddles as I walked along the driver's side of the pretend car. I dropped my gaze to the asphalt, looking for any clue the police might have overlooked. After hearing a bump, rattle, and clatter, I diverted my stare to a runaway grocery cart, headed without a care in the world toward the great beyond. I shifted the umbrella to my right hand and held out my left to stop the orange plastic buggy's great escape.

Dressed in a yellow slicker and resembling a duckling, an employee held his cap's bill low over his forehead as he ran after it.

He grabbed the handlebar. "Hey, thanks."

I released my hold. "No problem."

The Super Saver employee pointed at the parking spot. "Lots of spectators came by."

"Really?"

"Really."

"Maybe because nothing ever happens in Sommerville"—I looked at his nametag—"Elmer."

Elmer stroked his chin. "Could be."

I side-stepped a small wet spot. "Anything found?"

"Don't think so." He shook his head. "The police canvassed the area."

*Canvassed?* Sounded like lousy television terminology.

"You seem way nice," he said. "The murdered guy wasn't."

*The kid saw Jonson?* I wondered had he seen Tracey, too. "Thank you. I hope I am, at least, my friends say I am. Did you know the man who parked here?"

"Know him? Sure. Saw Mr. Leggett all the time." The cart retriever pulled the basket toward his hip with his toe. "Didn't miss the pretty blonde lady in a white coat sock him."

I gulped. *Wow. Elmer might have seen Tracey. Great news.* "You saw her?"

He nodded. "I sure did."

"Blonde nearly white spikey hair?"

"That's her. I was like 'you go, girl.' " He punched his fist skyward.

Relief hit my body. I felt like screaming and dancing. "How well did you know the man in the car?"

"I helped with Mr. Leggett's groceries many times. He rarely tipped and griped about how I stacked the bags in the rear. He didn't like stuff rolling around. I wanted to tell him, 'Well, why don't you buy plastic crates to stick your bags in?' "

I didn't use crates either; maybe I should start. "Nice tip."

Elmer shook his head. "I dunno. People like him would rather complain. Act…superior."

"I know the kind you mean."

He shielded his mouth with his cupped hand and checked over each of his shoulders. "None of us liked him, just tolerated his sass. Kinda loud."

I knew the Super Saver kid was bang on—Jonson always spoke loudly. Deafeningly.

Elmer rolled the cart back and forth.

The wheels squeaked like nails on a chalkboard, and the right front one wobbled. I suppressed the urge to cover my ears. I couldn't while holding my umbrella anyway.

"You know, whatcha call obnoxious. The manager said the 'customer is always right,' but the boss was all show. He didn't like the, uh, dead guy either."

Elmer glanced at me.

"Sorry," he said.

When a gust lifted one side of the umbrella's canopy, I regripped the handle.

He tightened his grasp on the cart's handlebar, the blast weaving the rain poncho he wore around his thighs.

I tilted my head. "Did he stay in the car?"

Elmer wiped the water from his face. "No, ma'am, I'm pretty sure he went inside. And I'm pretty sure he bought an ice pack, you know, the kind for a cooler."

"Okay." I considered why Jonson needed an ice pack. Maybe because of Tracey's punch. "But a cold pack is important because…"

"When I rolled a cart by his car a little bit later, he was holdin' it…"

Elmer demonstrated how Jonson pressed the cold pack above his eye.

Now, all made sense. Tracey hit Jonson right above his eye. And regrettably, I hadn't given it to Jonson. But my sister did. Bully for her. *Wonder if the police studied his face?*

"I'm bettin' he got a nasty bruise," Elmer said.

And something nice to share with Detective Wellborn. "Sounds about right."

"Need anythin' else?" he asked.

"No. Wait." I raised a hand like a rent-a-security guard at a concert event. "Did you tell the police what you saw?"

"No, ma'am."

*Ma'am. I must look one hundred five years old.*

"My shift ended 'fore they came."

If Elmer hadn't been interviewed by the police, his news needed to be shared. "Would you do me a favor? Would you call the Sommerville Police Department and ask for Detective Allan Wellborn—"

His mouth drooped as he shook his head. "Don't want no trouble—"

I knew what Elmer told me needed to be passed on to Allan ASAP. "You won't get into trouble. I promise, Elmer. The detective's a great guy. Truly, one of the good ones. Please ask for Detective Allan Wellborn. Please. He needs to hear your story. My sister, the one who punched Jonson, is in trouble."

Elmer dipped his chin, then raised his head. "Your sister's the woman in the white coat?"

"Yes."

He dropped his gaze to the pavement.

When I saw he lifted his head, I knew he would help me.

Elmer thumbed his chest. "Sure. You can count on me."

"I appreciate it and here"—I dug a precious twenty out of my pocket—"have a pizza. My treat."

With a smile, Elmer stuffed the bill inside his pants pocket. As he walked away, he saluted. "I'll phone now. My break's comin'. See ya, and thanks." He corralled another wayward cart and combined it with two more, rolling them to the store and shoving them in their designated spot by the entrance.

I stood for a long time, watching the young man work and thinking about what he said. The rain splattered lightly on my umbrella. A drop slid along the shaft and onto the back of my hand. I looked up and found a hole at the apex of the canopy. *Great.* A glance at my watch indicated my lunch break ended, and I better fast-track to Wedding Wonderland.

As I turned toward my car, the stores in the retail strip across the street from Super Saver Grocery hooked my eye, one being Little Egypt, a pizza joint, although the name implied something different and exotic. Joe Josephson's Jewelry—*I wonder if crime is up. He added burglar bars to the front windows.* And Dee's Delicious Donuts. *Dee has a new window display of stacked confections.* An imaginary fried dough scent wafted my way, making my mouth water. Donuts rocked.

*No time to stop at those businesses now.* I promised Miss A. I would return in an hour. Perhaps, a visit to

Dee's in the morning would be a most excellent idea.

So would buying donuts.

**\*\*\*\***

After work, I tossed together lettuce, tomatoes, and feta cheese to make a salad for dinner, adding a buttered and toasted ciabatta roll to the plate. I set my food on the coffee table where I propped my feet on top, put the plate on my lap, and tucked a napkin in my collar.

Between bites, I scrolled through the contacts on my phone. When Stuart's name popped up, I paused and considered my promise to Mom and Dad. Conversations with Stuart were never normal. He was easily distracted. But I swore I would speak with my future brother-in-law to determine the status of his relationship with Tracey, ask about the wedding, and any other little ol' thing.

I exhaled a long breath. *Is meddling anyone's forte?*

Stuart proposed to Tracey, albeit they hadn't known each other for an extensive amount of time. But he did, and they seemed pledged to one another.

Strange things did happen, and her current predicament could be one. If Stuart was aware of her side of the Jonson story—and I hoped beyond hope Tracey had told him everything by now—they should have a happy ever after. After all, as my mother often said, "Honesty is the best policy."

Before I could stop myself, I hit the green button to connect with Stuart. While the phone buzzed one-two-three times, I readied myself to leave a message. Tracey said the accounting firm had assigned Stuart to an out-of-town oil and gas audit. Reaching him might be…iffy.

Before I could state my name and phone number, I heard a brisk, "Stuart Steems."

*The epitome of professionalism.* "Hey, Stuart. It's Hattie."

"Hi, Hattie, soon-to-be my favorite sister-in-law."

Favorite—*ha!* "'Cause I'm your only sister-in-law?"

"True and a nice surprise. By the way, how are those tango lessons going?"

*The nerve.* The vision of Stuart's shoulders shaking with laughter got under my skin. "Fine. They would be a whole lot better, bub, if you hadn't paired me with you know who."

Stuart chuckled. "As if I could've paired you with anyone else. The other couples are dating or married. You and Allan are the only two who aren't, except for Trixie. Besides, he paid me."

*Paid?* Shocked, I bit my lower lip. *Definitely puzzling.* "Allan *paid* you?"

"Paid. Coffee for life."

I twitched my nose. "I get it. However, I still don't have to like it."

"You'll get over being embarrassed."

I swear Stuart borrowed a page from Allan's phraseology book—"Gotta go." "Tell me about it." "You'll get over it."

Stuart blew his nose. "Sorry, allergies. He asked me to—" He blasted another sneeze.

"He—who—Allan? Allan asked you what?" I nearly screamed.

"God, Hattie, I'm gonna lose the hearing in my left ear."

"Sorry, Stuart. Allan asked you what?"

A loonng pause of nothingness.

"Stuart." Nothing. "Stuart," I said louder. "Talk now, or I'll stick my arm through the phone line and grab you by the throat."

"All right already. Allan called after Tracey and I announced our plan for the reception dance and asked if he could be paired with you. I was being nice, you know, like your mom's little speech on 'Being Nice to Other People.'"

*Oh my God, has my mother brainwashed Stuart already? He isn't even family yet.* "It's okay, bud. Her talks tend to—"

"Hattie, I hate to cut you off, but I need to get back to work, especially if I want to come home soon. Tracey needs me."

"About Tracey…" As I crumbled the roll, I let a space of silence blanket our conversation. "I don't know how to say this; I'm just blurting it out. Are you okay about my sister?"

"What do you mean by okay?"

An image of Stuart with his close-cropped black hair, him wiping his nose with an over-sized hankie, his white button-down shirt, and ugly green tie formed in my head. "Well, I, er, we, er, the family is…uh, wondering if you plan on going forward with the, uh, marriage, you know, in light of the, uh, murder?"

"Of course," Stuart said. "The ex… Well, I can't use profanity in mixed company."

"Don't worry, Stuart. We all have the same thoughts."

"He and Tracey were an item long ago and have nothing to do with us today."

I forked a piece of tomato. "True."

"I'm sorry she went through what he did the first time. Who can imagine him as a"—Stuart harrumphed—"gentleman?"

*Very true.* "Unlike you, my friend."

"Thank you. You know Jonson sent an email and propositioned Tracey? That's the reason she went ballistic at Wedding Wonderland the other day."

Casually, I let the fork drop. *Yup, she did act unnerved. Deservedly so.* "Can you tell me what he said?"

"It's not…nice."

"Nothing about him ever was," I said.

"Let's just say if I had socked him, he'd be sporting more than one black eye."

*Oh, the visual.* I giggled. "Stuart, you're so…dangerous. How attractive."

"I know you're kidding, Hattie. But I honestly believe he took advantage of Tracey. A part of me feels sorry for his fiancée—what's her name?"

"Barbie."

"That's it."

"I know what you're saying, but don't worry about Barbie. She's not nice either." I sipped some water.

"Oh. I do have one question—"

*Lordy.* "Yes?"

"About my tux—"

*Here we go.* I threw my napkin on the table and let my gaze drift to study the ceiling. Stuart rattled on with a few choice "ums" interspersed before he paused for a breath.

*Shouldn't talking fashion with Stuart be Tracey's job?*

Chapter Seventeen

As I readied for work the next morning, I skipped breakfast to hit Dee's Delicious Donuts for one of my favs—er, two…no, three—buttermilk cake donuts with vanilla glaze. In case someone snagged those before I did, I could settle—not a hardship—for the chocolate cake variety.

I slipped into my Jeep and drove to the strip center across the street from Super Saver Grocery Store's parking lot. My family and I were donut fanatics and visited Dee's hundreds, almost thousands, of times. Lately, I skipped an indulgence or two so the bridesmaid's dress would fit. I tended to snag a granola bar and slam down a glass of milk instead of a healthy, first meal-of-the-day. Jenny banned me from bringing home my favorite food group—cake—as she was dieting as well. Since I didn't have to be at the store until nine thirty, I usually indulged in extra shuteye.

I slotted my car in a space next to an oversized, crew cab truck with a huge lift kit. The tires were comparable to those on an 18-wheeler. I'm fairly tall, but even I would have to use a stepladder to climb inside this truck. I hoped-prayed-wished the owner didn't ding my Jeep baby when he hopped in his ride.

The breeze ruffled the ends of my hair across my lipstick as I exited the Jeep. I spluttered them away, tamed my flyaways, and headed for the donut store.

Once inside, I opened the tall refrigerated case by the door to grab a carton of low-fat milk. I stepped in line behind a mom and her four-year-old, most likely on their way to daycare, determining which treats they couldn't live without. At his age, I would have been overwhelmed by the selection, too. They should take one of each and be done with it.

Finally, Dee cashiered out mom and tot.

A gentleman, approximately my dad's age, stepped forward. Cropped white hair styled into a businessman look, charcoal suit, lean frame. He picked two sausage rolls and ordered a black coffee-to-go.

I bet the man visited the store habitually, like a coffeehouse regular.

Dee dumped three, extra donut holes in his bag and smiled. Another satisfied customer on his way to nine to five.

Finally, my turn. "Hi, Dee." Instantly, overwhelming, yet happy, feelings caused by all the deliciousness behind the display cases transformed me into a child. I fought the urge to press my nose to the glass and lick my lips.

"Hattie!" Dee tucked escaped hair strands under her red kerchief. "You haven't visited in a while."

I bobbed my head, resting my hands on top of the case. "I know. I guess a girl can't live on donuts alone. And I must fit in the bridesmaid dress. Tracey's picked a pink, skinny sheath number."

"Pink is your color, girl. You'll look fab. You always do."

"Thanks." I looked out the window and found the big truck had moved on. Must have belonged to the guy customer before me.

Dee slid open the display cabinet door and grabbed a bakery tissue. "What'll you have?"

I pointed to my selections, ordering two vanilla and one chocolate buttermilk confections.

Dee dropped the treats in a white paper bag embellished with a dancing donut cartoon. "How are the wedding plans? Is your mom arranging for a huge shindig?"

"Lordy. Parents. Especially my mother." I rolled my eyes. Everyone I went to school with knew stories about my mom, just as I knew stories about theirs. "My mother is driving everyone crazy. Dad keeps wondering how he'll pay for the wedding, even though Tracey and Stuart are pulling their weight financially."

Dee walked over to the cash register and pushed buttons. "Three donuts. Six ten."

I held up the carton of low-fat. "Did you get the milk?"

"Oops." She worked another button. "For a total of eight thirty-four. What about you? Any wedding bells in your future?"

With a snort, I passed her my debit card. "No wedding bells in my future."

Dee made the "all-knowing sideways" look. "I hear…differently."

I lifted one eyebrow and slanted my head. "Who have you been talking to?"

"Your mother said something to my mother over grapefruit at Super Saver."

Dee handed over my card. "Just a minute. I want to hear more. But first, let me help Mrs. Scott."

I nodded to Mrs. Scott, another Sommerville Library Board member, and an intimate friend of my mom and Mrs. Wellborn. After her sedate "Hattie," I sat at a café table by the door. Picking up a napkin, I dug my hand in my bag and lifted one buttermilk cake. I took a big bite, then glanced at my shirt. I wore a black silk top, and sure enough, white icing decorated my chest. I shifted the donut to my other hand and brushed the spots. Undoubtedly, I would be sporting the "flocked" look by the time I finished indulging. *Totally worth it.*

Mrs. Scott paused by my side with another "Hattie."

Geez. "Bye, Mrs. Scott."

The shop door dinged after her.

"I'm back." Dee sat across from me. "Rumor says you and Allan Wellborn are quite an item." She cradled her chin in her palm. Her eyes took on the I-remember-when dream gaze. "In high school, I used to have a crush on him."

*Wow. Who knew?* I took another bite. "You did?"

"I did." She kicked back her chair and went to the backroom. She returned with a roll of paper towels and spray cleaner. Spying something, my friend unwound a paper towel from the roll. "Lots of us did. He was two years older and even with those glasses, the pocket protector, *and* the trombone—he was hunky."

*Goes to show, everyone has different tastes.* "Dee, I have a question."

Spritz, spritz. Wipe. After she cleaned the register area, she changed her course to polish two tables opposite me. Dee set her bottle on the empty chair and toweled crumbs and bits into her hand. "Ask away."

"You know Jonson Leggett the Third—"

"Who doesn't? The moron."

"Gee, Dee." My eyes rounded and my brow lifted. I was surprised my friend expressed herself out loud, but she stated what I believed. "Tell us how you really feel."

"It's true." Dee shook her head. "Jonson met his doomsday across the street. The Sommerville Express reporters camped out in the lot for most of the day." Spritz. Wipe.

I didn't utter the descriptive words I wanted to. "I know."

"Ya." She pushed the paper towel roll against her hip. "I remember reading the article about Tracey's split from him in the paper. Scandalous for Sommerville."

I bit into a chocolate cake. While chewing, I said, "Mom hibernated when the story broke. You know, the gossip."

She shrugged. "She shouldn't have. Since nothing much happens in Sommerville, their divorce was big news. Didn't something about a rabid raccoon in Sandy Sanders' backyard supplant it?"

"Could be. Mom lives the old ways of personal business being personal." I brushed my hands on a paper napkin. "Changing the subject, Dee. I wondered—do you have security cameras?"

She halted her polishing on the chrome trim at the coffee bar. "Why?"

I looked over my shoulder and out the window toward Super Saver Grocery and pointed. "You know how Jonson died?"

"Of course." Dee lifted her chin. "But what does that have to do with my security cameras?"

I looked at my friend. *How do I explain about*

*needing her help?* "The police questioned Tracey about his murder."

"Nooo waay." She shook her head. "You girls are the essence of Miss Goody Two-Shoes."

I let loose a short snort. "You might be the only person who believes so."

Dee giggled, then spritzed. "I know the truth. I joined some of your escapades, mostly toilet papering. Mild stuff."

I trailed my finger along the table's edge. "Is it possible your cameras recorded something?"

She walked to the front door and rested her hands against the glass, leaving fingerprints. She squirted and mopped. "You think maybe my security cameras—I have two, one aimed at the door and one focused on the parking spaces—maybe-maybe-maybe someone else might show up, the someone who could have possibly murdered Jonson, and hopefully, exonerate Tracey."

"Bingo."

Dee pivoted and walked behind the counter. "I can look. I want to look. Anything to help your sister. Just as soon as the morning rush subsides."

"Thanks, Dee. Would you mind sending the file to my email?"

She narrowed her eyes. "Sure. Same address?"

"Same." *Yipee!!*

Dee pursed her lips. "Think once the police see the video, and someone else will be on it, Tracey'll be out of the hot seat?"

"I pray daily for good news. The police haven't finished interviewing. They'll check with a lot of stores and people. You know." I waved a hand toward the outside.

"I'm guessing sooner or later"—Dee returned to the register, stowing the spray and tossing the used paper towels in a trash can under the counter—"they'll come by here, wanting the same recording."

Remembering my conversation with Allan and what he said about the police checking out the strip center's cameras, I pressed a napkin to my lower lip. "If they do, Dee, don't say you shared with me...okay? I wouldn't want you to get into trouble."

Dee batted her lashes. "But if it's your hunky detective, I might be persuaded."

I gave her the "you hussy" look.

"Just kidding. Mum's the word." She swiped the age-old finger zipper across her mouth. "By the way, the photo of Tracey leaving jail—priceless. Cool handbag, though."

*Oops.* Wonder what Mom would think about that?

\*\*\*\*

In my car and on my way to work, I crammed the rest of donut number two in my mouth and chomped, washing all down with a healthy swallow of low-fat milk. I used both hands to maneuver a right-handed turn. I didn't want to be late for work. Once settled at a traffic light, I glanced to my left. A cop car with two police officers inside had stopped next to me. They stabbed fingers my way and laughed.

*Jerks. Bet they're friends of Allan's. I'll show them.* Removing donut number three ever-so deliberately from the bag, I very slowly and deliberately teethed a bite, then ran my tongue very slowly and deliberately along my lips with my eyes mostly shuttered, all the while watching them from the corner of my eye. From the look on their faces and the one they shared, realization punched them. The moment the light changed, they made a fast u-turn in the direction of Dee's.

*He-he-he.* The power of donuts. If I did visit Dee's more often, I should negotiate for a percentage from the new business she garnered. I shoved a chunk in my mouth, drank, and fished my hand in the bag for a clean napkin.

I parked my car a few rows back from Wedding Wonderland's entrance. I carried the now-empty bag between my teeth. Before exiting, I grabbed my almost-empty milk container and my handbag. With a glance at my watch, I bumped the door with my hip. Three minutes to spare.

Inside the store, I dropped my things at reception, dumped the trash in the can, and pulled out the credenza drawer. "I'm here, Miss A."

"Good morning, Hattie," she called from the fitting area.

I stuffed my handbag inside the drawer. "Morning."

"I'm such a klutz, dearie."

I took a few steps in her direction, noticing her bent over. "Oh?"

"Yes, well"—with her hand on her lower back, she straightened—"I dropped a container of straight pins."

"Which could happen to anybody."

"Still frustrating. I have no explanation. The box exploded, sending pins everywhere."

"Need help?"

"No, thank you," Miss A. said. "I am mostly done. I wouldn't want anyone to step on one accidentally. I'll run the vacuum to be sure."

Returning to my desk, I set my morning diet cola caffeine-fix next to the monitor.

Miss A. plugged in and turned on the sweeper.

I hit the computer's power button, hearing the hums and beeps resurrect it to life. After a few more clicks, I found today's updates and forwarded reminders to the soon-to-be brides.

The vacuum shut off.

Miss A. had finished retrieving the pins and joined me, leaning terribly close to my shoulder, obviously monitoring my tasks. I could smell the coffee she drank on her breath. Popping the soda tab, I imbibed a reviving swallow. As I raised the can to my lips for a second shot, my phone dinged.

I checked. Dee's name popped up. I nearly danced a jig and opened her message. "Just sent security camera link." I shuttered my phone. "Yay."

Miss A. straightened the business cards for Wedding Wonderland in the silver-plated tray on the desk. "Good news?"

"I think so. My parents are frantic because my sister was once married to Jonson Leggett. The police have questioned her and not in a good way."

"Oh my. Of course, your family is upset. The police talk to everyone." Miss A.'s hands fluttered. "No sister of yours could perform such a heinous act."

Maybe I could share the rest of my news with Miss A. "My grade school friend owns Dee's Delicious Donuts across the street from Super Saver Grocery. I wanted to talk to Dee about her security cameras and if they might have recorded something." I shrugged. "You never know."

"A sound plan."

"My friend sent me the security video."

"Great news." Miss A. rested her hand on my shoulder. "I'm sure you're eager to look."

"Do you mind?" I opened my phone. "It won't take long."

A shake of her head sent her tight curls bouncing. "Not at all. Can I peek over your shoulder?"

"Absolutely." I rotated the device where she could see, too.

I swiped back to the home screen and found my email icon, pressed the button, and my messages appeared. I scrolled to Dee's name and opened her note.

Dee wrote, *Here's the link, Hattie. I hope it helps.*

I muttered a small prayer something miraculous would materialize, and even better, a view of someone in the vicinity of Jonson and his car parked in the Super Saver lot. Now or never, and bam, the video link opened to what I identified as coming from the front entrance of the donut store. I observed many customers who passed into and out of Dee's Delicious Donuts.

"I don't see anyone near Jonson," Miss A. said.

"Me neither. Wish I could zoom in." Pensive, I twisted my mouth to one side. "I believe this image is from the front entry and customers."

Miss A tapped the screen. "Could she have sent the wrong link?"

I turned off the video. "You know, Dee did mention something about having a second camera, one aimed at the parking lot. I want to check my emails one more time to be positive."

I glided my finger over the Back To Mail words in the upper left-hand corner, which took me to the list of emails. I eyed them, looking for a second email from

Dee, but no, nothing. Nada. Zip. Not a thing.

"Rats."

Miss A. set her finger on her chin. "Ask your friend for the other view. She probably sent the first one without looking."

"All great minds, Miss A... I'll do so and then get back to work."

"I'd like to see it, too, if you don't mind, just in case I can help." She straightened, sending her gaze to the front door. "It's nearly ten. Time to open Wonderland."

"Almost done." I concentrated hard on composing the email, hit Send, and waited for a moment while my message winged its way to Dee.

I tossed my phone in my handbag, which I locked in the credenza drawer and pocketed the key. *Waiting is hell.* I tapped my toes. *Come on, Dee.* Situations like this tried my patience.

****

Wedding Wonderland was super busy all day. And the popularity thrilled Miss A. More prospective brides and friends and family investigated the store. From their comments, Miss A. would have a huge success on her hands—a good thing.

After the shop closed and in my car, I took off my shoes for the drive home. My feet hurt badly, especially the toes. I ached to massage them. Once parked in the apartment lot, I put on my heels to stagger to my door and inside, kicked them off. Then I let loose and plopped my body on the khaki sofa, propping my feet on the coffee table. Funny how a little elevation made them feel better. Grabbing my toes, I rubbed. I closed my eyes. Catching a few winks sounded like a superb idea.

"Hey." Jenny shut the door I hadn't closed properly. "You're home on time."

I cracked open one eye. "For what?"

Moving to stand in front of me, she stuck her hands on her hips. "Dinner's ready."

Both of my eyes went wide. "You…cooked?"

"Don't act so surprised."

"Let me get this straight. You cooked by yourself. No one helped you. No delivery. No takeout."

Jenny pointed a spatula at me. "Give the girl a Kewpie doll."

I scrunched my nose. "You know what a Kewpie doll is?"

"I get around."

"Where did you hide my friend?" I slid deeper in the couch cushions and let my eyelids shutter. I mumbled, "I'm pretty hungry. Better be good."

"It's awesome." Her shoes clacked as she walked to the kitchen and did the same when she returned. "Dig in."

Jenny set a plate laden with homemade enchiladas on the coffee table. A napkin fell in my lap, and she stuck silverware in my fist.

Reluctantly, I roused and moved my feet off the furniture. "Do you want to feed me too?"

"Lordy, no."

The tantalizing aroma of cheese and chili sent me to Mexican food heaven. I hovered the fork over the food while deciding where to dive in. *Cheese or chili? Chili or cheese?* As I shoveled a bite in my mouth, I caught Jenny watching.

Her light laugh trailed her back to the kitchen. She

returned, carrying a pitcher filled with a pale green liquid and two glasses containing limes and crushed ice, the rims coated with salt. "I prescribe margaritas on the rocks. You need it."

"You're a saint." Never one to turn down a good cocktail, I took what she proffered. "Pour away."

Jenny filled my glass.

I squeezed the lime, stirring the juice with the end of my fork. After licking the liquid off the handle, I imbibed deeply. "Great food takes the edge off a long day."

"Tell me about it."

I squeezed my eyes into thin slits. "I swear you've been listening to Allan Wellborn too much. He utilizes the 'tell me about it' phrase all the time."

"You've made that comment before, and like before, I don't consciously mean to copy him." Jenny waved her glass. "So, are you eatin'?"

I plowed my fork into the enchilada a second time, scooping all the melty cheese, onion, and chili. What I tasted exploded delightfully with delectable deliciousness in my mouth. I took a third bite. "Really yummy, Jenny. You've surpassed yourself."

"Yup, the family recipe. Never fails."

"Since your family's from the country, shouldn't you fix the traditional fare—cornbread and beans? Fried bologna sandwiches?"

"I've never eaten fried bologna and don't plan on it either." Jenny studied the bite she'd forked. "If'n I'm eatin' calories, they'd better be good ones." She slid the food in her mouth and shut her eyes. "What was the best thing about today?"

"Word is getting out about Wedding Wonderland.

Business is growing—a lot. I've never worked so hard. Like Christmas time at Tucker's." I patted my mouth with a corner of the napkin. "Changing the subject... This morning, I had an idea about checking the security cameras at Dee's to see if she had footage of Super Saver's lot and Jonson's car. Dee told me one of her cameras points that way."

Jenny took another mouthful. "Why haven't the police talked with Dee?"

I shrugged. "Don't know. Dee said no one contacted her. Maybe SPD needs manpower. They seem to be behind. Anyway, she sent me a link, but from what I could tell, the camera's aimed at the door, not the one looking at the lot."

Jenny scraped her plate for the last bit of food. "Emailed her back?"

"Yes." I drank from my cocktail. "No answer—yet."

She dropped her silver on the cleared plate. "Sometimes, no news isn't good news. Dee's probably sleeping by now."

"Undoubtedly. I think she's at the shop by the ungodly hour of four a.m."

"Ick. Early mornings are against my constitution." Jenny motioned to my plate. "Finished?"

"No, one more little...bit." I ate the last speck and let the utensil clatter on top of an almost spotless surface. "Done, and thank you."

"More for tomorrow." Jenny set my plate on the coffee table and reclined in her chair. "You get to do dishes."

I nodded. "Fair trade."

Jenny sipped her margarita until nothing remained

but cubes. She held the glass to the light, looking for more to drink. "Hattie, does Allan know about Dee's footage?"

"Not from me."

My statement got me The Look—a sideways glance lined with skepticism. She plopped the empty glass on the coffee table.

"Seriously, Jenny. Wipe the 'you're gonna be in trouble' off your face. Like I *told* you, Dee *told* me no one from the Sommerville PD has called. She said if Allan asks, she'll send him a link, too. I just happened to be first. I want to update my family."

Jenny pleated her forehead with her forefinger and thumb. "We need some good news for Tracey."

"Finding good news for Tracey also means good news for Jonson by identifying his killer." I tilted my head. "I might try Little Egypt, the pizza joint next door to Dee's—"

"Isn't it funny a pizza store is named Little Egypt?"

"A local legend about the second owner not wanting to spend money on a new sign—something about him being a tightwad. I can say so with all honesty since I've known them before babyhood. The current owner is a longtime family friend. I doubt they have cameras."

Jenny's cellphone beeped. As she read the text, a long gradual smile shaped her mouth.

*My friend is in love.* A large hollow space in my chest formed. I envied how her boyfriend captured her heart and soul. I missed what she experienced. I wanted what she experienced.

I licked the rim of my glass before swallowing the last lime-y drop. I studied the depths. "Mr. Who-Uses-

All-The-Hot-Water?"

"Maybe." Jenny rose, giving me an enigmatic grin. As she made her way to the kitchen, she said over her shoulder, "Maybe a fifty-gallon water heater would be a good idea."

I swung my feet to the floor and stood, gathering the plates. She didn't hear me mumble softly, "Especially if he's a permanent roomie."

Chapter Eighteen

Somewhere in sleepy time, a tiny "ding" roused me. Grappling for my phone charging on my night table, I looked at it—not Mom. *Thank God*, and I let my head drop on my pillow.

What seemed like a little while later, but in reality was four hours later, the phone's alarm sounded. I stretched wide my eyes. I stood and lifted my arms overhead. On autopilot, I shed my nightie as I slogged my way to the shower. The prickling pinpoints of water stirred me to life, and by the time I finished the soap and hot rinse cycle, I resurrected like Frankenstein, only cleaner and not grungy green with bizarre hardware implanted on my body.

I blasted my hair into a sleek 'do and shaped the ends with a curling iron. After slapping on war paint, I stepped into a slim black skirt and matching jacket with black heels. I deemed a fiery red handbag with scalloped trim to be the perfect accessory.

While standing at the island and eating toast, I checked on the email ding and found a new message from Dee. She'd written "Number 2" in the subject line. I clicked on the link and boom! Super Saver's lot filled the entire screen. Jonson's luxury SUV sat front and center. I studied the video longer until what appeared to be a woman approached his car. She wore a white jacket with a matching skirt and sported a short haircut—

The video buzzed into an alternative universe. I clicked a button on my phone. Nothing. I played "the wait it out" game. Eventually, the static-y thing disappeared, and I could refocus on the woman.

Jenny shuffled into the kitchen and poured a cup of freshly perked coffee. She sipped with her eyes closed.

"Morning," I said. "Late night?"

Looking up, she took another drink. "Finished a book around one."

An excellent read captivated me, too—glorious and worthwhile. "Must've been an extraordinary book. I treasure the feeling."

"I read the ending twice. Only done that once in my short lifetime." Jenny smiled. "Whatcha doing?"

"I got Dee's second video."

She lifted her brows. "And?"

"*Annnd* a woman in a white coat stopped at Jonson's vehicle."

She wrinkled her nose. "That's all?"

"Yes, but I can't tell who the person is—"

"Can't see who it is?"

"Not really. White jacket. Short hair. Heels. Then the recording drops."

Jenny lifted her cup. "It does sorta sound like Tracey. She has a white suit. Short hair. Wears high heels."

"It does. But lots of people wear white." I crooked my mouth. "Surely, I schooled Tracey better in clothing choices. So not the correct color for this time of year."

"Totally. Did Trace wear hers the day Jonson was murdered?"

I frowned, shifted my stance, and crossed my arms.

"She did. She said none of her other clothes were clean. Filthy greasy grime streaked the chest—according to Tracey. You know, from where Jonson yanked her against his car."

"I'm surprised he let his car get dirty."

"Me, too." I rose and stuffed a granola bar in my handbag, then added a second one and a diet drink.

Jenny sampled her brew. "Now, where are you going?"

"I think I'll go see Mr. Ryan, the owner of Little Egypt, to ask about a video. He plays tennis with Dad. He acts like a penny pincher, yet nowadays, everyone has a security camera. He's...careful." I dropped my voice. "The long-time Sommerville rumor is he's connected to the Mafia."

"Like in *The Mafia* Mafia?" Her eyebrows morphed into peaked rooftops. She looked over each shoulder like a bad dude lurked behind her. "In Sommerville?"

"I guess so. That's why it's a rumor."

Shaking her head, Jenny strolled toward the hallway toward her room, drinking more of the reviving brew. "Those small-town connections..."

I shouldered my bag and walked to the front door. "Maybe I'll score a pizza."

"One with cholesterol?"

"Would I buy any other kind?"

****

Lunch ran late at work because every bride-to-be visited the store during the noon hour. Around two, when the furor subsided, I took a break to drive to Little Egypt to ask about the video. Without a doubt, Mr. Ryan would help his long-time family friend.

Sommervillians believed Little Egypt's thin crispy pizza comparable to the kind found in Italy. The perfect amount of house-made sauce on top and covered in my favorite toppings, usually Canadian bacon and bacon.

After the founding patriarch passed to the Italian cathedral in the great beyond, Mr. Ryan, the son, took over the business. When younger, he oversaw a pricey French restaurant in the nearby big city and relocated back to Sommerville to care for his mother, the widow. Very early every Saturday morning, he played tennis with my dad and his cronies.

Mrs. Ryan sat on the Sommerville Library Board with Mom and Mrs. Wellborn.

Since no other cars had parked in the spaces in front of Little Egypt, I found a slot easily. Dee had already closed her shop because her hours were from six A.M. to two P.M., which meant I couldn't thank her in person for her help nor snag a few more donut treats. I was a worthy cause for all things in the donut leftover category.

I shouldered open Little Egypt's restaurant door upholstered in burgundy vinyl and decorated with nail heads in a Moorish design. I crossed the threshold, peering into the dimly lit space, hoping to spy someone who could help me. The lack of bright light gave the restaurant a fifties-looking Godfather ambiance, yet made it challenging to locate Mr. Ryan. Since the lunch hour passed, not many people were hanging about. I stared harder.

Booths with bench seats, covered in the same deep color as the door, lined one wall. A mini jukebox was mounted above each table, ready for quarters. Four-tops sat in the middle section of the restaurant. The seats were upholstered in the same vinyl. A checked tablecloth covered every tabletop for easy wipe up.

Nothing ever changed. The typical Italian scenery prints decorated the pale gray walls. In the background, music from the seventies gave a cheerful ambiance.

I cruised my gaze over to the bar, where I saw Mr. Ryan dispensing instructions. When a waiter pointed toward me, he turned, raising his hand in a friendly greeting. I returned the gesture.

Mr. Ryan walked toward me, arms extended, and wrapped my body in a huge hug. "Hattie, it's been too long. Why isn't your boyfriend treating you to dinner? Doesn't Allan eat pizza?"

Mr. Ryan rivaled my family and friends in the gossip department. I shifted back and gave him my best-est "whatever" look accompanied with an eye roll. "I'm sure Dad's told you about my lack of dating life lately."

Letting go of me, Mr. Ryan stroked his chin. "He did mention Allan—"

I thrust my hand in a policeman halt. "Let's not go there, Mr. Ryan."

"I get it. Private. I hear the same thing from my kids." He put his hands on his hips. "Question. What brings you by, young lady?"

"The body found in the car at Super Saver." I pointed toward the front door. "I'm hoping you have security cameras and one's aimed at the parking lot."

Mr. Ryan narrowed his eyes. "Are you asking because of Tracey's ex's murder?"

"Yes." I bit into my lower lip. Mr. Ryan was a family friend. He would be discreet—crossing fingers. "The police have focused the investigation on her."

"Morons." He snorted. "They haven't a clue."

"I'm out to prove she didn't do it."

He looked at the floor, shaking his head. "Tracey wouldn't. She might dress weird, but she doesn't have an unkind bone in her body." He lifted his gaze. "Does Detective Allan Wellborn have any ideas?"

"Well... You know how it is sometimes, Mr. Ryan. I haven't said anything about anything"—I rubbed my forehead. If Allan found out how I went behind his back, yikes—"you catch my drift?"

"Absolutely." He waved his hand toward a hallway behind us. "Let's go to my office and check the feed."

I trailed after Mr. Ryan through the back hallway lined with well-organized boxes of paper goods and canisters containing soda fountain fixings.

He opened a door on the right labeled "Office" in black-and-gold lettering, the stick-on variety found at the local hardware store. He circled his desk's L-shaped peninsula and sat in an ergonomically designed desk chair in lime.

*Lime?* Somehow, the color didn't match the burgundy vinyl look going on throughout the restaurant. Maybe he wanted to escape the fifties. I set my handbag on top of the files covering the seat of the only other chair.

Mr. Ryan mouse-ed to an icon and clicked. The image of the exterior door of the restaurant appeared as well as the sidewalk and several cars slotted in front. We stared hard at the screen.

Instantly, my hopes dived to my feet. The camera didn't focus on the Super Saver lot.

Mr. Ryan slid on bifocals and peered harder at the screen. "Hmm, not what we're looking for. Let's go to view two…" He clicked again.

Voila! Super Saver's view of the lot became visible. Setting my hand on Mr. Ryan's shoulder, I leaned closer to see what was what. I tapped an area on the monitor. "That's Jonson's car."

"Wow," he drawled. "Some fancy ride."

"Yeah, we're wondering how the heck Jonson afforded it."

"He always acted like he had money but not a dime behind him."

I straightened. "How do you know about Jonson's finances?"

"Small town stuff. Ask the right people in Sommerville about his family, and they know. His mother didn't, probably couldn't, pay her bills on time. Felt sorry for her." I went still and considered. Mothers, but especially my mom, could be tightlipped when need be. "Mom never said."

"Probably didn't mention it to you kids. Kids never keep secrets." Mr. Ryan wiggled the mouse. "Now, this is looking good."

I rapped the screen. "Can you zoom in?"

With a click, Mr. Ryan enlarged the picture. "From the rear of the vehicle we think is Jonson's, we see a woman approaching wearing a white coat."

"Darn." Tracey's outfit. My heart sank to the bottomless pit of damned souls. The incriminating evidence mounted, and my brilliant plan maybe didn't seem so brilliant after all. "Well, crap. Your video is exactly like Dee's."

Mr. Ryan's brow lifted as he twisted my way. "You asked Dee for her security videos?"

"Yes." I crossed my arms. "She has the same one

featuring a lady in a white coat."

Frustration fell over me. I stepped back and rubbed my forehead. "Tracey has a white suit; however, nobody could say for sure if it's her because the image isn't clear." I huffed, blowing a hair strand from my eyes. "I'm so not catching a break here."

Mr. Ryan removed his bifocals. "I'm no computer expert, but maybe you could consider hiring an audio-visual professional to examine the footage. He'll restore the image, and possibly you can identify the person with Jonson Leggett, and specifically, if the person"— he touched the screen with his glasses' earpiece—"is Tracey."

I dragged my index finger over my chin. "Interesting. Would a pro cost a lot?"

"Hattie, are you worried about the money to pay for the expert?"

Sighing, I didn't say anything for a while. I wished what we viewed had been as clear as day and not like mud. My family needed answers now—*now* so we could clear Tracey. *It's always something.* "I'm sure Dad can bankroll me."

"Old man moneybags to the rescue." The side of Mr. Ryan's mouth lifted in a sarcastic, joking grin. "Seriously, your father would do anything for his girls."

"I know." I fisted my hands on my hips. "Mr. Ryan, would you mind sending me the security file?"

"Sure can." He did some voodoo on his computer. "What's your email?"

I recited my address.

He typed, then hit Send. "Sorry I couldn't be more help."

"We know more from your security video than we

did. I can't say enough how much I appreciate you taking the time to help, Mr. Ryan."

"Anytime, Hattie. Anytime."

I shouldered my handbag and walked to the office door. I smoothed my hand over the burgundy vinyl, which covered the inside of his door—*what is it with the fabric?* Maybe someone held a huge sale—and like the front one, studded with decorative nails in a pattern.

I paused before entering the dining room. "Mr. Ryan?"

"Yes, Hattie?"

I firmed my lips. "My parents are so worried."

He patted my shoulder. "I know. Especially when the implicated criminal could be their child."

"Well"—I shifted from one foot to the other—"I'm positive the, er, police will come by."

Mr. Ryan shoved his shoulder against the door, waving his hand for me to pass through. "I'm catching your drift about the police—standard operating procedure. I won't say anything to them about sharing with you, not unless I have to. Now, young lady, it's long past the lunch hour. How about we get your favorite pizza to-go…on the house?"

My favorite pizza. No way on earth would I pass up a pizza offer. I nearly smacked my lips. Canadian bacon and bacon with extra cholesterol—nothing tasted better. I smiled like a half-moon slice of cantaloupe. "Yes, sir."

"By the way"—he pivoted my way—"terrible photo of Trace in the paper. What did your mom say?"

\*\*\*\*

Later that night, I attended another dreadful tango lesson… *Dear Lord, how many more?*

Ms. Yolanda shifted the boys in one line and girls in another, facing each other.

I had no partner. Good, because if I did—especially the one Ms. Yolanda paired me with—I'd kick him in the kneecap. No, I'd kick both kneecaps, just for Tracey.

Our teacher moved to the center of the room. "Class. Since something has delayed our happy twosome—"

*Delayed, my ass.*

"—tonight," Ms. Yolanda said, "someone will have to take their place. Any volunteers?"

The happy chatter died to cricket chirping. The other dancers faded into the walls lined with mirrors so they wouldn't be prevailed upon.

I didn't move quickly enough.

"Maid of honor"—Ms. Yolanda pointed—"where's your partner? The good-looking young man." Her gaze swept the room.

Allan blew in, his hand raised like a kindergartner. "Here."

The members of the bridal party melted off the walls.

My body took on a nervous rigidity.

"Yes, you, young man." Miss Yolanda pointed a neon red talon toward Allan. "You're a little tardy."

"I apologize, Ms. Yolanda." Mr. O Saintly One bowed over her hand. "Please, forgive me."

*Lordy.* Ms. Yolanda nearly dissolved into a puddle like the Wicked Witch. A pleased smile shaped her mouth.

"No worries. Our lesson just began. I selected your previous partner."

Ms. Yolanda took his hand, led him toward me, and set my right hand in his and his right on my waist. She tented her fingertips together and bounced on her toes. "Perfect."

She circled about, beckoning the others to come forward. "During the dance, for a moment or two, you"—she stabbed her finger at the bridesmaids and groomsmen—"will pause and form a circle around the bride and groom. They will dance their sequence, specially choreographed for the wedding, and then, all of you will join, er, Stuart and Tracey to finish the number. Any questions?"

Realizing I lifted my hand in the same manner Allan had, I dropped my hand. I spoke up. "So, Miss Yolanda, how will we practice without Tracey and Stuart—"

She drew a curvy "S" with her finger. "Not a problem. And explains why you're the maid of honor, Miss—" She paused as her brain Rolodex-ed through names. Then bing! "Cooks. Tonight, you can substitute for Tracey with the best man."

Ms. Yolanda gestured for the others to form a ring.

She held a long-stemmed blood-red rose. "Do you remember when you practiced with the rose?"

*Only amnesia would allow me to forget.* Rose stem in mouth—check. Uncomfortable—check. Icky taste—check. I twirled the flower. "Yes, Ms. Yolanda."

"Excellent. Then repeat what you've learned. Places, everyone," she said. "Good. Anda one. Anda two."

I stuck the rose between my teeth. I would never resemble a tantalizing lover, not with my lips locked in a grimace. Finally, I glared at Allan.

He stared back.

I muttered, "I'm a wittle wague on the wovements."

He bit back a laugh, probably because I sounded like a cartoon pig.

"Maybe they'll return."

After two glides, the steps did come back. Allan bowed me over his leg in a lunge.

Allan asked, "So, what did you see on Dee's videos?"

My mouth fell open, and the rose dangled from the corner before falling to the floor. I rescued it. *He has some nerve interrogating me here.* "What…videos?"

Without any explanation, he pulled me to my feet.

I regripped the stem with my lips and executed a few steps. In an artful pause, he tipped me back and took the rose from my lips with his mouth. His breath bathed my cheek, and his five o'clock shadow roughened my jaw. Butterfly fluttery feelings took flight in my chest. My eyelashes involuntarily batted like a schoolgirl.

Allan's gaze locked with mine. Time and space evaporated. The tango music faded into oblivion. A little dazzle in my brain transported me to the love dimension, the one filled with daisy chains, puppies and kitties, and rainbows.

"Excellent."

Ms. Yolanda's claps jarred reality to the forefront.

Allan guided me around the room.

When I seemed steady, I felt him let go of me. My heart beat hard. I fisted my hand, released, fisted again as if to capture whatever passed between us.

"Thank you, Mr. and Mrs. Steems' stand-ins. Let's repeat the beginning sequence," Ms. Yolanda said.

The troupe fell into place.

Allan sighed and took the rose from his mouth. He wiped the stem with a white hankie.

I held in a giggle as we had swapped spit on other occasions. I took the flower.

"Don't play games with me, Hattie," he said. "I know you spoke with Dee, and I'm positive you visited Mr. Ryan, your dad's tennis partner, as well."

*Lordy.* Allan's superpower must be X-ray vision. I twirled the stem between my fingers. "How do you know that's true, if, indeed, it *is* true?"

"I'm not even trying to interpret what you just said."

His mouth shaped into a smile.

"I'll boil what you said, or didn't say, down to one question—how *do* I know?"

With a curt nod, I suppressed the urge to slap the smarmy grin off his face.

"I know you know how I know. Dee told me. I turned on my secret agent charm, and she spilled the goodies. Specifically, she told me about your chat and how she emailed you security footage."

"Funny, how you never said a word. I was wounded"—Allan smiled, setting a palm to his heart—"but not for long. Dee gave me a box of my favorite donuts. Cured everything." His brow bounced with his grin.

Traitor Dee. She gave him a whole freakin' box of donuts—for free. I paid for mine. I gave a bare shrug. "I knew you'd go to her store sooner or later." I poked his abs, which weren't squishy. *Lordy.* "You didn't eat all the donuts at once, did you?"

"Nah, I shared with the guys."

*Sharing donuts with other people*—oh, hell no. Struck momentarily dumb, I didn't utter a word.

Allan asked, "So guess what I saw?"

*Not my sister. Not my sister. Not my sister.* I pressed my lips together. "Oh. On the video? I haven't a clue."

His eyes squinched and his brown irises darkened. "Liar. A lady. In a white suit."

Allan's hand measured near the top of my head.

"A tall lady with white-ish blonde-ish hair. Someone who resembles your sister—which you already knew."

I stumbled against his chest. His hands circled my upper arms. I gulped. "A-And?"

He dropped his hands to his sides. "Bad news for your sister, Hattie."

I went hot. My blood boiled. "You." I locked my arms like steel girders and curled my hands into fists. "You-you moron."

I did what any red-blooded, all-American sister would do. I did what I had thought of doing earlier—I kicked Allan's kneecap and ran to the exit. At the door, I paused long enough to see him dancing—*haha*—on one leg while he rubbed the injured limb.

****

As I fast-walked through the parking lot to my car, I fumbled through my handbag for the key fob. Glancing up, I caught Allan exiting the dance studio.

Our gazes connected.

Allan picked up speed.

I redoubled my efforts and bounced the unlock icon multiple times, heard a beep, and jerked open the door. Just after I climbed inside and about to pull the door shut, I saw he pressed his hand against the door frame. No way could I close it now.

"One minute, sweetheart," he said.

Over his shoulder, I spied the entire wedding party at the windows and door, their noses and palms pressed to the glass, their mouths gawking as if they hadn't seen two people about to go to war.

The wind whipped inside the car, sending a cold chill to swirl over my body. I pulled on the door handle to break Allan's hold but to no avail. "Seriously, will you ever stop calling me sweetheart?"

"Probably not. But if you want to try and stop me, go for it. Most of the time, I don't believe you want me to." He tilted his head and shifted his body. "Something is between us, and one day, we'll explore it."

Another cool breeze blew in the car. I yanked again.

The door bumped his side. "Ow."

"God, you're stubborn."

"Slow down, Hattie. Let me finish."

He crowded me and not in a good way. He blocked the draft—a plus. "Why, Allan? You've already said you won't stop with the sweetheart stuff. You've already tried and convicted my sister with Jonson's murder." I gave him a hard squinty look. "By the way, a nice feather in your cap. Maybe a promotion, too."

He jammed his body between the door and the door well. "Is that what you think? You think I want your sister to go to jail, and I get some big career advancement?"

*The guys on TV do, but I didn't use those exact words.* I let my hands plonk in my lap. While I collected my wits, my chin drooped to my chest. I raised my head. "All I *want* is my sister to not go to jail. You seem intent on sending her."

Allan touched my shoulder and squeezed.

I fought the impulse to rub my jaw against his fingers.

"No one has arrested your sister."

I shot up my head up. I knocked off his hand like it was a buzzing mosquito ready to draw blood. "Is this a trick question?" I rubbed a finger over the V crease that shaped my brow. "I'm having trouble believing anything right now."

"You forget. We have the fingerprints from the car doors. And FYI—we found others besides Tracey's."

*What??!!* Other fingerprints, not just Tracey's? *Thank God.* I tilted my head. "Then, whose are they?"

Allan hit his waist with his hands, shoving aside his coat. He looked past the parking lot to the other stores along the street. "I don't know. Just let me do my job and quit interfering."

I bristled. "I. Am. Not. Interfering."

Allan angled his brow. "Says who?"

"Says me."

He gave me the "so not believing you" look.

"I'm not."

"Then tell me, please, who talked to Dee and Mr. Ryan before me?"

I rubbed my finger along my nose and across my mouth to my chin. I needed to speak with the right words, not babble like an idiot. I did enough babbling on ordinary days. "I had a…necessity. Yah, a necessity." I pulled my lower lip and sank deeper into the front seat.

"I can't wait to hear your explanation."

"Yes, a necessity. Because—because—"

Allan rolled his finger. "I don't have all day."

Sigh. My stall tactics didn't work. I lifted my chin. "Because I needed donuts and pizza. Besides, Dee's a family friend. So's Mr. Ryan. I can talk to whomever I want."

Allan said, "Didn't say you couldn't talk to your friends."

I bobbed my head. "I *had* to have Dee's donuts. Our chat turned to Jonson's murder. She graciously supplied me with—"

"Recordings from her security cameras. Imagine that."

I ignored Allan's answer. "And Mr. Ryan's a long-time family friend. He gave me a pizza—"

"I know. I know." He huffed, his arms crossing his chest. "Your favorite. Canadian bacon with crispy bacon—"

"And during our conversation, he mentioned the"—I looked in the distance and pulled a stray curl—"security cameras. One thing led to another." I tapped my fingers on the steering wheel. "Did you use thumbscrews?"

"Not necessary." Allan buzzed my forehead. "Just flashed my badge, like normal cops."

He stepped away and closed my door with an irresistible grin sure to stir my flustery feelings to life again.

Chapter Nineteen

The next morning, I dragged myself into Wedding Wonderland. Pictures tornado-ed through my head, like ones of Allan and me hot and sweaty in a body-lock, which kept me from sleeping most of the night. When shut-eye finally came, I dreamt of us tying the knot. I grew restless. The tossing and flailing turned my body black and blue. Cue hot shower and two ibuprofens.

At Wedding Wonderland, I hollered a greeting to Miss A. in my usual way.

She called her "hello, dearie" reply from the belly of the stockroom, her typical routine. A few moments later, she opened the office door and bustled to the front of the store with a long, satin gown draped over her arms. "Hattie, I'm so excited. Your sister's dress arrived. Can you ask her to come for alterations?"

I doodled on a scratchpad, then dropped my pencil and frowned. "Miss A., you know how the police are investigating Tracey?"

She laid Tracey's dress on a reception chair. "Still?"

I nodded, picked up my pencil, and twisted windmills on the desk. "My sister's not doing so well."

She tutted. "Oh, dear. I'm so sorry to hear."

"I don't understand why my sister's not fighting back." I palmed my chin. "Tracey's hibernating in her bedroom at Mom and Dad's. Drastic, I say. Is it possible… Can we wait…on the fitting?"

Miss A. pulled off her cheaters. They dangled by a chain in the vicinity of her ample chest. "Hattie. We must do it now, or the dress won't be ready. We have very little time—"

"You're right." I scratched my temple. *How to solve my problem*? I sighed. "I see no other alternative. I'll phone her."

Grabbing my cellphone, I pounced on Tracey's speed dial number, but instead of my younger sibling answering, my mom did, which nearly sent my body into spasms. Mom's implications about hooking up with Allan to *persuade* him to help Tracey still annoyed me. She bridged a line no mother should cross. I didn't say a word in case I needed to disconnect.

"Hattie? Hattie!" Mom asked. "Is that you?"

*Lord, save me. My reflexes have dulled.* "It's me. Mom, let me speak to Tracey. She needs to try on her gown for alterations."

"She's…um. Well, she's, uh… Yes, she's indisposed."

*Indisposed? What the hell?* "Last night at tango lessons, I subbed for her because Tracey and Stuart did a no-show. That kind of indisposed?"

"Well, yes, you could say that."

Mom's pause went on forever. From the corner of my eye, I saw Miss A. continued to watch me, and I sure as hell knew she thought my sister's wedding could and would be the stupidest on record.

"How did the lesson go?" Mom asked.

"Very well—aw, Mom, not the point." I picked up the pencil and slammed it on the desk. "Tracey should've gone."

"You know how she feels."

"If anyone does, it would be me. Ask Tracey to talk to me right now." I hated to beg anything from my mother. But I had to. "Please."

"Fine. I'll check again."

I rolled my eyes and rotated my neck. My spine released a satisfying unkinking pop. In the background, I heard someone—most likely Mom—murmur. She even sounded like she pleaded. *My sister needs to get over being an ass.*

"Hattie?" Mom asked.

"I'm still here."

"Tracey says she wants you to try on the gown."

"She what?" *Ridiculous.* "Mother. I'm taller than her."

"You and the seamstress will figure out what to do."

I flicked my left hand toward the ceiling. "But—"

Mom disconnected. *What?!* Still holding the phone to my ear, I turned to Miss A. I was stunned. Outraged. Infuriated. How could she? My mother hung up on me, her oldest daughter.

Miss A. scooped Tracey's dress in her arms. "Hattie? Is your sister coming?"

I pressed the phone to my chest. *I still can't believe what Mom said.* "I'm supposed to—"

"—yes, dearie?"

"—*I'm* supposed to wear the dress *for* her." *Guess who is beginning to feel like The Bride. First, the tango lessons and second, the alterations.* Who knew "maid of honor" meant "bride in training"?

Miss A. frowned with a pout. "I'm not understanding. You're a stand-in for your sister?"

241

"Yes." I nodded. "Mom insisted." I bit my lower lip before asking. "Is it bad luck to wear your sister's wedding dress?"

"I don't…think so."

"Maybe we should do a search on bad luck and weddings." What would be the point besides knowing the minutiae about wedding day karma? I clenched the phone and walked toward the changing rooms. "Let's get this over with."

Turning in my boss's direction, I touched her arm. "And please, Miss A.—"

She paused. "Yes, my dear?"

"No photos."

*Why is she laughing?*

\*\*\*\*

Later in the afternoon, Miss A. called me to the office. "Have a seat, Hattie."

I lowered myself into the chair across from her desk. A strong aroma of coffee found my nose. I checked the room, noting the samples, the rack of freshly altered gowns, the white mug by her phone inscribed with "Wedding or Bust" in a flow-y script.

"Is something up?" I asked. "Did I do something wrong?"

"No-no-no. No worries." Miss A. took a sip of her high-octane brew. With a dainty "aah," she set the cup on her desk. "I wanted to discuss with you about possibly attending a wedding conference with me. All the latest trends, fashions, etc. will be on display. We might connect with the hottest new vendors and find exclusives for Wedding Wonderland."

A business trip? *How fabulous.* "Where is the conference?"

Miss A. shuffled through a stack and selected a piece of correspondence. "I'm sorry, I should have said. In Smithville. Of course, we will stay overnight, and I will cover the room costs, meals, and conference fees. We can drive to Smithville Saturday evening, stay, go to the event all day Sunday, and drive home on Monday."

Miss A. peered over the rim of her blue-framed bifocals, the same color she had used to embroider her name on her white coat.

"What do you think?"

I thought for a bit. Not costing me a dime computed. So far, working for Miss A. and learning the wedding business was ideal. No weird monkey stuff. She was a great mentor. And a three-hour drive wouldn't be a hardship. "What about the shop?"

Miss A. tapped her calendar book. "We would only miss Sunday, and Wedding Wonderland's closed on Mondays. A problem for you to go out of town?"

"Not at all. When do we go?"

"I'm a tad late in registering." Miss A. manipulated and clicked the mouse. "The date is next weekend, three weeks before Tracey's wedding. Any problems?"

I shook my head and stood. "Shouldn't be. Everything wedding-related should be done—thanks to my mom—and snap-snap-snap, fall into place like clockwork."

Miss A.'s mouth drooped a bit. "Are you having a bachelorette party?"

"Jenny said something about hostessing one the night before the wedding at our apartment. She hired someone to give us massages, do our nails, and ordered a hot fudge sundae bar, which I'll have to pass on because I need to watch calories to fit in the pink dress."

"Ice cream sundaes sound terrific. Let me know how I can help." Her eyebrow quirked as she waved the information sheet. "Do you want to attend the convention with me?"

Deeply, I wanted to go with Miss A. to Smithville. I would learn tons and be a better asset to Wonderland and beef up my resumé. "I'm a definite yes."

Miss A.'s face beamed like a new morning sun. She pressed the phone to her ear. "Great. I'll make the arrangements now."

I hit speed dial two on my phone. "I'll just let my mom know what's going on. I don't want her to have a panic attack when I'm a no-show for what she considers important."

Miss A. paused. "Aren't the mother of the bride's worries the pits?"

\*\*\*\*

Twilight settled in as I steered my Jeep into a parking spot steps away from Kella's apartment.

I sensed my phone vibrate. "Yes?"

Dweller Kella asked, "Are you on your way?"

I killed the engine. "Just parked."

"Did you remember to buy the glass votive holders?"

"Yes, ma'am. Two for a dollar at the 99-cent store." I scooped up my handbag and the plastic grocery sack containing the requested items. I asked the clerk to wrap the candle holders individually as I would never hear the end of the Funsisters' grief if I showed with broken or chipped ones.

"Good. That's all we need."

I rang her doorbell, and Trixie let me inside. The Funsisters came together to make tabletop decorations—Jenny's idea—for my sister's rehearsal dinner. Another way to help Allan Wellborn throw the party Stuart's mom should be hostessing.

After I entered, I felt a brush along my arm—Trixie.

"Before we start on our project, we need to know if Tracey and Stuart are getting married for real."

I knocked aside her hand and gave her my best "what are you talking about" look. "Of course, they are. Trace'll be exonerated, and all will be copasetic. Besides, Stuart told me so."

A small look of confusion swept Trixie's face. Her head slanted and her mouth pursed. "You're sure?"

"I pinkie swear positively positive I'm sure. We talked." I crushed the bag in her arms and proceeded to Kella's kitchen. The Funsisters promised dinner, and my stomach vocalized its hungry noises. "The detective on the case said some of the fingerprints weren't hers."

Maggie joined us, tossing her hands. "Just say his name."

"Whose name? Allan, like in Allan Wellborn?" My friends loved to irritate me. I dumped my handbag in the center of the table and motioned for Trixie to add the plastic bag.

Maggie gave a bare nod.

"All right, fine. Allan said so."

Maggie's shoulder knocked my shoulder. "Hard to say?"

Jenny waltzed in and handed me a glass of iced tea. Spying the dollar store bag, she took out the votive containers, unwrapped them, and held each to the light for imperfections. She polished a few on her jeans to erase the smudges. "These look perfect."

"Thank you. Seriously"—I set down my glass—"someone pass me food before I collapse."

Trixie passed me a plate loaded with a hot croissant filled with ham, gruyère cheese, and green apple slices. A bag of gourmet potato chips followed. She pressed a napkin in my free hand. "Happy now?"

I bit into the sandwich. Hot, smooth, and crisp at the same time. *Delicious.* I took a second bite. Around crumbles of bread, I mumbled, "Yes, and thank you."

"Enough with the chitchat. We need to get busy." Trixie scrubbed her palms. "Jenny, what's first?"

The Funsisters sorted the supplies for the decorations into piles. Jenny passed Kella a piece of paper printed with the faces of Tracey and Stuart. "You cut out the heads. And please do a good job. Sometimes, your cutting—"

Kella snatched the scissors and trimmed a Tracey head. "I'm not in first grade, you know. My mother says I've improved."

I noticed how everyone stared at her. Improving her scissoring technique sounded funny.

"Fine." Jenny rolled her eyes ceilingward. "Trixie, you glue the heads on these paper dolls I copied."

Trixie took the glue stick from Jenny and saluted. "As you command."

"Hattie."

I shoved the rest of the sandwich in my mouth. *Boy, I needed more time to eat.* "Yes?"

"You hot glue the pipe cleaner to the back of the paper dolls. I made twelve of each sex. One groom and one bride for each table."

"Ten-four." After the face was glued on the paper doll, I applied the pipe cleaner to the back. When finished, I held it for everyone to see—a Tracey paper doll. "One word—adorable."

"Wait until you see what I do." Jenny coiled the lengthy leftover pipe cleaner into a button-like shape and hot glued it to the votive, which she'd tipped base-side up. She added the groom to another votive. She set them side-by-side and waved her hand over the creation. "What do you think?"

Kella clapped her hands and bounced on her toes. "I like it. Like-like-like. We should save them and reuse when Hattie marries Allan."

Holding the glue gun in mid-air, I froze. "Wh-hat?"

Trixie waved her hand in a flighty way. "It's just a matter of time."

"But-but-but we haven't dated like normal couples do." I slid my hand over my mouth. "We haven't had"—I lowered my voice—"s-e-x."

Consumed by hysterical giggles, Trixie doubled over. "Even I know how to fix that." Hiccups followed, and she ran from the room. "Water. Water."

Kella said, "Look. The Stuart doll doesn't have feet."

"I'll add a doily and feathers and stuff." Jenny rummaged through another grocery sack and located a package of paper doilies and feathers. "No one will notice."

"So, Hattie…" Kella manipulated the scissors around Tracey's photocopied head. "Why haven't you two done the nasty? Seems like you had plenty of opportunities. I'd be all over him—if he was my type."

"One." I ticked my finger. "We seem to be angry

with each other."

"Two." Jenny raised two fingers. "His cell phone interrupts."

"True," Kella said. "Three. He dated Blonde Bimbo."

"Four." I signaled with four fingers.

Everyone looked at each other.

Their expressions read, "There's a four?"

"I don't know if he's in love with me."

"Dimwit. Who said anything about love? A major orgasm is the goal. A giant one." Trixie returned to her spot and looked at her sticky fingers. She picked off a stuck paper sliver. "We know Allan cares for you. The whole world knows."

"I'm begging…" I pressed my palm to my chest. "Move on. Surely, somebody has a more exciting love life." I flung my hands skyward, only to stop when the glue gun's cord didn't extend far enough. "Like Jenny and Mr. Who-Uses-All-The-Hot-Water—"

My friend gave a curious eye and a subtle shake of her head.

She wanted to shush me about Mr. Who-Uses-All-The-Hot-Water—which was fine. But why was she reluctant to tell the other Funsisters where their relationship was headed?

"Ladies." Jenny studied the bride and groom paper dolls. "These decorations aren't getting done."

Trixie passed a completed groom. "Here you go, Hattie. Maybe you should have snagged Stuart."

I jerked the paper from her hand. "Not in this lifetime."

\*\*\*\*

Another banner new day at Wedding Wonderland.

"Hattie, dear?"

I followed Miss A.'s call to her office. If I remembered correctly, several brides-to-be scheduled appointments. Perhaps, she wanted to discuss them. "Morning, Miss A. Whatcha know?"

Miss A.'s shoulders slumped as she returned the phone to its stand. "I have some news which might compromise our trip to the wedding convention in Smithville."

I didn't like the sounds of "compromise." Hopefully, her small problem could easily be solved. "What's wrong?"

"You see, dearie, I had to take my car to the shop this morning. The service manager phoned a minute ago, and well"—she smoothed her hand over her forehead, pushing back the springy curls—"I have a huge, oh, what's the right word? Drawback. I feel awful about this."

"Car problems are no fun, Miss A." I nodded. "I don't know what I'd do if someone hurt my Jeep baby."

She smiled. "Your car is so darling. Someday, you'll have to let me cruise the parking lot."

I choked back a laugh. Who wouldn't want to see Miss A. handling my sporty vehicle? We could take the top off. Her white curls flying helter-skelter in the breeze. A goofy smile shaping her mouth as she wheeled about. "Anytime. What's wrong with yours?"

She flicked her hand. "I didn't understand everything the mechanic told me—you know how the service department is. He clearly said the part was on order, which means—"

"We can't take your car to the convention."

Her head nod affirmed my comment.

"I hate to ask, but could we go in your Jeep?"

I gave a small smile. "Of course. Just be warned the ride's a tad bumpy, and the car barely has enough room for our suitcases." I set a finger to my chin. "Maybe I could borrow my mom's larger SUV."

Standing, Miss A. rounded the corner of her desk. "No, no, we won't bother your mother. We don't need much for overnight. I'll take one suitcase only. And anything I buy at the conference can be shipped to the store. I will gladly reimburse you for gas, etc."

"Perfect. If there's nothing else"—I walked to the storeroom door—"I need to check on the alerts for today."

Miss A. waved me on. "Absolutely. And Hattie—"

I turned back. "Yes, ma'am?"

"Thank you so much."

I saluted. "Sure, Miss A."

\*\*\*\*

Miss A. and I scurried like squirrels all week. Preparations for our trip to the wedding convention in Smithville were finalized. As prearranged, I drove to her townhome Saturday night after work to pick up her. I made space to stow her bag in the Jeep's back seat while she locked her front door.

She wheeled her enormous suitcase down the driveway.

"Hi, Hattie," she said with a wave. "Shall I load my belongings? Did you remember to pack a tote to fill with giveaways?"

I lifted a nylon duffle bag. "Think mine is big enough?"

Miss A. shrugged. "If not, some vendor will have one. No worries. We'll figure it out."

Together, Miss A. and I hoisted her red rollaway into the back seat, where it smashed mine against the car frame.

I closed the back hatch and looked at my car, then her. "I think I have everything. You?"

"Splendid. I do like your fun ride," Miss A. said. "I can't wait to have an adventure in it."

"I promise you"—I crossed my chest—"three hours later, and you'll beg me to let you out. The car's fun, but a long ride isn't for everyone."

She bobbed her head. "Good to know." And with a grandiose wave, she said, "Shall we go?"

The drive passed fast. Miss A. asked a lot of questions about my family and life in Sommerville. After a peek at her watch and then a consult with her phone's GPS, she said, "We exit here and take the first right. The hotel is on the corner."

I steered the Jeep onto the correct street and turned into the hotel parking lot. Miss A. had booked a large room with double beds. We checked in, and the receptionist informed us where to find the convention center and how it opened the next morning.

After unpacking, Miss A. said, "Let's get some dinner."

Miss A. and I returned to the lobby and located the hotel restaurant, a low-key affair.

A woman behind the counter asked, "What'll it be, ma'am?"

Miss A. ordered a hamburger, which sounded so yummy, I did as well.

The girl passed plastic cups and pointed to a beverage dispenser. "Help yourself to your favorite drink."

I filled my glass and found seats at a small round bar top. Miss A. sat as well with napkins fisted in her hand. After a few minutes, the young lady set a tray on the counter. The food emanated a wonderful smell, which made my tummy gurgle. I spread ketchup on the meat, dashed on black pepper. The pickles, lettuce, tomato and a thick slice of white onion topped all. I dipped a fry in the ketchup and savored how delicious it tasted.

"Are you excited about the convention, dearie?" Miss A. asked.

I wiped my hands on a napkin. "I am jumping out of my skin with excitement. You teaching me the ins and outs of the wedding business is much appreciated."

"You're welcome."

Miss A.'s playful smile made me grin back. "I know I'll be overwhelmed with everything. Market at the Apparel Mart exhausted me, yet I was thrilled. Selecting the new clothes, seeing the people—"

"You told me how sad you were to leave the job." She drank from her iced tea.

I waved my hand. "Yes, and the stupid temporary jobs since—"

A frown crossed her face.

"I'm sorry, Miss A. I sounded rude. Please don't think I meant Wonderland—"

"Of course not, my dear. I am the one smart enough to hire you." Miss A. patted her lips with her paper napkin. "Shall we get some shut-eye and hit the convention early?"

"Yes, ma'am."

\*\*\*\*

A huge "Welcome to Wedding Extravaganza! Find

your Blissful Ever After" banner hung over the entrance of the Smithville convention center. The prospect of a new adventure excited me. I had to contain my enthusiasm to keep from dancing like a two-year-old.

Miss A. gave a small laugh. "Blissful Ever After— how cute. I should find a slogan for Wonderland. Do you think they coined theirs for the convention?"

I parked the car and killed the engine. "Makes sense."

"How about—Find Your Dreams in Wedding Wonderland?"

"I like your slogan—a lot. I think you're on to something. We could put it on the business cards and in our ads."

"As always, Hattie, you have great suggestions."

*Yeah!*

Miss A. and I removed our totes and laptops from the car. Inside the convention center, a helpful receptionist handed us our badges and cheerfully pointed out how to access the venue. Miss A. and I stepped past the entry to study the layout and plot a course of action.

She nodded. "How about I go to the right, and you take the left. I'll text you when I'm done, and then we can exchange information over lunch. If we aren't too tired, we'll reverse. I go to the left, and you go right."

"Excellent idea," I said. "Later."

Slowly, I perused the vendors. I snagged business cards and stuffed goodies in my extra tote. After each stop, I took notes and some pictures of items I thought would work well in Wedding Wonderland. Talking with people about the latest and greatest trends brought back the good ol' days at Tucker's.

Two hours passed, and aches and pains consumed my body with every step. I *had* to sit soon. My phone buzzed—my boss. "Hi, Miss A. Ready for a break?"

"Oh, dearie, too much to see. I'm thoroughly"—she inhaled—"exhausted."

"I kinda wondered. When I attended the menswear market for Tucker's, often, I couldn't take another step. I know, let's get some food. Once our tummies are filled, and we rest, our sanity will return." I rose to my tippy toes to locate her. "Where are you? Can you see me?"

Miss A. stood and signaled.

I waved, turned off my phone, and weaved my way through the convention-goers to the table she found, where I dumped my bags at her feet. With a hand pressed to my spine, I arched my back. "I need some pain relievers, like now."

Being a boon compadré, Miss A. passed a travel-sized tube labeled ibuprofen.

"Thanks." I swallowed two tablets without water. Not ideal, but I wanted fast relief. I canted my head. "Darn it. You're wearing your Wedding Wonderland jacket. I should have done the same." I bit my thumbnail. "I'm sorry, Miss A. I don't know what I was thinking. Not thinking is more like it."

Miss A. wagged her finger. "No worries, dearie. I snatched mine at the last minute. I thought I would look more professional, and it would fight off a chill in case the air conditioning felt cold, which it is. You know how conventions are."

"I do." I pulled a pink pashmina from my tote and draped it over my shoulders, hunching into the warmth. "So how about a Caesar salad and a cup of tomato bisque for lunch?"

"Splendid. And a bottle of water, please." Miss A. slid two twenties across the table.

"No, ma'am." I pushed the bills back. "You paid for the trip, the least I can do is buy lunch."

She didn't protest.

I smiled and made my way to the counter. Within two shakes, our order was ready. Carefully, I carried the tray with my eyes on the table and Miss A.

I chastised myself a second time for not packing my white jacket. My work at Wedding Wonderland made me proud. I probably could have made super contacts by advertising in this small way. *Can't be helped.*

As I approached our table, I overheard a woman exclaim, "Anna Holcomb—it *is* you!"

The color drained from Miss A.'s face. She set her hand to the column of her neck. "Pardon me. Do I know you?"

"Of course, you do, silly girl," the stranger said.

*Girl?*

"I'm Ivy Bush, Hon. Don't you remember? I worked with you in Honolulu." The silver-headed, tightly permed, and skinny-as-a-stick lady patted the top of Miss A.'s hand and sat in my chair.

I set the tray on the table, placed Miss A.'s meal in front of her, and stuck out my hand. "How do you do? I'm Hattie Cooks. I work for Miss A. at Wedding Won—"

"Oh, thank you so much, Hattie, for lunch," Miss A. interrupted. "Now, if you will excuse us, er, Ivy. We need to eat and get back to work."

By the squirm of her butt in the chair, Ivy wasn't

about to go anywhere.

"Anna, just last week," Ivy said, "I told my mahjong friends about you. Do you recollect the fun day in Cancun?" She snapped her fingers. "I must be getting old; I can't remember the name of the hotel. Anyway, we had a blast on that trip. Remember when we pretended to be well-heeled ladies from L.A. and settled ourselves on one of those lounge beds by the pool? Girl, how we flirted with the cabana boys." She fanned her face.

*Cabana boys? Flirting?* I stared at my boss. *I suppose anything is possible like Miss A. flirting.*

"And the mai tais," Ivy smiled.

*Mai tais?*

Miss A. didn't utter a word except dip her spoon in the bisque and let the liquid drip into the bowl.

"And the dancing. My heart still races over the conga line on the beach. Surely, it was a mile long." Ivy flopped back and waved her face with the convention brochure. "Aw, those were the days."

Ivy barely swallowed from her drink. She didn't need any more caffeine.

I raised one eyebrow. *Dancing? Conga line?*

She fixed on me an all-knowing look. "Oh yes, young lady, Anna can shake a rug. She was once a Rodeo Girl."

*As in THE Rodeo girl? Like the famous dance team who performed every year in the Thanksgiving Day Parade in New York City—Miss A.?* Crazy! From her white curls, perfect diction, and prim outfits—I couldn't envision a trim Miss A. with shapely legs doing high kicks and contagion ripples.

Ivy leaned in. "It's a shame our boss at Miss

Misty's fired you when the till was stolen."

A hard, angry look shaped Miss A.'s mouth.

Before anyone could say anything, someone called a "yoohoo" to Ivy, who returned with a wave and stood.

"I'm so sorry we couldn't chat more, Anna," Ivy said. "Here's my business card. Let's reconnect. Email me sometime."

Ivy blew a kiss in our direction and skimmed toward her friend. She pointed us out to her companion and filled in the woman. Eventually, they melted into the crowd.

"So," I said as I sat, "Ivy. Old colleague, friend Ivy."

Without missing a beat, Miss A. swept the business card off the table and crushed it under her foot. She smiled. "Shall we continue?"

Chapter Twenty

On the Friday evening, two weeks before the wedding, I drove downtown to the church my family attended. Tracey and Stuart selected the smaller chapel set apart from the rest of the church complex.

I loved the building, as well. A mossy brick walkway linked the chapel to the main sanctuary. Limestone archways provided a unifying architectural detail. Two dark-stained, heavy oak doors opened into the inner sanctum. The chapel walls soared from floor to ceiling with stained glass windows. In the afternoon, light filtered through the glass, painting the floor with jewel colors. Tiny gold tiles covered the wall beyond the altar railing. A wooden cross dangled from the ceiling in front of the gold-ness.

I arrived before the others for the rehearsal, which slightly bothered me. Agitated, I checked around for them. *Why hasn't the rest of the wedding party shown?*

Who *needed* a rehearsal nowadays? What could go wrong? Everyone knew the basic routine. My maid of honor duties included:

—Help with hair and makeup.

—Be supportive.

—Walk the walk.

—Smile.

—Stand just so.

—Hold the bride's bouquet.

—Adjust her train.

—Carry spare tissues.

I ruffled my hair at the crown and slipped into the second from the front pew to wait. And to think. Think about Tracey and Stuart, their ordeal, my frantic parents. The whole sordid enchilada. *How can a problem like my sister's be in any typical suburban family?*

I heard crunchy scuffs on the carpet but didn't look. When someone paused by my side, I looked up— Allan. "Hey. Why are you here?" Then remembering, I tapped my temple. "Best man."

Allan set his hand on the back of the pew. "I guess you don't know."

*Did not sound good.* "What?"

"Over kumquats at Super Saver, your mom told my mom, Tracey felt…let's say…ill."

I jumped to my feet and glanced toward the building door. "Tracey's sick?" *Very newsworthy.* "She didn't say a word yesterday. Did she go to the doctor?"

Allan shook his head. "I…don't…think…so."

"Because…" I rolled my hand.

He didn't utter a word, just glanced at his shoes and lifted his toes.

*Maddening man.* I squinched my eyes into slits. "Something's going on, and you better tell me. Now."

Allan sighed. "Here's the short story. Your mom, dad, Stuart, and Tracey are, er, missing the rehearsal. We're"—he motioned from himself to me and back— "standing in for them."

*Un. Be. Lieve. Able.* My jaw dropped. *This wedding will be the death of me.* "Stand in for them— again? You've got to be kidding."

259

He leveled on me his best no-nonsense look. "Do I look like a comedian?"

*He didn't.* Fanning my hands wide, I paced six feet to my right, spun about, six feet to my left. "I've tried on Tracey's dress. I've stood in for their tango dance…" I rotated fully to face him. "No. I won't do it. I won't be a stand-in at her wedding rehearsal. Period."

"Our mothers say Trace is a little…embarrassed."

"Embarrassed? What'll she do on the day of the real I Dos?" I stood and brushed past Allan to the altar railing. Once there, I paused and studied the cross, praying for divine wedding intercession. I wheeled about and stepped closer to him, so close, I nearly hugged him and almost forgot why I was so mad. "I'll show her embarrassed—"

Stepping back, I smacked my hand against my forehead. "How could I forget. I know why. It's because of you. You questioning Tracey at the station and your ineptness in finding the real murderer." Did I say murderer in church? *Lordy.* I set an evil eye on him. "Thanks bunches…pal."

Allan walked to the first pew and sat. He dropped his forearms to his thighs and stared near the vicinity of his perfectly polished oxfords. He raised his head a fraction. "You know, Hattie, your blame game is old."

*Blame game?* Before I could speak one word, the chapel door burst open. I snapped my gaze toward the entry. In walked the rest of the party—at a high-octane chattering pitch—followed by the minister, Reverend Walsh, the same guy who baptized Tracey and me, all sober and dressed in a no-nonsense dark suit.

"Hi, Hattie." Trixie pointed at Allan, who stood and faced the group. "Oh, look, everyone. It's Allan

Wellborn—"

The girls tittered. Truly, tittered.

"Detective"—Trixie sauntered down the aisle—"Allan Wellborn, the dirty rotten rat."

Mr. Saintliness glowered.

Calling him "rat"—not popular.

Jenny, who followed Trixie, looked at Allan, then me. A glance of understanding passed through her eyes.

She mouthed, "You okay?"

I nodded.

I stepped past the bridesmaids collected in the aisle, still giving Allan their best "go to hell and burn" glare.

Looking way too cheerful, Reverend Walsh smiled, scrubbed his hands, and placed himself in front of the altar railing. "Shall we get to it?"

Allan stood, jamming his hands in his pants' pockets.

Trixie looked to the entry. "What about the other groomsmen?"

"We have one; he'll have to do. I'm sure you ladies have played the role before and can help the young men when need be. All standard stuff." Reverend Walsh waved to the Funsisters. "Please, take your places in the narthex."

Leisurely, Kella and Jenny led the way up the aisle to the narthex, sharing silly stuff the whole way.

Trixie shot Allan another from her Book of Nasty Looks, then followed our girlfriends.

With a tight smile, Allan watched them.

*So not a proper wedding.* I lagged behind the others. Anger issues over Tracey and Stuart and Allan made irritableness consume my head. Who wouldn't be irritated with everyone's interference in my life?

In the foyer, I skirted my friends to stand by the door. *Yup, time for a vacation. An extended retreat to a Pacific island with no phones, a state-of-the-art spa, and glorious sunny days. Never mind not having the money to go. I'll figure something out.*

At "uh hum" and a signal from Reverend Walsh, the bridesmaids aligned themselves in the predetermined order to advance down the aisle. Once he saw us organized, the minister raised his finger like a conductor. "Ready?"

The Funsisters nodded.

He sang, "Tumtum ta tum, tumtum tat um."

Trixie proceeded first. She stood regally while holding her pretend bouquet. One by one, the other bridesmaids marched slowly and intently in perfect time as the minister hummed the traditional wedding march. Their hands clasped nonexistent bouquets at their waists. Mostly, they looked demure, except for Trixie. She never looked demure. She still looked…pissed off.

When they stopped at the altar and took their spots, I stepped forward.

"Hattie, fix your eye on me, please," Reverend Walsh said.

Shifting my gaze meant I couldn't ignore Allan, who stood to the minister's left. But I did my darndest. *Damn Jonson Leggett the Third. How could Tracey get dumped in such a pickle right before her wedding?*

I expected to find Allan's eyes sparkling with a twinkle, one which relished in my discomfiture. But I didn't. His irises turned nearly black. And on his face, his expression read "mine." I sensed my heart kick in extra beats.

I continued to face the, er, faux groom side. Blinking rapidly, I pretended the whole thing was a dream or nightmare—it depended. Maybe whichever would pass quickly. Simultaneously, Allan and I rotated to face the minister.

Reverend Walsh said, "Perfectly executed bridesmaids and grooms"—he took in only Allan and harrumphed—"groomsman who's substituting for the groom. And now, we'll practice the vows." He grasped our arms and turned us to face each other.

I wriggled away. "I don't want to be the bride—"

"Hattie, it's not a big deal. Not a lifetime commitment. Not legal. Just a re-hear-sal." Reverend Walsh rubbed the top of his bald head. Over his wire rims, he studied me with the lift of one brow. "Unless, perhaps, you want it so? Maybe the lady protesteth too much?"

I shook my head, but through my lashes, I saw Allan gulp then square his body. *The big horse's patootie.*

"Now, we're settled." Reverend Walsh tucked his chin and let his gaze rove those of us at the altar. "However," he said softly, "I expect your situation will change…one day soon."

*What I'd like to know is if my situation would change before anyone else knew.*

He lifted his Bible. "Dearly beloved…"

Before long, I zoned out. I zoned to a faraway land of another church. Beside me stood a groom dressed in a black tux with a pink cummerbund. Blush dahlias and stargazer lilies, spreading their scent, decorated the urns by the altar railing. I wore a white flowing gown with an off-the-shoulder look. The music soared through the loftiness of the sanctuary—

Someone jabbed my ribs. I pushed aside the daydream and joined in with an, "I do."

Sounding like happy fledglings, the bridesmaids twittered.

I didn't dignify it. I didn't look. I didn't comment.

"I now pronounce you man and wife." Reverend Walsh closed his Good Book. "You may kiss your bride."

Again, significant twittering from the birdie chorus.

Allan held my hand—*How did that happen?*

He dipped his head lower, then lower until we were a lip lock apart.

I stared into his chocolate irises. *Kiss me—kiss me—kiss me.*

He did, but not on my mouth, which throbbed and ached for him. Nope, he played it safe and smacked me on my hair.

More significant twittering.

"Please turn and face the congregation," Reverend Walsh said. "May I introduce you to Mr. and Mrs. Steems."

The bridesmaids clapped.

Allan twined my arm with his. Jenny passed me an invisible bouquet. We, the poser newlyweds, strode arm in arm down the red carpet, mostly because Allan held me in place with his hand on top of mine when I tried to jerk away.

From behind us, I heard Reverend Walsh say, "Shall we repeat?"

Allan's shoulder brushed against mine. "I do."

My breath caught. *Lord, save me.* And then, my prayer was answered.

Trixie said, "No way in hell."

*Isn't Trixie the epitome of a best friend?*

\*\*\*\*

I drove from the church to the Waterworks building by Sommerville Lake for the rehearsal dinner, which had morphed into a party. Lots of family and friends had been invited. Along the small street which wound along the curves of the lakeshore, I found direction signs inscribed with "Steems-Cooks Rehearsal" and red arrows, which indicated the way to turn.

So far, Allan did a meticulous job.

*Duh.* Of course, he would.

After parking the Jeep, I entered the building through an archway formed with teal and pink—the bride's colors—balloons. I dragged my finger along one, hearing a rubbery squeak. Allan's penchant for balloons popped in my mind.

As I rounded the corner to enter the party room, I stopped abruptly. Smack dab in front of me stood life-sized cutouts of a bride and groom, the kind where people stuck their faces in the holes to have their picture made.

Surprise! I didn't know about the photo prop.

Surprise! I knew what was coming.

The wedding party and family guests circled the stand-ups to admire the handiwork. They clamored for a chance to poke their heads in the cutouts. A family friend jumped into position while another friend held a camera-ready smartphone.

Rubbing the length of my nose, I readied myself.

Some well-meaning person would inevitably pair me with Allan for a goofy portrait. I would slap a smirk on my face and let them snap away until the giggles had subsided. Then run for—well, anywhere else but here. Mount Rushmore seemed like the perfect spot. Tons of crevices were carved in the Presidents, making them the ideal location for hiding.

I dreaded the whole thought behind this-this coupling with Allan. Yes, I wanted to kiss him and do other romantic things. But part of me held back because he always, always put work first, like his questioning my sister. And our so-called romance seemed to play in front of everyone. I wanted to hold our affair for myself. To cherish the newness of discovery. To know at any moment, images of us would form in my brain and make me squishy-wishy.

Until the little issues were resolved, I'd guard my heart.

Sigh. *If only...*

I would pose for pictures for Stuart's and Tracey's sake—*just once*—to maintain a cool status quo and not make a scene. But later, I would eliminate the person who dreamt up the little enterprise, and dollars to donuts, the mastermind was…Jenny.

Jenny helped Allan.

She tugged me into the hallway.

"I'm gonna kill him," I mumbled out of the side of my mouth.

"No, you're not. You can't. Allan's a cop. Cops don't like people who hurt their cops."

I pulled my arm free and crossed them. "Ya, whatever. Besides, I'd get off—extenuating circumstances."

Jenny waved toward the cutouts. "You didn't know?"

"About these? Nope. Not a thing." I sent my head from side to side. "I ordered the food and the tables. Allan ordered the hay."

"Did he do the cutouts on purpose?" Jenny pulled on her bottom lip. "I don't think he's creative. Someone helped him."

"And which of my best friends would help him?"

Jenny proudly thumbed her chest. "Me."

I rolled my eyes and tossed my hands. "Of course, you would."

Arms lifted, Jenny twirled, then tilted back her body. She looked mighty happy with what she'd done. A savvy grin with a smart-ass gleam fired in her brown eyes. "He seemed…inundated."

"Inundated? Allan? Wrong." I fixed on her my most extraordinary evil eye. "I thought you were my friend. Why-why-why would you embarrass me?"

"Remember way back when Mrs. Steems threw the rehearsal dinner on Allan, and you said he needed lots and lots of help?"

I bobbed my head. "He roped me into riding to the rescue."

"Ride 'em cowboy."

I stared so hard, Jenny should be bleeding from the piercing holes.

"Fine," Jenny said. "Allan needed other ideas to make the reception special. Someone at work attended a wedding and the cutouts"—she waved her hands over her idea—"were at the reception. I liked the concept and told Allan. The rehearsal dinner seemed to be a fun place to do it. I contacted a rental company, and for a mere one hundred seventy-five dollars apiece, you can take them home."

I stuck my hands to my hips and swiveled to check out her triumph. "As cute as they are, I'll pass."

"Me, too."

"Mr. Who-Uses-All-The-Hot-Water might have other ideas."

"Don't go there."

"How come we can talk about Allan and me ad nauseum and not you and Mr., er, you know—the guy you're dating?"

"Because"—Jenny stabbed my shoulder with a finger—not too delicately—right where the bone met the soft tissue—"I'm me, and you're, you know, you."

*Okay.*

"I love you like a sister, Hattie. If you suppose my intent with the cutouts was to pair you with Allan, fine. Despite what you may believe, there's not any huge Conspiracy Theory, except in *your* head. I only wanted to help a friend—"

"I *am* your friend."

"I had no ulterior motive."

"As you say."

Jenny liked Allan; she always had. She always seemed to take his side, and today was one of them. "Sorry," I said. "I'm grumpy."

"Apology accepted. For what it's worth, here's my short opinion." She raised her index finger. "I think it's time for you to get over your hang-ups. He didn't get you killed; you didn't get him killed. No one's out to get you. Admit your feelings for him."

Jenny pulled me close, so close her forehead met mine.

"Hattie, it's time for a heart to heart. You're in love with Allan Wellborn. Everyone knows you care for each other."

"Everyone?" I gulped, then considered. "Of course, they do. Everyone in little ol' Sommerville knows everyone's business. I'm no exception. Nothing's ever private."

"Then own it. Own it in your heart. Say 'I love Allan.' Maybe the town'll find another hot item."

Jenny could be right. I considered some more.

"Hattie?"

"I'm thinking."

"I can't stand here all night with my forehead stuck to yours. You're sweaty."

Straightening, I gulped deeply and said softly, "I l-love Allan."

"Doesn't sound much like owning it. Nor heartfelt."

"You heard me."

"I'll turn on my hearing aids."

*Fine.* Louder, I said, "I. Love. Allan."

Just like in the movies, the proverbial dropped pin pinged like a bomb, and by coincidence, exactly when everyone stopped talking. Sensing all turn our way to stare, I closed my eyes. *Thank God, my backside is to the crowd.* I could feel holes drilling into the back of my swanky little black dress. Their hot looks melting my zipper to my spine.

The quiet seemed overwhelmingly profound. I peeked through my eyelashes and barely shifted my gaze to the left and then to the right. I very, very quietly asked, "How bad do you think it is?"

She lifted her hands just enough to reveal

hopelessness. "Oh, you know…"

*Great.* "No possibility of an earthquake swallowing and spitting us out somewhere else?"

Jenny smiled. "I don't think so—not today. But you never know. Seems some new gas wells have created heave-ho issues."

"No molten lava cascading from a nearby erupting volcano, causing the need to evacuate and mass pandemonium?"

She giggled. "No."

"No drug bust because someone caught a bunch of teenagers smoking weed on the balcony?"

"No, Hattie."

"Damn." I bit my lower lip. "It's a good guess everyone knows something's up?"

"Yep."

"Is my mom here?"

"Can't tell from this angle." Jenny lifted her chin and adjusted for a better view. "Yes, and Mrs. Wellborn and she are whispering furiously."

*Darn. Those two and their matchmaking. Why didn't Mom stay at home?* "Allan?"

"I see him. He's"—she peeked past my shoulder— "he's moving our way…"

Could I be any more mortified? I bounced into an upright stance and squeaked, "Allan's coming over here?"

Jenny rose to her toes and looked over my shoulder to check again. "It's hard to say. A crowd of people is between us, but I *can* see his head. He's zigzagging around them to find you."

Allan heard everything. Everything. Every. Little. Thing. *Awkward. Uncomfortable. Embarrassing. No privacy.*

"I know." Jenny grabbed my elbow. "Let's escape to the ladies' room."

A good plan, way better than any I had now. "Brilliant. Allan wouldn't dare go in."

"Ready?" She propelled me from the reception room.

I let her take me. I could hide indefinitely in the ladies' room, especially if I locked the door. No one would bother us, especially Allan.

Check that. *He might.*

However, his mother raised him to be the perfect gentleman. *He might not.*

My tummy grumbled. *Can I order a plate of fried chicken to be delivered?*

**** 

Pale pink and black tile decorated the women's bathroom walls and floor which looked like a flashback to the forties. In an alcove, women could check their makeup and clothing in tall pier mirrors gilded in gold leaf. Large upholstered chairs and ottomans in a pink trellis pattern were scattered about for comfy seating.

I picked up a soap dispenser and sniffed— lavender—my favorite. I circled the rest of the room— *unexciting, but then, what public bathrooms are?* Crossing my arms, I rested my backside against the vanity. "So, exactly how long do we have to stay out of sight?"

Jenny turned the lock. "Work with me. We've been in here all of two minutes."

"An eternity."

"I'm thinkin' "—she stared at her phone—"twenty more minutes should do it. Do you want me to see where Allan's at?"

I turned to look at my reflection in the vanity mirror and grabbed a tissue which I dabbed to the corners of my mouth. "Yes, please. Being stuck in a restroom is as boring as dirt."

Jenny harrumphed. "I've never been compared to dirt before—"

"Sorry—"

"I know what you mean." She twisted the doorknob. "Maybe if the coast's clear, I can scarf up food. I love fried chicken."

"Excellent plan. Don't forget the peach cobbler with ice cream."

I turned and let my rear end rest against the counter again. I didn't exactly count out how many minutes, but after a long while, I believed Jenny had disappeared forever. Then, the door creaked with a squeak.

My friend entered backside first, carrying a tray. "Look what I have. Texas sheet cake."

I grabbed a plate of cake and a utensil, forking a hefty bite with no consideration about fitting into the bridesmaid dress. Around the crumbs, I said, "I. Love. Cake."

"I know. Sorry, no cobbler. The caterer took her time replenishing it."

"At least someone is eating something." When hearing the door rasp a second time, I stuffed a large bite in my mouth. "Did you lock the door behind you?"

Jenny cringed and checked over her shoulder. "Umm. Maybe not. I was cake distracted."

Another squeak. Somebody pushed a metal utility cart—the stainless kind used for industrial purposes—into the room.

In better lighting, Allan materialized.

"Hi, ladies."

His wide toothy smile looked brilliant like his pinpoint white shirt over which he wore a sport coat.

The man excelled in dressing, but I bet my last dollar he used toothpaste guaranteed to whiten teeth. I'd seen a tube when I searched his house a few months ago. I stared at the toilet doors. *Sometimes, I don't know what to think about him.*

I shifted my gaze back to Allan. "Shouldn't you be entertaining your guests, oh sainted one?"

"All's cool. I left the party in Trixie's and Kella's capable hands," he said.

"My friend? Trixie? She'll demand everyone join the limbo contest. Kella'll will make sure all is okay." I dropped into a chair. "I see you brought food. Are you hungry? Were all the chairs taken in the boy's restroom?"

Allan locked the door. "I might get a warmer reception in the men's room."

How…unexpected.

He looked around. "I've never been locked in a women's restroom at a rehearsal dinner before. A real first."

Someone pounded on the door.

"Out of order," Jenny hollered.

"Hattie, are you okay?"

I mouthed, "Mom."

When my mother banged a second time, Jenny's shoulders shuddered with laughter.

I raised my palms and said in a soft voice, "Help."

"Can you unlock the door, Jenny?" my mom asked.

Jenny moved to the door where she pressed her ear

to it. "Something's wrong with the hot water, Mrs. Cooks."

"Shall I find the Waterworks building manager?"

I rolled my eyes.

"No, ma'am. Shouldn't be much longer."

"Thanks, Jenny," Mother said.

"Sure, Mrs. Cooks." Jenny wiggled her smartphone in my face. "I have Kella on the phone. I'm telling her the downstairs restroom's out of order and, in case of an emergency, to send the guests to the upstairs one."

"Good plan," Allan said.

Selecting a plate, she set a chicken breast on it. "Looks yummy. Thanks for organizing the food for…er, us."

"My pleasure. Good eats shouldn't be missed. Go on"—Allan flicked a finger at the rest of the tray—"mac 'n cheese. Salad. Biscuits and strawberry jam in the basket."

"Don't mind if I do." Jenny heaped the sides on her plate.

After she snagged a baked goodie and topped it with butter and jam, she looked over. "Hattie, would you like me to fix you a plate?"

With a sigh, I stood and walked toward her. The gurgles in my tummy sounded very unladylike. The chicken smelled divine. I extended my arm. "Just a small piece will do."

Jenny passed me a full plate. "Here you go."

I returned to my chair and, when settled, bit into the chicken. Closing my eyes briefly, I savored the lovely crunch of the perfect golden crust. Slowly, I took a second and third bite.

Allan set a glass of iced tea on the table.

I glanced up. "Thank you."

His smile framed the perfect teeth. He took a swallow from a beer. "You're welcome." He munched on the entrée, too. Between mouthfuls, he met my gaze. "Good choice on the caterer, Hattie."

I nodded. For a while, the three of us concentrated on filling our bellies.

Jenny looked over the room, then giggled. "I don't think I've ever eaten in a women's restroom before. Nor the men's, either."

"Me neither. Before you ask, beer isn't food." Allan pointed to the platter of chicken. "Seconds?"

Jenny took a drink of tea and wiped her fingers. "No, thank you."

I shook my head and followed with a clearing of my throat.

"Something on your mind, sweetheart?" Allan asked.

*Sweetheart.* That would be me. "Well—"

Jenny blurted, "We want to know what you're thinking about the videos."

"Videos?" He scrunched his brow. "What videos?"

"Don't play dumb, Allan." I set my empty plate on the vanity and rubbed my hands on a pink paper square. "We talked about how I've been to Dee's Donuts and Little Egypt and watched their security tapes."

"Oh. *Those* videos." Allan nodded. "No comment."

I moved to stand in front of him, crossing my arms. I stared at every nuance in his face, his lips, and his eyes. *He knows more than he's saying. He always does.* "I can remind you if you need me to."

He waved his piece of chicken. "Tell me what you think."

275

"Dear God," Jenny said to no one. "Not again."

Allan and I looked at her.

She raised her palms. "What? You will go at it until one of you gets mad."

Allan and I acknowledged each other. Together, we nodded. "Probably."

I circled the cart. "Both Dee's and Little Egypt's tapes show someone in a white suit approaching Jonson's vehicle."

Allan rubbed his chin. "Okay—"

"But"—I paused and raised my finger—"I see differences."

His eyes narrowed. "Like what?"

I ticked off my right hand. "From what I've seen, size-wise, the person is bigger than Tracey. Hair is whiter than Tracey's. The coat doesn't exactly match Tracey's."

Allan drank deeply from his beer and abruptly stood. He picked at a corner of the label and then took another swig.

The interesting look he placed on me made me shift away, but not for long. In the past, I learned he might be a cop, but his work behavior would never intimidate me. I firmed my stance and leveled my shoulders, noting his delicious lips—

*Delicious lips?*

"Anything else?" he asked.

I cocked my head to my right. *His lips are delicious, and he knows how to use them.* "No. Just pointing out what was recorded. The police will probably want to review, you know, to be sure."

"You're correct. The police will review with more detail in mind. We're requesting lengthier footage."

Allan leaned closer. "So…you love me?"

Jenny's eyes widened with Dear-God-Help-Me-Cause-I'm-in-the-Wrong-Place. She quivered with a slight head jiggle and did her best to become one with the wallpaper in the alcove.

*Like anything could stop her from listening.* Stepping closer, I sensed the toes of my shoes touch his.

Allan tilted my chin toward him.

Words escaped me. The urge to delve into his eyes—dark irises like a ninety-percent cocoa bar with a flash of golden light—pushed to the front. I swallowed long and deep. *Lordy.*

Allan nodded. "Thought so." He broke away and returned to the cart, wheeling it to the door. "Ladies, thanks for a memorable rehearsal party."

"Thanks for the food, Allan," Jenny said.

He winked. "Anytime."

The tension slipped from my legs to collect at my feet. As the door swooshed closed behind him, I blinked and swayed.

Jenny glided to my side and nudged me with her elbow. "I didn't know Allan could read minds."

Planting my right hand against the wall for support, I bit into my lower lip. "I did."

\*\*\*\*

Over the next few days, my time was consumed by a flurry of tango lessons, work, and subbing for Tracey at her shower—what a non-event that was. No bride-to-be. No exclamations over gifts. Jenny had salvaged the Stuart and Tracey paper dolls from the rehearsal and set them around Kella's living room and dining table. The best part? Eating two lemon cupcakes.

I kept busy with organizing Wedding Wonderland.

I cleaned the shop more than I cleaned my apartment. First, I vacuumed the dressing rooms and then arranged the gowns in the gown room. Dusted and swept the reception area and the raised platform. Finally, I tackled the storage and office area.

On a bookcase shelf behind Miss A.'s desk, I shifted the toolbox to wedge new bridal magazines next to it. A hammer sitting on top of the hard, plastic case caught my eye. *Is it the one Miss A. lost long ago?* Even though Miss A. replaced the misplaced one, she would be happy about my find.

"I found it," I said a little loudly, "Miss A."

"What is it, dearie?" Miss A. moved to the front of the store where she polished the glass door panes fingerprint-free.

"I found the hammer." I walked to the storeroom door and held high the tool so she could see it. "The missing one. What was lost is now found."

"Good job, Hattie. I saved the receipt and can return the replacement I bought. The cost of a new one—it was ridiculous how much the hardware store charged. Did you put the old one in the toolbox?"

"Sure will." Swiveling, I stepped to the shelf and lifted the toolbox lid. I dropped the hammer inside, and I took the new one and put it on her desk.

After snapping shut the lock, I saw a brown-ish residue on my palm. Resisting the first urge to rub my hand on my skirt, I sniffed my hand. *Yuck.* I couldn't determine the scent, but pleasant did not come to mind. With a second sniff, a faint…metallic odor found my nose. Confused, something about the smell nagged me. I tried to remember, but the memory wouldn't resurrect.

I reopened the box and checked out the

hammerhead on the old tool. Nothing weird, just beat-up and used. I studied the new one, then the old one. Wisps of light brown fuzzy lint were stuck on the nail driver of the new one. No clue what that could be.

While I considered, I focused on Miss A.'s white jacket, which hung from the brass coat hook screwed onto the back of the office door. I set the new hammer on her desk.

Somehow, I needed to unravel this conundrum. I studied the coat, its size, and the blue embroidered name. The pockets. I was struck by how similar it looked to Tracey's suit coat.

While my head wrapped around "coat," I compressed my lips. Something filtered through my thoughts, and I envisioned Miss A. at the crime scene wearing *her* white jacket. And wham! I knew. I really, really knew.

Miss A. went to Super Saver Grocery wearing her white coat to buy a hammer.

My heartbeat intensified. Wheeling, I walked to Miss A.'s desk and sank into her chair. I cradled my chin in my propped hands and deliberated. I'd seen the videos, and the person didn't look like Tracey in her white suit and short hair. The person looked like…Miss A.

-Both wore a white coat.

-Both had light-colored hair.

-Both were near Jonson Leggett's car.

My feminine intuition told me Miss A. murdered Jonson. I bet twenty bucks she used the new hammer I just found. Allan said someone left fingerprints on Jonson's car—beside my sister. *Do the prints belong to Miss A.?*

Ey, yi, yi. *I should call Allan. He knows what to do.*

I heard a rustle from behind me, and before I could check, I felt something flung over my biceps. In an instant, I felt my arms pinned against my body. I pushed to my feet. I fought, twisting from my right to my left to get loose. In the struggle, the hammer jostled off the desk. The clank on the floor caused me to jerk. My legs were kicked out from under me. Off-balance, I face-planted on the cement floor.

I couldn't focus. My head circled to la-la-land. When the pain subsided, an awareness of my surroundings filtered in. I attempted to flex my hands, but they didn't move. Turning my head, I looked about barely able to comprehend how my arms and ankles were bound.

I wriggled to no avail. In the shadows, I saw an outline of Miss A. stooped over. She pulled on the knot around my ankles.

My boss had trussed me like a damn turkey.

I croaked, but nothing came out. Trying again, I forced out a hoarse, "Miss A."

She hoisted herself upright and walked to stand by my head. After she pulled a hankie from her pants pocket, she fluttered the folds apart, then patted her forehead as well as the back of her neck. Her plump chest palpitated with the exertion. "Oh, my dear, Hattie. I am so sorry about everything. Things have gone from horrid to horrible.

"I didn't think very clearly when I left the new hammer on top of the toolbox. When your friend, the detective, visited—the morning after Jonson died—to interview me, I had to move quickly and hide it. I shoved the paper bag under my desk. The other day, my foot kicked it, and I remembered what I'd done. I thought, 'You're in a pickle, Anna,' and had no idea of what to do next. A splendid notion came into my mind—what better place to hide a tool temporarily than on a toolbox?"

Miss A. twisted the fine cotton square in her hands. "Everything has been so confusing and hectic and-and I guess I forgot the hammer was on top of the toolbox."

*God, no words.* "I…don't…understand."

"You don't, dearie? Looks like you are the dimmest bulb in the store." She tilted her head. "Shall I explain? It is all so simple—really. I killed Jonson Leggett the Third."

*Oh. My. God.* Miss A.—a work colleague I admired, and whom I believed was a friend, and my mentor—killed my sister's ex?

But her dispatching Jonson made no sense.

Concentrating on what was unfolding made my head hurt. I needed to focus on her. "You-you did? You killed J-Jonson? W-why?"

She lifted a shoulder. "What a prick. A slimeball like you said. Repeatedly."

"Lots"—I swallowed profoundly and rubbed my jaw against my shoulder—"of people…are slimeballs, but most humans don't murder them."

"True." Miss A. frowned. "Jonson and I appreciated a different philosophy about marriage. His track record—not on par."

She propped one hand on her hip in the teapot stance all pre-teen girls learned in deportment classes.

"You and I know his marriage to Barbie wouldn't have worked out, and she would have divorced him, and down the road, he would have married again. He didn't value the sanctity at all. A serial groom similar to a serial killer." She snorted. "Serial groom. Ha-ha. Funny if I do say so myself."

Miss A. was right. Jonson Leggett the Third only valued himself and sex. The whole world knew of his narcissism. And *serial groom*—an appropriate appellation.

*But is Miss A. a serial killer? Oh my God. This is horrific.* I felt my belly roil and not in a good way.

Miss A. bent over and pulled on the knots hobbling my hands to confirm their tightness. Standing, she brushed the dust from her palms. "Jonson's devil-may-care attitude toward marriage rubbed me funny. He was walking the aisle for the *third* time. I couldn't let him. His awful pattern would continue, and it just made me so angry.

"You see, my dear, I know all too well his type. My ex-husband did the same thing. Married six times, he found his final resting place with the Lord." Miss A. crisscrossed her chest in the fashion devout churchgoers did.

I didn't know people could be married so many times in our state. I mumbled, "S-six times?"

"Absolutely. Where I lived before, my understanding is there's no limit to how many marriages. All that's needed is proof of divorce."

"Who would want to marry someone after two or three or five times?"

"As I said, you're only partially dim." Miss A. scuffed the toe of her shoe against the desk leg. "Back to my ex, he had an, oh, let's say, an accident."

*An "accident"—like Jonson's?* Miss A. posed as a

sweet, older woman; yet, inside that façade housed a psycho insane one.

*Lordy.* Some people were never who you thought they were.

*What about me attracts weirdoes?*

In my DNA, I must possess one of those syndromes the talk show hosts on television described. Probably the "Be Kind to Everyone" my mother instilled in me with her oft-repeated little lectures.

"It was a long time ago." Miss A. ran her fingers over her forehead. "I bumped into my former husband at the grocery store, and things got out of hand. I let him seduce me in the back seat of his Cadillac."

Her mouth shaped a vague faraway smile. She bounced lightly on her toes, flouncing her hankie.

"Ooh, how we tested the springs," she said. "Such a charmer. Good thing it was nearly dark out."

The daydreamer look on Miss A.'s face—a pleasing sweet gleam in her eyes and a happy countenance—while she remembered her ex and their, er, affair, made a bilious churn in my stomach creep up the back of my throat. I swallowed multiple times to avoid throwing up. It was the last thing I ever wanted to do.

She waved her hand. "Did you know it rains almost every day in Seattle? But one particular Friday—if I remember correctly—simply glorious." She clasped her hands to her chest and sighed. "It had been a long while since I had good sex, and my ex-husband performed— well, good, just like the old days." She assessed a distance with her hands, which looked to be twelve inches.

*Ick. Ick. Ick.* Did Miss A. just rate the size of her

ex-husband's man-part? I sooo didn't need to know that.

"Afterwards, I freshened myself with the handkerchief he passed me while he sat in the front seat. He strummed his fingers on the steering wheel impatiently. Then he said, 'Hurry, Anna. God, you're slow. I've got people to see.' I took 'people' to mean 'other women.'

"Well, dearie, his lack of consideration infuriated me. No way to treat a lady after sex, except maybe a prostitute, and I have no doubt he would have been kinder to her. I was no prostitute. Not a hooker. Not a whore. I am above that. And he cleaned out our bank account, most of which was my money. My money. Mine. I became infuriated."

"Are you still alive?" She nudged my foot with the toe of her sturdy navy-blue heels. "Where am I?... Oh yes. Thinking about the harsh words he'd spoken made the sting of them grow and grow. A hurt developed in my chest. My brain seized in a white light."

The corners of her mouth drooped. Furrows as deep as canyons between her brows developed. *How in the hell am I getting out of here?*

"I went to take my purse"—she showed me how she stretched her hand toward the floor—"and instead of my bag, I, somehow, ended up...with...a hammer, one most likely from the tool kit he deposited on the back-seat floorboard. I guess it fell out.

"I stared and stared at the hammer in my hands. I rolled it in my left, then the right hand. I raised my head when I heard him say, 'Seriously, Anna. What's taking so GD long?' Before I could utter, 'One Mississippi,' I hit him on the head.

"Oh my God, the sound—like a hideous clack— nothing else like it. The blood spurted. I-I recoiled. Everything was so shocking. The smell. My mind snapped into another zone. His skin color faded from pink to gray. His eyes shut. His limbs—limp. What happened? What did I do? I had no idea he would die. Then, I noticed the blood. The blood on the hammer, my arm, and the car. Something possessed me to clean. Clean the car's interior. Clean my arm. Clean-clean- clean everything I touched."

No amount of cleaning could fix her problem.

"With my slip, I wiped my arm and the interior and eased my way out of the back seat. I took the hammer with me, which I disposed of in a pond at a nearby park. I even took his—"

I couldn't plug my ears so I couldn't hear—

"—handkerchief, the one I'd used. I held it between my—"

*Don't say teeth. Don't say teeth. Don't say teeth—*

"—fingernails." She pinched her fingers.

I could hardly blink. My eyes seemed super-glued to open.

"No one ever figured out what I did… Oh, Lord. The police interviewed me because I was the ex. But they had a lot of other ex-wives to contend with besides me. Later, I reasoned I did the world a great service by ridding humankind of the slick philanderer. I shouldn't have done what I did with him. Still, a long time had passed since good sex came my way."

Miss A.'s face glowed with the remembered orgasm. "Lordy. He still had it. All…twelve…inches."

*Again, with THE Number.* I wondered about older men and how he got it up without Viagra and thinking of what old-man penises look like. My imagination took me to ugly, bumpy, stumpy sour pickles, like the king-sized ones in white plastic buckets sold at the movies. I shook my head. *Gross.*

I did not want to know. I did not need to know. I needed to leave Wedding Nightmare-land. I wiggled like a landlocked earthworm.

Miss A. yanked the knots tighter, then turned me over.

Because of the awkward bend to my body, my arms strained in their sockets. My feet grew numb. Her handiwork cut deep ridges in my skin. The pain? All encompassing. I held my eyes shut until the agony passed.

Miss A. straightened. "Those knots should hold you, my dear." A moment later, she added, "Sorry. I really am, Hattie. You were the best I ever employed. Now, I must go."

"You're leaving me…here?"

"I have to, dearie," Miss A. said. "I don't want the police to catch me. I'm pretty sure a little old lady like me wouldn't do well in prison." With her gaze fixed on me, she stepped toward the exit.

I wanted to plead, beg, scream, cry, but I couldn't. I lay on the floor, dumbfounded, knowing my boss had transformed into the classic villain.

Miss A. stepped beyond the threshold and pulled the door to.

Perhaps, regret, caring—who could say, and at this point, who cared—but something made her pause.

"I should phone your friend Jenny and let her know you'll be late while we catch up with paperwork. Since my car is a direct tie to me, I will take yours—"

*No-no-no.* My eyes rounded like saucers as I vigorously shook my head. *Not my beloved Jeep.* "Nononononono—"

"—I'll get the keys from your handbag."

Miss A. slipped out of view, then returned, jingling my car keys. "It's regrettable your sister Tracey was implicated in Jonson's murder. I went to Super Saver to purchase a new hammer—isn't it great how that store has everything—and on my way back to my car, Jonson pulled into a parking spot a row ahead of me. I sat in my car, watching, and remembering what you said and how he acted. A young woman passed, and I wondered who was that girl?

"When she stepped closer to Jonson's car, he reached out the window and grabbed her, pulling her body against the door frame. Her face turned all red like a boiled lobster. She looked scared. What words I heard Jonson say sounded…disgusting. Your sister tried to get away, but he held her tight. Jonson said something, and she socked him with a left jab. He grabbed his head and yelled as she ran away.

"Tracey's anguish reached me, but what could I do?" Miss A. shook her head. "Jonson went into Super Saver, presumably to clean his wound, and while inside, something possessed me to try his car's back door. Luckily for me, it was unlocked."

*Did Allan check the security tape's additional footage and see Miss A.?*

"I crouched on the floorboard—which was hard for this old gal's knees."

She tucked and untucked her bottom lip. "I remembered the newly purchased hammer in my hand. Jonson returned. He reached to start the car. I sat up and hit him in the head. No muss and no fuss would be wrong—blood and brain matter everywhere. I was a mess, and his car was, too."

Miss A. looked at the imaginary red stuff supposedly coating her palms. "Guess I went a little crazy."

*No shit. Good thing she wasn't holding a hammer right now.*

"You were in the wrong place at the wrong time, Hattie. Simple as that. Toodles." The storeroom door slammed shut.

Chapter Twenty-One

*Toodles?* Who said *toodles* nowadays?

I lay on the floor for a while. How to get out of the mess raced like the Indy 500 in my brain. *Damn, damn, damn.* I was stuck and I had the urge to pee and I hurt beyond hurt. I rolled around and contorted my body so I could finger the fabric tying my ankles. Miss A. used tulle to tie me up, and the tulle wouldn't budge. The little "old lady" tied a tough knot.

As I stared at the industrial light fixture hanging from the joists, I felt the cold from the concrete floor seep into my shoulders. No one would think to look for me for a long while, especially with Miss A.'s phone call to Jenny confirming we were working late, the "closed" sign on the shop door, and my car missing from the parking lot.

I needed to get out of here. I couldn't miss my sister's wedding. My friends and family knew I would be front and center.

Maybe Allan could read my mind. He'd done so before. If I focused on him and let the brainwaves do their magic… Something could happen. *Better than nothing.*

I closed my eyes and transmitted, "Please come get me, Allan. Please come. I'm in the storeroom. Please. Please. Please."

I waited for what seemed like an eternity, but

probably was only a minute. Nothing. *Didn't the hunky cop rescue the damsel in distress in the movies?* The one time I asked for help through his telepathic capabilities, and I got a Big Fat Nothing.

The nothing knowledge caused tears to leak out the corners of my eyes. I blinked hard and fast. *I will not cry. Will not cry. Will not.*

Anger flared in my soul. *Where is my hero?*

*Cut Allan some slack, Hattie. Who in the wide world can read minds? Maybe he doesn't do telepathy. Or perhaps enough time hasn't passed.*

*Damn, damn, damn.*

I was stuck on the storeroom's floor for more time than I knew. I rolled to my side, tucked my knees to my chest, and maneuvered my tied arms along the back of my bent legs, scraping my skin with the tulle rope. I paused to shove back the pain. Over my bottom, around my ankles, until my arms were in front of me. The ringing of the phone on the desk above my head caught my ear. Hope unfurled in my chest. I turned my head toward the sound. I wished I could answer. I butt-scooted to the desk, lifted my legs, and smacked my bound feet against the side. The desk wobbled, a high heel flew off and bonked me on the forehead, but the phone didn't budge.

Eventually, the rings ceased, and the answering machine turned on. I heard Jenny say, "Hattie, what's going on? Miss A. left an odd message, saying you're working late. I don't get it. I vaguely remember you said something about coming home early—right? Isn't tonight the last tango lesson? I'm positive you wouldn't miss the fun. He-he-he. Anyway, I tried your cell and left a message, too. Call me. Now."

Being tied up meant making phone calls impossible. At least, Jenny figured out something strange brewed. Maybe *her* brainwaves could connect with Allan.

In the meantime, I thought. I needed an escape plan because staying in this shithole of an office and waiting endless hours until someone could ride to the rescue— *not happening.*

*God, I'm exhausted.* I lifted my shoulders off the floor, then flopped back. My heart raced. Maybe I had low blood sugar. Maybe weak from the blow on the beaner. All I knew, the world whirled. And then, I blanked out.

****

I woke with massive spasmodic coughing. An oddly different, sharp acrid odor permeated the room. My nose scrunched. Definitely not the lovely lavender scent I usually sprayed in the store, the one the girl at the Sommerville Soap Company said imbued an "atmosphere of relaxation and harmony."

When the smell passed through a second time, I coughed, and concern filtered in my head. The smell continued to roll in, longer and more defined like-like a wood fire, which would be possible because the temp outside could turn a little nippy as the days drew closer to Christmastime.

And then, the most horrible thought of all creation burst through my brain. *Is Wedding Wonderland on fire?*

Panic seized my chest. *Surely not.* I'd be in big trouble. *If so, where's the fire department? Where are the sirens? Where's Allan?*

Moisture clouded my eyes. I would've been missed

by now. *Jenny, did you connect with Allan?*

Bam, bam, bam. My pity-party disappeared as I stared at the office door. Someone outside hammered the shop's front entry. Could this person be my rescue?

"Hey. Hey. Help. Help. I need help." The louder I shouted, the more I coughed. The smoke grew thicker. My throat scratched like scrubbing brush bristles. Unable to utter a word, I choked. My gaze shifted over the storage room. Everything appeared blurry like pale gray shadows shaded the shapes. The smoke alarm blared a loud alert siren with the warning for "everyone to exit the premises." The sound stung my ears.

"Help!"—*Cough, cough.* I believed no one heard me. No one knew what happened.

The shop's door crashed open. "Sommerville Fire Department. Hattie Cooks. Hattie Cooks. Are you here?"

"You circle that way," another someone said. "I'll go to the back. Be careful. This place could collapse soon."

Faintly, I cried a gravelly "Help," which bordered on useless. At the back of the store in a room with a closed door—*who would hear* me? *Cough, cough.*

"Hurry. The fire's spreading."

"Ceiling is about to fall. Let's go."

When I recognized the sound of retreating footsteps, fright gripped my chest. My heart squeezed so hard, it hurt. *Will I make it out of here alive?*

"Did you check the whole store?"

That voice. *That's Allan's voice.* Allan. It sounded clear and strong. He did hear me after all. Like a germinating seed, possibility curled throughout my body. *He's here. He's here. Come to me.*

"A preliminary check."

"My girlfriend, Hattie Cooks, works at Wonderland," Allan said. "I have a funny feeling she's inside the store."

"We'll go in again, detective, but it's gonna be tricky."

A great cloud of smoke seeped in the gap at the bottom of the storage room door—*cough, cough.* I shifted my body, so my feet rested against the wood. If only I could stand up. I rolled to a nearby chair, lifted my legs, and banged them on the seat.

"Hattie Cooks. Sommerville Fire Department. Are you here?"

I sure felt pathetic. I screamed one last time. "Allan."

*Nothing.*

"We can't find her."

*Allan, I'm right here. Please, please, please, don't leave me.*

I kicked the chair again. My legs collapsed. Rolling to the door, I punched it with my feet once, twice. My energy was zapped. I could barely lift my lead-filled legs. Live? Or die? I had to try.

As I struck the door a third, then a fourth time, I sent *help me* to Allan. Could he read my mind?

"Hattie's in the store. I know it," Allan said.

I gave one last bam and dropped to my side. I wiggled my body like a caterpillar to put my mouth at the opening between the door and the threshold. "Help."

All of a sudden, someone shoved the storeroom door. I found myself smashed between the door and the wall. The hard push against my body knocked the breath from me. Heaviness settled on my chest. I couldn't move. I couldn't speak. Not even mumble.

"Nobody's in here. I don't know what the cop's talking about. I don't see anyone. We gotta get out of here before the ceiling caves."

As I lay on my side, trapped behind the door, I determined the only choice I had—save myself. The wiggling like a caterpillar worked a while ago; however, it didn't get me far fast.

*I am out of options.*

I wormed my shoulder forward and pressed my knees against the floor. Bit by bit, I somehow crept from behind the door. Then I bunched my arms and legs to my chest in a ball, rolled sideways to the doorway, and over the threshold.

Pain shot through my shoulder. *God.* Tears flooded my eyes. I batted them away. I had to continue.

A flickering glow from the opposite side of the store where the wedding gowns hung captured my eye. The flames licked along a dress's hem and fast-crawled to the waist in a huge swoosh.

*Shit.* I looked to the blue sky visible beyond the front door and back toward the dresses. *That would not be me.*

As the flames licked higher and the heat intensified, I slowly rolled and rolled past the side of the platform, past the blue velour banquette and the reception area. Behind me, the storeroom ceiling dropped in a horrendous crash. Flicks of ash flew around me. Cinders stung my arms and legs. I smelled burnt hair and prayed my whole head wasn't on fire as I continued.

Rolling while bound took plenty of stamina, but if I

stopped, I wouldn't survive. And this gal would cheat death with every ounce she possessed. I spooled past the desk—only twelve more feet—and finally reached the shop's front door. Grateful the firemen busted it open, I gulped and gasped. Behind me, I heard another crash.

I edged over the threshold. The concrete sidewalk tore my blouse. My scraped shoulder felt like raw meat. Coughs consumed me.

I made it.

I closed my eyes, not thinking, not feeling, only surviving. Waterworks of relief splattered my cheeks. My bound arms fell to my chest as my gaze turned to the dark sky. I needed to move a little farther along. Inhaling, I continued to creep my way to the curb bordering the sidewalk.

Ultimately exhaustion ruled, and I could move no more. I collapsed in a fetal pose, totally spent. I barely took in the grackles winging their way to the phone lines.

While I waited, I closed my eyes. I didn't dare open them to look for my Jeep because if Miss A. had taken my baby like she said she would, my heart would shatter in a bazillion pieces. I didn't dare open them to watch Wedding Wonderland go up in flames, knowing I could have been stuck inside. I didn't dare open them to see Allan's concerned face because if I did, I would cry again and I didn't want to hear him repeat the words, "another job," because he was right.

I heard the shouts of the firemen as they worked to save the men's store next to Wonderland. The hum of the fire engines. The sizzle as water extinguished the flames.

Footsteps stopped by my head. "Hey. Over here."

A stampede rushed to my side. Someone cut the tulle away. "Are you Hattie Cooks, the woman the detective asked us to look for?"

I fluttered my eyes open. I wanted to say *yes*, but only a sound, like from a goose with tonsillitis, burst forth. A paramedic swooped me into his arms and carried me to an ambulance. Someone slipped an oxygen mask over my mouth and nose.

"Ma'am? Ma'am?" someone else said.

I stared upwards, only seeing the outline of face shapes and eyeballs. All became...light.

Chapter Twenty-Two

"Ma'am?"

I must look like an eighty-year-old because "ma'am" sounded ancient. All I could manage was a blink.

"Ma'am."

At some point, the paramedics drove me to the hospital. When I raised my head a fraction, I discovered I wore a hospital gown with teal squiggles instead of my clothing. I lifted my left arm and winced, relieved to find the tulle binding gone. I stared at my right arm, stuck with an I.V. Machines beeped away. Gauze and tape covered the scrapes on my shoulder.

"Hello, Hattie." A young lady with her dark hair twisted and clipped on her head and wearing blue scrubs patted my fingers. "I'm Nurse Courtney. Nice rest?"

I pulled at the oxygen tube.

She batted my hands. "Not yet." She adjusted the tubing going into my nose. "You need oxygen. You inhaled a lot of smoke—"

"Sir. Sir. You can't go in," an authoritative voice coming from the hallway said.

"The hell I can't."

*Allan? He cursed?* I frowned. *He's here.* I stared toward the doorway sensing relief soar through my body. Tears came to my eyes. Surviving a life-or-death situation turned me into the proverbial basket case. The door to my room squeaked when he eased it open. I wiped my fingers over my cheeks. Dollars to ducks I looked atrocious.

"Hi." Allan moved to sit by my side and smoothed my hair from my forehead. He pressed a tissue in my hand.

I clasped it tighter than humanly possible.

"You're okay, sweetheart."

"Don't c-call"—*cough, cough*—"me sweetheart." My answer might have been automatic, but in truth, I wanted to be his sweetheart.

Allan handed me a glass of water with a straw.

I took strong, long draws, then coughed into the tissue and balled it in my fist. I removed the oxygen tubing from my nose. "Sorry."

I looked at Allan, then past his shoulder when a shimmery item caught my eye. A familiar brown paper sack with "Hattie" scribed on it sat at the foot of the bed. He had tied the neck of the bag with a Mylar balloon shaped like a pot of flowers. A *Get Well* banner swept across the pot. The man stocked an endless supply of balloons and bags. I knew for I'd found his stash on the top shelf of his closet. For once, "Get Well" actually meant something.

Unexpectedly, an unfamiliar and acrid waft pestered my nose. I poked Allan's arm. "Leave. Now."

"Why?" His brow creased. He squeezed my hand again. "Why? I want to help."

"I smmeeellll," I blurted a whiney wail.

Smiling, he snorted a tiny bit and let his hand rest against the side of my face. His thumb stroked along my jaw. "It's okay. You're just a little pungent. You can have a bath soon."

*Pungent?* I didn't like the sound of the word. Frowning, the last thing I wanted—anyone wanted—was to smell *pungent*.

Allan's eyes shaped into thin slits. He ran his index finger over the top of my hand. "I heard you."

I studied his face, swathed with concern. My love for him melted and fired like liquid gold in my heart. I could smell and look like shit, and he still cared for me.

*The beginnings of love are like this.*

I launched myself into his arms and held on tight. I shoved my face into his shoulder. He wrapped his arms around me. The heat from his body penetrated and blended with mine. Oh, how he filled my entire being and scared me at the same time. Moving a little away, I sniffed and picked at his sleeve. "Y-you did?"

"Loud and clear. Like you sent a message only I could hear. Eerie." He propped pillows behind my back and guided me to a recline. He patted the blankets. "Can you answer some questions?"

With a nod, I sipped water. "Okay." I motioned for a tissue. When I nearly hacked up a lung, he passed the whole box.

"Sir, you have to leave."

The Authoritative Nurse sounded mighty persistent, and she looked big, like the Abominable Snowman big. With her finger, she settled her red glasses into place, then rammed her hands on her hips.

I wouldn't mess with her.

The Great Detective, however, would always be a different story.

Allan glared at her and flashed his badge.

Doing so must have been convincing because she

made a "humpf," then backed out the door. It closed firmly behind her.

I covered my smile with my hand.

Hearing my barely suppressed laugh, he swiveled his attention back and grinned.

My heart bloomed. Everything. Every little thing about him I adored. I smiled.

Allan tossed a paper grocery bag on the bed. "The firefighters found your handbag stored in the credenza behind your fancy desk. It's slightly singed but won't be the same. Sorry." He lifted out my scorched handbag—a particular favorite from my Rebecca Maine collection, one scored at a resale shop for pennies because a few faux jewels were missing.

I fingered one corner. Disappointment twisted my mouth. I wasn't happy about my treasure, but then, it was only a handbag. *Not my life.* I should remember being alive was more important. The stench brought back the nightmare. My shoulders shook. *Never again.*

I stuck the handbag inside the paper bag and put it on the bedside table. "Th-thanks."

Allan tilted his head. A twist of concern flitted through his eyes.

"Tell me about it."

His line, the one he used when he "chatted" with persons of interest. I shouldn't have been too surprised. First and foremost, *Allan Wellborn is a detective.*

I did the best I could in retelling my version. I attempted to weave all the mish-mashed pieces together. I stumbled and bumbled and coughed over my abbreviated story of Miss A., the multiple hammers, and Jonson Leggett the Third's death. "She left me trussed like a roped steer on the floor. And worst of all, she stole my Jeep. My car. My baby."

Allan raised his brow. "Uh oh. Which explains why we didn't find your car in the lot."

"I'll never forgive her. I told her how I scrimped and saved forever to buy it, and she still stole my…*MY*…car." Hoping to disguise any forming tears, I stared at the view outside the window and recited the tag number.

"Got it." Allan wrote furiously in his notebook. "We'll find her and your Jeep baby."

"She took mine because her Mercedes is in the shop—so she said. We drove the Jeep to the wedding convention in Smithville."

"Wedding convention?" He shook his head. "Spare me the details."

I studied my hands in my lap. "Can I leave the hospital in time for Tracey's wedding?"

"I think way before then. Want me to find out from the Dragon Lady Nurse who wants to get rid of me?"

The unmistakable gleam in his eyes looked adorable.

I ducked my chin and shook my head. "I'll ask…later."

He slanted his head. "Fortunately, you aren't too bad. The doctor's primary concern is making sure your lungs are clear. I'm sure he explained everything."

I inhaled and exhaled. "I feel like I'm breathing easier."

"Good." He grasped my hands.

I let the emotions exchanging between us consume me.

Finally, he pulled back. "You were very brave, Hattie. You didn't surrender. I don't know how you did all the rolling with fire about to incinerate the whole joint. You're amazing. And your hair will grow."

*My hair?* I shot my hands to finger my hair and examined the ends for damage. If Allan thought I looked incredibly bad, he would have told me. I dearly wanted to go to the restroom and make sure I didn't resemble a lunatic. Good thing I scheduled a trim before Tracey's big day.

Collapsing against the pillows, I settled the oxygen tube into my nose and tucked the flannel-like blanket under my armpits. Resting my hands on top of my belly, I let my gaze meet Allan's.

Nothing was said.

Everything implied.

My heart thumped so loudly, I could hear it. By the grace of God, I lived through a nightmare and wasn't charred toast. Water welled in my eyes with the remembering. I didn't want him to see me look so terrible. Embarrassed, I slid my hands over my face.

"It's okay. It's over, sweetheart." Allan tugged my hands down and dipped his head to stare into my eyes. "I called your mom and dad and Jenny. They'll be here shortly. I have to go."

"Please...don't—"

"I have to, sweetheart. I must get the bad lady. She hurt my girl." Releasing my hands, he stooped over.

He kissed my forehead softly, sweetly, gently, and despite the eau de stink-ola drifting from me.

I gripped his wrists, never wanting the moment to stop.

Eventually, all good "hold yous" came to an end.

Pulling away, Allan walked to the door. His hand lingered against the frame. Over his shoulder, he glanced at me. "I'll be back."

A rushing consumed my entire being. I more than desperately wanted him to return. "P-Promise?"

"Cross my heart."

His sweet grin comforted me.

"Love you," he said.

"Love you."

But Allan departed before he could hear me say so.

I stared at the television mounted near the ceiling, where a home improvement show blared and slowly smiled. The man I loved wasn't a cartoon superhero. He was my man, *my* crusader. And he would be back because he loved me.

Chapter Twenty-Three

After my lungs cleared, the hospital released me. I recuperated at the family homestead. But didn't get the hovering I expected. Instead, Tracey and Stuart's plunge into matrimony kept Mom preoccupied. She rushed around like a crazy woman to placate my sister and lift her spirits.

To stay out of the way, Dad found refuge in puttering in the garage.

After a few days of no tender loving care, I asked Dad to drive me to my apartment. I'd mended nicely. Jenny experimented with her homemade lasagna. *Yum.*

When all the ruckus died down, I located another job, still not in my preferred employment as a retail buyer. I found work on my own as a highway department flagger.

To say I knew the realities of what the job encompassed as a flagger would be wrong. I read the description on the website. The position sounded relatively easy with decent pay, and probably with minimal danger-danger element.

Nor did I take the job because of the marvelous apparel—steel-toed boots, thick socks, industrial-strength blue jeans, and a white twill shirt. Over those clothes, the Highway Department gave me a yellow-green fluorescent safety vest with wide reflective bands in orange, and a hard hat, which, from the black scuffs, had long passed the days of brand new. Safety glasses became the preferred eyewear.

Potholes magically appeared after the cold and rain, and the department kept them filled—our tax dollars at work. I was assigned to a crew working on a county road connecting the large cities which bordered Sommerville. In the chilly morning, I stood on the streets while the crew repaired-and-slash-or-replaced the roadway. I firmly gripped a STOP and SLOW sign-on-a-pole in one hand. I directed vehicles to bypass the equipment and the site. The drivers ranged from friendly wavers to kill-me strangers.

The dust raised coated my body. Every evening, my hair required several shampoos to purge the gritty filth.

Because the temperature was cold, I wore a T-shirt under the company shirt, then a hoodie over the whole lot, donning the safety vest last. Cheap knit gloves covered my hands, but in my pockets were hard-core leather ones from the home improvement store—just in case.

Today, I motioned a car through which hit a pothole filled with the brackish, brownish water left over from an overnight rain shower. The spray dumped on my head and clothing. Everyone knew what the image of drowned rat resembled. I looked beyond drowned and rat. I wiped my face with a blue paper towel, purloined from the roll on the back of the service truck. Luckily, I'd tucked my knotted hair in the hoodie.

While I brushed drops from my chest, I saw a car stop on the shoulder right next to where I stood. I looked over and locked eyes with Allan. Mortification flooded me. I shared with no one about my latest employment opportunity. And now…

Allan tightly clamped his lips.

A steely Clint Eastwood glint shaped his eyes.

He didn't like what he saw.

Without a doubt, Allan would tell his mother who would tell my mother as they scrutinized artichokes at Super Saver Grocery while the Mothers Always Know Network convened.

Allan fixed his hands on the steering wheel, flexed, and regripped several times as he stared out the window, collecting thoughts. The driver's window lowered. A moment, two, and three passed. "Hattie."

I bit into my bottom lip. "Allan."

Staring out the front windshield, he drummed the steering wheel. He slanted his eyes toward my direction. The drumming halted. "Another job?"

The STOP and SLOW sign pretty much gave me away. I shrugged.

"Hey, mister," my supervisor said. "Get a move on. Chat up the girl on your own time."

Allan waved and turned on his right indicator. He slotted the cop car deeper in the dead grass bordering the shoulder. He exited and stepped on the edge of the asphalt, closer but not too close.

He crooked his finger. "Can we talk, sweetheart?"

*Oh boy.* I turned to my coworkers and signaled between Allan and me. The youngest one who also worked the pole—aka Dickhead because he acted like a know-it-all—at the supply truck whose red hair stuck out all over, let his head drop to one side.

Dickhead had already complained about how many bathroom breaks I took—a vast total of two. I didn't know what he expected. No way would I ever, or could I ever, utilize an empty milk jug as the guys did.

Blowing a sigh, Dickhead jogged over and jerked the sign from my hand. "Make it snappy."

I walked toward Allan and grasped his arm to redirect us to the weedy lot. "Talk fast. I have a job to do."

"Surprise. Surprise," he said. "I didn't expect to see you on a road crew. Why?"

"Isn't it obvious? I'm working. Bills to pay. You know, et cetera, et cetera." I flickered my fingers.

"More than obvious, sweetheart. The more important question is, does your mom know?"

I snorted. A glance toward the road told me a large SUV turned our way. "Like I'd tell her. Besides, she's too busy with Tracey and Stuart to care."

"I doubt that. I know your mother cares." Allan overlapped his arms and relaxed his stance. "She'll find out from my mom over eggplant at Super Saver, especially when I tell mine."

I squeezed my eyes into reptile slits. "You wouldn't dare."

"Huh." He stroked his chin. "Maybe I would."

"Traitor."

Allan smothered his grin with his hand. "Did they"—he jerked his head toward the work crew— "train you for this? It's dangerous."

I didn't answer him for a while, just scuffed the toe of my boot to loosen a dead weed twiglet embedded in the black goo.

"The answer should be yes."

I lifted my left shoulder. "All right already. Yes. The basics of signage. Nothing else required."

"And how did you get here without a car?"

I set my hands to my waist. "If the police would *find* my Jeep, I'd have a car."

"I think your Jeep is long gone."

A beat, two, and three more passed.

"Sorry, sweetheart." Allan dipped his head.

"Not good news, Detective. And don't call me sweetheart."

"An investigation takes thirty days before the case is closed. Then you can notify your insurance company so you can get a replacement. You have a couple of weeks to go. Are you"—he glanced at my co-workers—"carpooling?"

"No. My insurance covered"—I pointed across the road where a small, barely silver compact sedan from a rental company rested in the shade of mesquite trees. *So not my preferred ride.* I avoided looking at or driving it as much as possible.

Allan took in the cheap vehicle with a sizeable dent in the bumper. "Not...your...style."

"A lot you know." I lifted a shoulder. "All I could afford."

"Hattie." My red-headed antagonist waved vigorously. "Time's up."

*Kids these days.* I scrunched a face his way. He didn't retreat.

Allan took three steps in Dickhead's direction. His hands parted his khaki blazer to rest on his hips. "Excuse me."

Certainly, his gun showed because my co-worker shook his head and backed away with a "never mind."

I shifted from one foot to the other. "I need to get back to—"

Allan returned to his place in front of me, his lips formed into a firm, seamless line. "God damn it, Hattie. You make my blood boil."

*Yikes.* I gave him my best "see-if-I-care" look. "Noted."

"I have more news."

I crossed my arms and arched a brow. "I'm sure it's riveting."

"Maybe. We caught Miss A."

I gasped. "What? Where?"

"Outside Kansas City."

"No way."

"Yes way."

"She'll stand trial?"

"Here and in Seattle. She's gotta lot to answer for."

"But not my Jeep?"

"No. Sorry."

I rubbed my forehead, then looked to my left. "Thank you. Anything else?"

"Don't move." He went to the cop car and flung open the door. He rummaged for a while, scribbled, then slammed the door.

With determined strides, Allan returned and thrust a rectangular piece of paper toward me.

"Here."

I clasped my hands behind my back. "What—"

"Just take it."

With a cautious and curious eye on him, I took the slip. My eyes rounded. A check. In fact, a check with the humongous number of five thousand dollars in the amount box.

I rubbed my finger across my lips, then frowned. "Um, this check's written for a big chunk of change.

Why?"

"For you. To use. To start your business. Time to quit jumping from one job to the next and get serious in your career. Open your own goddamn store."

I couldn't take Allan's money. I stuck the check inside his sport coat's breast pocket and patted it. His piney soap scent found my nose. Pausing, I fought the urge to shut my eyes and fall into the fragrance of him. "Look, buster," I said. "I know you mean well; however, I don't take handouts. I can't repay you. Thanks for the offer. Dickhead is getting impatient. Gotta go."

I turned, and as I did, I felt his grip on my bicep. I looked at his steady hand and didn't try to shake him off. "Please, Allan. Let go."

"I will but listen first." He shifted slightly and loosened his grasp. "You aren't happy as a highway flagger, are you?"

*Shit no.* I rolled my eyes. "What do you think? What matters is, the crappy job pays the bills."

"For now. What if you get hurt?"

I pulled away my arm. "I was almost french fried at Wedding Wonderland, which everyone believed was a stupendous place to work. I'm willing to take the risk."

Allan took the check from his coat pocket and crushed it in my hand. "Take. The. Check. You don't have to cash it. Just take it and think."

"Hattie!" Dickhead called.

*God, I hate this job.* I looked at my slouched co-worker, staring with one hand on his hip. I learned early in the world of the highway department, flag duty was beneath him.

I looked at my hands and unfurled the check, and

possibly, my future.

"Okay." I lifted my gaze to meet his. "I'll think. Now, I have to go." And being my mother's daughter, I halted long enough to say a very polite "Thank you, Allan."

"Oh"—he bounced his brow—"I'll find a way for you to pay me back, like washing my clothes, pet sitting, cleaning my car."

*Lordy.* I'd signed on as his personal assistant.

Chapter Twenty-Four

That evening, I slugged through my apartment doorway. I kicked off the boots and literally dragged myself to the kitchen. I threw the helmet on the island. I ought to hurry and shed my work clothes and hop in the shower before Jenny came home and discovered what I'd done. She would ream me out 'til Hades seemed palatable. After Allan's lecture, I didn't need another one. I touched my jeans' front pocket where I'd stashed Allan's check.

*Think about it.*

I couldn't *stop* thinking about his check. I held the ridiculous pole with the absurd signs and daydreamed about owning my own business. However, all I seemed to do was think. Fanciful pictures of a cute boutique with large windows and the name in a black flowing script filled my head. I planned exactly what kind of inventory I could buy, too.

Until one of the kill-me strangers laid on his horn and jerked me from the moment.

*Sigh.* I dug Allan's check from my pocket and set it on the kitchen counter. Although generous, I needed more to make my venture a "go."

I snagged a granola bar from the pantry, and just as I chomped into the peanuts and oats, I heard an "ahem."

I rotated slowly and found my good bud, Jenny, standing behind me. Then a colossal realization smacked me sideways—she came home early, and I hadn't cleaned up.

One big fat *oops*.

"Nice outfit." Jenny gestured toward the helmet. "Killer."

"Thanks." I took a bite. "You know me, always prepared."

She slid onto a barstool. "For Halloween."

I popped open the trashcan and tossed the filmy covering of the granola bar inside.

"Exactly when did you plan on informing me—or any of the Funsisters—about your job?"

"Hey, I hadn't got around to saying anything to anyone." With my mouth stuffed with crunchy bits, I shrugged. "How I pay my rent is none of your concern."

Jenny passed me the "whatever" look.

"Okay. Fine. I'm tired of the crazy temp jobs and found one with the highway department." I thumbed my chest. "I'm a flagger."

Her brow lifted. "Hmm. You look as if you have been shoveling ditches."

I leaned against the wall. "A little road grime never hurt anyone."

"Don't touch—"

"I'll clean it." I found paper towels and a spray bottle of soap under the sink. I covered the spot with liquid and wiped the smear. "And abracadabra."

"Lovely. Now take off your shirt and pants and put them in the washer before you contaminate anything else."

Jenny sounded exactly like my mother when I worked at Amazing Adventureland theme park with my

313

friend Maggie. A day of sunshine produced sweaty pits and stinky feet. I'd parked my Keds outside the garage to air them.

I unbuttoned my shirt, toed off my socks, and slipped off my jeans when I remembered Allan's check on the counter.

Jenny dragged the paper closer. "What is this?"

*Uh-oh.* "Pretty self-evident. A gift. From Allan."

"Interesting." Jenny took the check and read. "And a whole lotta moola. What for?"

I tossed the grimy pants in the washer. I stood in front of Jenny in my bra and panties, the ratty ones, barely covered by the unbuttoned shirt, exposed in many ways like the naked adventurers in the TV survival show.

I overlapped my arms over my chest. "Allan said I'm supposed to—quote—think about it—unquote."

"Think about…what?"

"My future. A store."

Jenny nodded. "Gotcha." She dropped his check and disappeared into her room. She returned with a paper of her own, which she placed side by side with Allan's. "Here's mine. For your future."

I pressed my lips into a level line and held back the overwhelming emotions which threatened to make me weep like a two-year-old. "I can't take it, Jenny."

"You can. It's time."

I examined the check. The dollar amount—notable. Hers matched Allan's—five thousand dollars. "This is your life savings."

"Some. Not all."

"I-I"—I brushed my hand over my forehead, feeling the asphalt dust on my fingers—"I hate the

314

highway job."

"Of course, you do. It wasn't the career you were meant to have."

Jenny circled the peninsula and barely patted my shoulder. "Maybe I'll quit Tuckers and join you. We can open a store. We can develop a business plan. Who knows?"

My eyes went large. "You'd leave your buying job and join me?"

Rubbing her chin, she nodded. "I might."

"Okay, we can talk. Think. But first, a shower."

"The water bill says you've been taking looonnng ones," she said. "You're wasting precious resources."

"The drowned rat has resurrected." I laughed. My prospects had changed. With a best friend by my side and money from another one, I felt empowered. "Hey."

Jenny swiveled about.

"Want to go somewhere with me?"

She squeezed her brow. "Depends. Where?"

"Wedding Wonderland."

"Oh." She crooked aside her head. "Back to the crime scene?"

I nodded.

Jenny pursed her lips. "Okay. Give me a sec."

****

After I showered away the road dirt and dressed, I let Jenny drive us to Wedding Wonderland in her car because she vowed to never ride in the scary rental. She steered into a spot near the storefront and killed the engine.

Amazed, I stared into the blackened abyss. I opened the car door and exited. Jenny did the same thing. We circled the front end and leaned against the front bumper. I couldn't take my gaze off the overcooked remains.

Jenny knocked my side with her hip. "You got the willies?"

"I should." A chill raced up my arm. *Scary.* I nodded. "I do."

"Wouldn't blame you if you did have them. I do even now. I grew a few gray hairs when I heard how you escaped. Luckily, I have an excellent hairstylist."

I shifted my gaze to the area of the storeroom office and gulped. A terrifying pain rooted in my chest and made my pulse pound. If a few more minutes had passed, I would have been a goner. "Looking at it, I'm amazed I got away. Not an experience I want to repeat."

Thank goodness I'd been determined to save myself.

The ruins of the men's haberdashery couldn't be missed either. All the wet, charred, broken remains. *Can't work at that store either.*

I rubbed the scar on the top of my hand where a cinder did its best damage when the gowns flamed and spouted. "I think I trust people too much."

Jenny tilted her head. "Being kind is a virtue. Your mother raised you to be so. To work hard. To respect others."

I gave a negative toss of my head. "I'm naive. I trust easily."

"You won't go through this again."

"No. Never."

Another car rolled into the lot and parked beside Jenny's. I looked over and saw my mom— *What is she doing here?*

Mom exited her vehicle and moved toward Jenny

and me. "Hi, girls."

I stood straighter and kissed her cheek. "Mom." I did my best not to choke.

"Mrs. Cooks."

"I was headed home when I saw you two." She crossed her arms over her chest, almost transfixed by the devastation. Then she turned. "You okay?"

"Yes." I went back to rest against the front bumper and stare at Wonderland.

"Jenny, is she?" Mom asked.

Jenny wobbled her head. "I think so. However—"

"I can't wait to hear."

"You should ask about her latest temporary job."

*Label my best friend a traitor.*

Mom's perfectly plucked and outlined eyebrow arched. "Oh?"

"Highway flagger." I said out the side of my mouth for Jenny's ears, "Bigmouth."

Jenny barely giggled.

Mom huffed a sigh. "I need a moment." She dropped her handbag on the hood of Jenny's sedan and took out…her checkbook. After she scribbled for a bit, she ripped off a sheet and folded my fingers over it.

I looked at the paper. The amount written— *Whoa!* My heart flipped over. "Mom?"

"For you…to open your store."

"How funny," Jenny said. "I gave her a check. Allan did, too."

I passed back Mom's offering. "I can't take your money."

"Why not?" Mom asked. "You took Allan's and Jenny's. You can take mine."

"I'm just thinking about theirs. I didn't commit."

"Maybe you should. I have faith in you and so do your friends." Mom grinned.

"You people don't get it." I so didn't want to confess my innermost truth.

"Get what?" she asked.

"What-what..." And from God knew where, I blurted out, "what if I fail?"

"You think we'd let you fail?" Jenny snorted. "Not in our lifetime. Besides, failure isn't such a big deal. People who fail learn something."

"You've never failed."

The corner of her mouth lifted. "I did fail a long time ago."

"When?"

"At sixteen. I took the driving test three times. Parallel parking's a killer."

I raised my gaze to the heavens.

"It was awful," Jenny said. "My brother drove me everywhere until I passed the driving section. My parents insisted I pay him, too."

Mom and I smiled at each other.

Mom nodded. "I failed once."

"You?" I pointed.

"Me. Pot roast 101. Raw. Your dad ate a huge piece and never said a word. Luckily, he didn't get ptomaine." Mom stuffed her check in my hand again. "Do it, Hattie. I have every confidence in you."

"In me?"

"More than you know." She recrossed her arms and looked at the building remains. "Now, we have another quandary. What to do about Tracey's wedding dress? As you know, the one she bought at Wedding Wonderland is all gone. Poof."

I stuffed the check in my front pants' pocket. "I have an idea—"

"What?"

Jenny and Mom looked at me as if I'd never had a brainwave before now.

"You're such alarmists. I could call the alterations lady, and we could do a nip and tuck on Mom's gown."

"My gown?" Mom bit her lip. "Would Tracey wear mine?"

"She would." I wound my arm with my mother's and laid my head against her shoulder. The scent of roses tickled my nose. "It's the best alternative. I don't know why we didn't think of it anyway."

Mom melted. "I would like her to. What can we do about the cake?"

I found a small stone at my feet and picked it up. I lightly tossed it in the air a couple of times. As Jenny opened the car door, I halted long enough to rest my hand on the top of the hood. "I have an idea about the cake, too. How about cupcakes decorated like flowers and arranged on tiered cake plates?" With a smile, I walked to the passenger side and slid inside the vehicle.

Jenny started her sedan. "Smarty pants. Guess you did learn something while working here."

Chapter Twenty-Five

Tracey looked beautiful as she glided along the aisle toward her hubby-to-be, her hand resting on Dad's right forearm.

The alterations lady had worked her magic on my mom's wedding gown. She transformed it into a slightly new style—off shoulders, minus the peplum. And for Tracey's veil, Mom and I took a headband of synthetic pearls and sparkling crystals and attached a simple fine net that trailed the red carpet behind her. Since Tracey didn't have many choices, seeing her now, what else could have been more perfect?

Dad's left hand covered Tracey's as he looked at her with adoration.

*Maybe someday I will feel like they do.*

From the bridesmaid's point of view spot at the altar, I glanced at Mom, who touched a tear with a vintage hankie edged in my grandmother's handmade white tatting. I knew her consuming thought—one down. And one to go.

*Whatever.*

I sent my gaze to Stuart, who looked the personification of the bridegroom with a grin rivaling a jack-o'-lantern's, except not ghoulish, just big and toothy. Shoulders squared, he was dressed in an impeccable black tux. After Tracey parted from Dad and joined Stuart, she tilted her gaze to meet his. Every emotion passing over her face showed how much she loved him. They clasped hands and turned to face the minister.

Looking past Stuart, I saw Allan solemnly observing the couple as they prepared to say their "I Do's." Then I noticed he watched me lean left and take her bouquet fashioned from grocery store roses and lilies. I'd tied them with a white satin ribbon.

Light danced in Allan's eyes and warmed my heart. Overcome with embarrassment, I dipped my chin and breathed in the perfume from the stargazer lilies.

Jenny nudged my back, which woke me from the land of daydreams. On the open Bible held by Reverend Walsh, I dropped Stuart's wedding band at the same time as Allan dropped the one he held. The rings clink-clinked together on the book's interior seam.

One by one, and then together, Reverend Walsh blessed the gold circles. Tracey and Stuart exchanged their vows and slid the bands over their ring fingers. Reverend Walsh introduced the radiant pair to the congregation. In a princely fashion, Stuart tilted to kiss his bride.

For a small moment, I imagined myself in my sister's place with the man I loved in Stuart's. I swore to myself things would change one day, and maybe-maybe-maybe it wouldn't be so far off either.

I set my hand on Allan's forearm and followed the newlyweds along the aisle to the narthex, where the party paused for cheers and hugs.

Allan stole a peek at me, and I winked back. I curled my fingers with his. I was all too aware of how good he felt and what I felt in my heart.

****

The wedding party gaily transferred to the church's banquet hall, where we found our places at the head table.

Mom and Mrs. Wellborn pitched in to drape the tables in white damask tablecloths, the kind all women of their generation owned. Pale teal napkins folded into triangles had been set in front of each chair. Shiny silver-plated forks on the left, knives and spoons on the right. Thankfully, Mom was able to hire the caterer originally booked.

The Funsisters and I had placed white Japanese lanterns in the center of the tables with battery-operated tea lights in each one. Long strands of twigs decorated with white, seed-like beads serpentined around the centerpieces and the length of the table. As the sun dipped into the west, the candlelight created an enchanting ambiance.

The bridesmaids and groomsmen alternated every other seat, and naturally, Allan and I sat side by side. Something compelled me to slide my hand along his thigh, which he promptly grasped, playfully shaking his other finger in my direction. But he didn't let go until the staff served our meal.

The guests dined on grilled chicken or salmon covered with lemon beurre sauce, an assorted wild greens salad topped with finely sliced apples and seasoned with a vinaigrette dressing, scalloped potatoes layered with gruyère cheese, and thin asparagus sautéed in olive oil and garlic. The food melted in my mouth.

As the dining portion of the evening ended, Allan offered up his best man's speech. I crooked my head to stare in wonderment. When I recited my maid of honor ditty, I brushed tears from my eyes and once—or twice—paused to collect myself.

Tracey and Stuart blotted their tears after my words.

Mother boohooed.

I lifted my flute filled with champagne.

The guests toasted each other and drank the bubbly.

My sister finally found the true happiness she deserved.

I returned to my seat and placed my napkin to the corners of my eyes.

"Good job," Allan whispered. "You gave them tears and laughter and no silly jokes."

"I'm fresh out of silly jokes."

The bride and groom walked hand in hand to the cake, which wasn't a cake. The Funsisters, Mom, Mrs. Wellborn, and I spent the prior afternoon creating white cupcakes with lemon curd swirled in the batter. Mrs. Wellborn used her cake decorating skills to fashion marbled pink and rose dahlias on the tops. I added three silver dragées to the flower's center.

Everyone declared our effort beautiful, and "quite innovative," whispered one of Mom's church friends.

Stuart fed Tracey and vice versa with no face-smashing mishap. Then with a nod to the DJ, they made their way to the center of the dance floor. The newly marrieds circled the room in a Viennese waltz, dipping and swirling artfully.

When the number ended, the rest of the party joined the couple and danced the exhibition tango number rehearsed with Ms. Yolanda, complete with a rose in my mouth.

Afterward, Stuart and his mom danced. Their talent

captivated every guest.

With a firm grasp on my bicep, Allan maneuvered a slightly breathless me onto the balcony, which overlooked the garden.

He jerked the tail of his bow tie loose and unfastened the top shirt button. Determination encompassed his face—flat lips and squinchy eyes. A man with a plan.

*Maybe I know his plan.*

I shook him off and pushed my hands onto my hips. "What's going on?"

"I have a plan, sweetheart."

*Ha.* "Of course, you do."

"My plan's better than your plan. Yours"—Allan nodded toward the banquet hall—"would be to dance to 'YMCA.' "

"Rats." I made a fake move to go back to the dance floor. "I can't miss my favorite—"

"Hold on, sweetheart." He grabbed my hand and circled me to his chest.

*Sweetheart. I love hearing him call me sweetheart.* "Whatcha want, cowboy?" I narrowed my eyes. "You sorta like dancing. Waiting for a specific song? By the way, what is your favorite song?"

"My favorite song is 'L-O-V-E' by Nat King Cole."

"An oldie but a goodie." I remembered Dad played the album all the time. I intended to use that song as my wedding dance.

Right then, the mentioned favorite floated out the door toward us. *Perfect timing.*

Allan wrapped his arms around me and edged his body closer. He swayed with the music and sang very softly in my ear, "L is for how you drive me crazy."

*Who would guess my man could be so romantic?*

I moved in sync with Allan and snuggled my mouth to the spot on his neck. I took a deep whiff of the piney soapy smell I adored and automatically pressed a kiss. "O means the obstinate one with me."

Allan dropped his chin and kissed my temple. "Thanks."

"You're welcome," I murmured. "V means the very vixen in me."

He laughed. "Vixen—funny."

"You know, you haven't answered my question. What's up?"

"I brought you out here because we haven't had time for an honest, one-on-one conversation."

"And?" I locked my arms around his neck. "You know we've been crazy busy getting Tracey and Stuart's wedding pulled together."

"I know. That's why I cut you some slack." Allan fixed his chocolate brownie gaze on me. "Did you quit the highway department?"

"You'll be glad to know my good news."

He lifted one brow. "What good news?"

"Yes, well"—I ducked my chin—"I'm no longer employed by the highway department."

"Excellent. Now, let's talk about…us."

*Showdown.*

I laced my fingers together to curb the unsteadiness flowing in me and looked at my shoes.

Allan and I stood toe to toe. With a finger, he lifted my chin. "I know what you thought once, but you were wrong. A while back, you wondered if I would propose."

Shamefaced and embarrassed, I dropped my head again and nodded. I'd slammed the door in his face after he asked me to "choose him."

"Not how I would propose," he said.

The glint reflected from his iris resembled old gold. "It isn't?"

Heat burned my cheeks. I looked into his eyes. All I felt and knew was hope and heart. Hope for the future. Heart to share with love. I prayed and prayed he still wanted me. I desperately wanted him.

"No, sweetheart. You deserve something special, like on top of the Eiffel Tower or the Empire State Building. On a hot air balloon ride or over a candlelit dinner at a French restaurant. I would not have asked you to marry me on my deathbed the way Stuart proposed to Tracey." He guided me against his chest.

His heat and scent encompassed my body. All man. *My man.*

"I've loved you all my life."

No surprise what he intended to do, and he knew I knew. With a little hesitancy, I glanced into his gaze. "Allan—"

"Hattie," he said. "You make my blood heat—"

*Oh God, not that blood boiling lecture again.*

"—in a good way."

"Yes!" I smiled right before his lips found mine.

His kiss touched tenderly at first, then devoured deeper and intensely, taking in my whole mouth. All cognition evaporated as his arms enveloped me even tighter.

I pressed into Allan. I glided my left hand over his shoulder to splay along the back of his neck, encouraging and urging.

And he gave.

I moaned.

"Get a room." Giggling and light clapping followed.

Allan broke the kiss. The dancing stopped.

I pressed my forehead to his chest. After a bit, I stole a look in the direction of the voice. *Jenny. No big surprise.*

Her countenance radiated pure happiness with a tinge of smirky-ness as she continued past with Mr. Who-Uses-All-The-Hot-Water. His arm encircled her waist.

As she passed us, from over her shoulder came "Told you so."

I snorted. Jenny had "after-party" plans. I returned to Allan. "Now, where were we?"

"E means," he sang slightly off-key, "everyone can see." He buzzed my lips. "I have a confession."

"Tell me."

"When you hung out with Sarah Ann, I would watch you."

I chuckled. The middle school years. "Seriously—"

The corners of his eyes lifted.

"—not a confession."

"But I didn't tell anyone."

"Lordy." I heaved a sigh. "Sarah Ann told me. Best friends share all secrets."

"Sisters." Allan shook his head. "You have a glow and a happy spirit I wanted to capture and carry with me.

"After I graduated from high school and went to college, I didn't forget you. I stole your picture from Sarah Ann's room and kept it on my desk. My roommates said I lusted after jailbait, but I ignored them." His mouth crooked a small smile. "I could touch the picture and feel you."

No one who knew his feelings had said anything. Not his sister and my best friend. Not my mother. Not my sister. No one.

"Mom told me about your college boy, and I wasn't happy. I dated other girls, and gradually, I changed. Then on the day I pulled you over for the citation, an old familiar feeling hit me. One last chance. One last chance to go for it. Go for you."

I tugged his lapels. "I'm not sure you want the same things as me."

"I want to marry and have kids." He inclined his head. "Don't you?"

My body hummed. I fashioned a bare nod. "I do, too."

"Hattie, love me. I don't ever want to let you go."

I lifted my gaze to meet his. A golden circle flared around his irises. Quietly, I affirmed, "I do."

Our foreheads touched. Allan and I slid to his right. Then back, and then, the song ended.

"Nice dress."

"Thanks. I helped Tracey pick the style." I wore a pink silk sheath with a V-neck, which I found on Tucker's online store after Wedding Wonderland burned. "You really like it?"

"I like what's underneath better." He slipped his right index finger into the V and stretched the bodice. He looked down the front. A grin teased the corners of his mouth.

Underneath my party duds, I wore my lacey panty and bra set—just in case.

"I like pink."
*He-he-he.* I knew that.

## A word about the author…

Award-winning author Vicki Batman has sold many romantic comedy works to magazines, several publishers, and most recently, three romantic comedy mysteries to The Wild Rose Press.

Avid Jazzerciser. Handbag lover. Mahjong player. Yoga practitioner. Movie fan. Book devourer. Chocoholic. Best Mom ever. And adores Handsome Hubby.

Most days begin with her hands set to the keyboard and thinking "What if??"

Visit her at:

http://vickibatman.blogspot.com

~*~

**Other Titles by this Author**

*TEMPORARILY EMPLOYED*
*TEMPORARILY INSANE*